All the Bodies Do

A Novel

William J. Cook

This novel is a work of fiction.
Any references to matters of historical record,
to real people, living or dead, or to real places are intended solely
to give the stories a setting in historical reality.
Other names, characters, places, and incidents
are the product of the author's imagination,
and their resemblance, if any,
to real-life counterparts is
entirely coincidental.

ISBN-13: 9798323496457

All the Bodies Do. Copyright © 2023 by William J. Cook. All rights reserved. Printed in the United States of America.

Cover designed and created by Roslyn McFarland (farlandspub@gmail.com).

Brief quotations are taken from:
The Little Prince, by Antoine de Saint-Exupéry, 1943.
The Stranger, by Albert Camus, 1942.

Other Books by William J. Cook:

Songs for the Journey Home, a novel of spiritual discovery
The Pieta in Ordinary Time and Other Stories
Catch of the Day, short stories
Before Our House Fell into the Ocean: Stories of Love and Death
The Driftwood Mysteries:
Seal of Secrets, a novel
Eye of Newt, a short story
Woman in the Waves, a novel
Dungeness and Dragons, a novel
Paper, a short story
Gallery of Gangsters, a novel

Table of Contents

Dedication	5
Author's Note	7
1. Moonlight Sonata	9
2. Cold Case	15
3. That 70s Place	25
4. Picture Perfect	31
5. A Shard of Sky	37
6. Visiting Cruella	44
7. All the Bodies Do	49
8. Spoofed	53
9. Close Encounters of the Mob Kind	61
10. The Cicada	66
11. Dancing in the Dark	77
12. Of Moles and Men	83
13. Home on the Range	87
14. Taking Down Empires	93
15. The Silver Fox	99
16. One Ring to Find Them	105
17. The Gentleman Winemaker	110
18. It's Willamette Dammit!	119
19. The Invisible Man	124
20. Flowers for Kate	129
21. Vigil	132
22. Cracks in the Foundation	136
23. Behind Enemy Lines	139
24. Rehab	147
25. The Interview	151
26. In the Vineyard with Thor	158
27. Binge-Watching *The Sopranos*	161
28. The Noose Tightens	167
29. The Existentialist	174
30. Ms. Pit Bull Meets Phantom of the Opera	177
31. Tanked	182
32. The Ferryman of Hades	186

33. The Undoing 191
34. All in the Family 203
35. Where the Heart Is 209
36. Oh, Henry! 214
37. The Apple Falls 221
38. In the Valley of the Shadow 227
39. Launching the Astronaut 233
40. The Going-All-In Caper 239
41. Of Chance and Necessity 244
42. Killing the Queen 248
43. Blood and Wine 255
44. The Lake Mead Murders 263
About the Author 274
Acknowledgements 275

Dedication

To my daughter Julie, who first told me about the bodies in Lake Mead and then inspired me to write this story. Throughout the project, I told her it was all her fault!

"God made Cabernet Sauvignon, whereas the Devil made Pinot Noir."

-Andre Tchelistcheff, Napa Winemaker

"If any grape would be at home in the pose of the femme fatale—smoke curling from its lips, long, irresistible legs crossed as another winemaker is sent to his doom—it would be Pinot Noir."

-Eric Asimov, Chief Wine Critic, *The New York Times*

"[Pinot Noirs are] the most romantic of wines, with so voluptuous a perfume, so sweet an edge, and so powerful a punch that, like falling in love, they make the blood run hot and the soul wax embarrassingly poetic."

-Joel L. Fleishman of *Vanity Fair*

"[Pinot Noir is] sex in a glass."

-Madeline Triffon, Master Sommelier

Author's Note

Lake Mead, the largest man-made reservoir in the United States, was formed in the 1930s by the Hoover Dam on the Colorado River. At its height in 1983, the lake was 1,225 feet above sea level. Assaulted by a two-decades-long megadrought in the West, however, by May of 2022, it had dropped to 1,049 feet above sea level, a staggering loss of 176 feet.

The receding waters exposed a World War II-era landing craft, a half-submerged B-29 plane, many wrecked boats. And bodies.

On May 1, 2022, human remains were found on the shore of Boulder Basin in a fifty-gallon drum near the Hemenway boat launch. Authorities identified clothing and footwear on the skeleton as coming from K-Mart in the mid-to late-1970s. As if being found in a barrel weren't enough, the bullet hole in the skull confirmed that this was a homicide. Television and the press had a field day. Speculations about "Hemenway Harbor Doe" insisted he was a "mob hit," likely related to the goings-on in nearby Las Vegas. Barbara Brock submitted a DNA sample to the police and said she believes he was her brother, Bobbi Eugene Shaw, who, she claims, disappeared in 1977 and was involved with the Mafia.

A week later, on May 7, 2022, paddle boaters discovered skeletal remains at Callville Bay. The remains were later identified as Thomas Erndt, a 42-year-old father who apparently had drowned in 2002 while taking his family on a midnight cruise.

On July 25, August 6, and August 18, three more sets of skeletal remains were found in the areas of Swim Beach and Boulder Beach.

Examiners are subjecting all these remains to rigorous medical assessment, including autopsy, radiographs, and consultation with forensic dentists and anthropologists. They will also attempt DNA analysis. Authorities acknowledge that it is often impossible to determine cause of death with only skeletal remains (Hemenway Harbor Doe notwithstanding!).

An article in the August 24, 2022, volume of *Newsweek Magazine* bore the disturbing headline:

"Lake Mead Has Hundreds of Bodies Waiting to be Found"

1. Moonlight Sonata

THURSDAY, SEPTEMBER 21, 1972. The man in handcuffs sat in the bow of the skiff and shivered in the cool desert air. His white shirt and dark suit pants were torn and dirty after the scuffle in the parking garage. His right leg was clamped to a five-foot length of anchor chain, the other end of which was fastened to a heavy cinder block.

The lake was a giant pane of glass, reflecting the near-full moon above and the few stars bright enough to withstand the star-quenching glow of Las Vegas in the distance. The only sound was the creak of the oarlocks and the gentle splash as the oars entered the water and propelled the craft forward.

The young man rowing moved with silent grace, his back and arms honed to iron fitness by daily workouts in Lucky's Gym, as his black T-shirt proclaimed. Sandy hair cascaded over his shoulders and gleamed silver in the moonlight.

The older man sitting in the stern loosened his tie and drew another cigarette from the pack in his pocket. After lighting it from the ember of his previous one, he flicked the spent butt far out over the water, a mini falling star that hissed and winked out. Engulfed in a cloud of fragrant tobacco smoke, his face was as pocked as the surface of the moon, the product of adolescent acne and a history of overzealous bar fights.

The man in the bow pleaded to the back of the rower. "Jeez, Bobby. C'mon. Don't do this. Tell your father it was all a mistake."

"Shut up, Harry!" growled the other man as he withdrew a pistol from the holster under his sports coat. "Don't talk to the boss's son. You got anything to say, you say it to me."

"Okay, Tom. Then listen. This is all wrong. I wouldn't think of cheatin' on the boss. You know that."

"I only know you been short six months in a row and Johnny is sick of it. He gave you every chance. Now the rumor is you want your Cactus Club to be the biggest on the Strip, even bigger than the Florentine. Not gonna happen. Johnny thinks your casino needs new management."

Harry's voice began to quiver. "I can pay you, man. Name your price. You let me off and you'll never see me again. I swear."

Tom leaned over and whispered in Bobby's ear. "You believe this guy? Next, you'll see him piss his pants just before I toss him over."

The shackled man rattled his chains. "I got three hundred large I can lay my hands on tonight. By tomorrow, I can have a mil. Whaddya say? We could do this. I'll disappear, you'll be rich, and Johnny'll never know." He was crying now, his tears shining rivulets down either cheek.

"Harry, Harry. That's not the way this works. Me and Bobby here are a good team. You could call us Johnny's Janitors." He laughed and looked at the twenty-year-old. "How many has it been over the last eight months, Bobby? Three? Four? I lost count." He raised his eyes to the hapless man in the bow. "We take out the boss's trash, and right now that means you."

Bobby frowned and shook his head. "Tom, I'm not sure I'd call us a team. I just row the boat."

"C'mon, Bobby, don't be like that. We work together. I take care of the bad stuff, and you're our captain and navigator. You get us where we need to be."

"But I don't like it, Tom."

"It'll be okay. Sooner or later your dad'll give you a casino, and you won't have to go on these midnight cruises with me."

"But when? Dad tells me I have to prove myself before he gives me a place. Says he has to be sure I'm man enough to make the hard decisions and follow through with them."

"Are you? Man enough?"

"If that means killing people, maybe. I haven't had to yet. I just row the damn boat."

Tom nodded his head. "We've racked up a pretty good score, you and me. And I sure like your company on the jobs. But you're young. You got plans. Dreams. College, maybe. Your old man could hire any dumb muscle like me for his dirty work. You should talk to him."

"I've tried, believe me. But he puts me off. 'I'm grooming you for the big one,' he says. 'After all, you're the crown prince of the Giancarlo Gemelli family. Someday all this will be yours.' It's all just crap. He doesn't trust me. And he doesn't like me. I think he likes my twin sister more than me."

The older man took a deep breath. "Don't be too hard on him, Bobby. After all, he helped put Vegas on the map."

The rower clenched his teeth. "I swear, if I hear that line again, I'm gonna puke."

"I hear you, Bobby-boy, but you know it's true. And he's juggling a lotta balls right now."

"What I know is I want out if he's not going to give me a casino."

"Okay." He clicked his tongue as he took another drag on his cigarette. "I'll put in a good word for ya, kid. The boss likes me, so maybe he'll listen."

"Thanks, Tom."

The man in the bow rattled his chains again. "Hey, Tom? Remember me? Don't make the kid do anymore of this. He don't need no more bad stuff. Give him nightmares."

"I told you to shut up, Harry." The big man scratched the side of his head. "Oh, yeah. I almost forgot." He jammed his left hand into his shirt pocket and withdrew a paperclip. He leaned over Bobby and handed it to Harry. It was a running joke he carried on with all of his victims, and it made Bobby cringe. "Just so you don't think I got no heart. If you can pick the locks on your handcuffs and chains in the couple of minutes before you drown, you get to swim away."

A quiet moan escaped Harry's lips. Then he gritted his teeth and clenched his jaw. "It ain't fair, I tell ya. Johnny takes the cream off the top, and we get stuck with the leftovers. He gets rich, and we're chasin' our tails."

Tom tapped Bobby's shoulder. "Put down the oars for a sec, will ya?" He climbed over Bobby and stood looking down at his captive. "Cops ever raid your joint, Harry?"

"No." Harry glared up at the man hovering over him, felt the chill of the gun barrel touching his scalp.

"Ever have any trouble with the IRS? Any hassles booking entertainment? Any problems at all running your shop?"

"You know I haven't, Tom." His lips curled in a defiant pout.

"You think all that was an accident? That you're as lucky as those schmucks who play at your tables think they are?" The man's voice grew louder now as he tapped Harry's forehead with the barrel of the gun. "That's all Johnny's work, you ungrateful shit! He's been watching your back while you've been stabbing his!" He bent down and pulled open Harry's shirt, snapping off the chain necklace that held Harry's prize possession—a Super Bowl III ring.

"Hey! C'mon! I won that fair and square at my club! My New York Jets ring."

The big man hunkered over him. "But you won't need it where you're going, Harry."

Suddenly, Harry leaped to his feet, butting the gun out of Tom's hand. Then he smashed the crown of his forehead into Tom's nose. The man yelped in surprise and pain as Harry twisted his shoulders and rammed Tom's chest. The gangster lost his balance and fell over the gunwale into the lake.

"Get him, Bobby! Get him!" he shouted, choking on a mouthful of water as he desperately reached for the side of the boat.

Bobby scrambled to retrieve the gun, which had fallen into the shadows on the deck. Just as his hand wrapped around the pistol grip, Harry pounced on him, looping his handcuffed wrists around Bobby's neck and yanking back as hard as he could. The gun discharged with a thunderous echo across the lake and fell from Bobby's grasp. A fountain of water began spurting through a hole in the stern. As the small chain linking the cuffs bit into his neck, Bobby reached over his shoulders, grasped Harry's upper arms, and used all his strength to flip the man over his head. The chain to the cinder block caught halfway through the maneuver, and the two men fell into a tangled, snarling mass on the deck. Harry clawed and bit like a feral cat, wailing in animal frenzy. Bobby wrenched himself away, turned, and landed a bone-cracking punch to the man's solar plexus. Harry lay helpless, unable to catch his breath. The boat began to list to starboard as it filled with water.

Tom clung to the gunwale, coughing and spitting, blood pouring from his broken nose. "Help me, Bobby! I can't swim!"

"We're taking on water, Tom! I've got nothing to bail it with. Hang on! I've got to plug the hole." He pushed Harry's quivering body out of the way and found where the water was gushing in. Ripping the T-shirt from his back, he tried to stuff a bit of it into the hole, but the pressure pushed back against him and thwarted his efforts.

Tom struggled to get into the boat. As he frantically tried to pull himself over the gunwale, the onboard water shifted to that side, and the weight was too much. Bobby leaped for safety as the boat slid under the water. The falling anchor chain snagged Tom's flailing arms. In less than a heartbeat, the cinder block dragged Harry and Tom down into the watery dark. The boat disappeared under rings of moonlit ripples.

An eerie stillness settled over the lake. The surface grew calm again. Only Bobby's head was visible as he tread water, gasping for breath, his heart pounding. He turned in a slow circle, looking for any trace of Tom or the boat. Overhead, the indifferent moon shone down, glinting off the two oars floating away in the shadows.

The glow on the horizon reminded him of Las Vegas, thirty miles distant, and all the people sleeping unaware in plush hotel rooms, restoring themselves for another day of mindless entertainment. He imagined the felt-covered tables in the gambling parlors, where the serious poker players stayed all night, certain the next hand would recoup all their losses, finally stumbling off to bed at six or seven o'clock in the morning, thousands of dollars poorer.

Will my father wonder what's keeping me? he thought. *Will he send someone to look for Tom and me, afraid something may have gone wrong with tonight's "garbage disposal?" Will he even notice?*

After a few minutes, his breathing returned to normal. Somewhere nearby a fish splashed in the darkness. Frogs along the shore resumed their belching chorus, and he swam in that direction.

2. Cold Case

AUGUST 15, 2022. Kate Temperance shook her head and thought, *If a classical composer were inspired to make a piece of music out of this nonsense, he'd call it 'Cacophony Number 22: From the Strip'.* Six lanes of bumper-to-bumper traffic, and nobody was going anywhere on Las Vegas Boulevard. It was pointless to honk horns, but impatient gamblers and taxi drivers leaned on them anyway. Pavements on both sides of the thoroughfare were jammed with tourists, eager to feed their money to hungry games of chance. Speakers blared discordant rock music from every open door, and Kate called the deep thrum of the bass "the heartbeat of the city." She was no psychiatrist, but it seemed like LV was in the throes of a massive manic episode after the depressive months of the pandemic.

Finally reaching Valet Parking at the Florentine Hotel and Casino, she got out of her aging Mercedes, took the receipt from a young man who didn't look old enough to drive, and walked toward the entrance. Not one but two marble replicas of Michelangelo's David flanked the enormous oak doors. *Ah, excess*, she thought, *the native language of Las Vegas.*

The entry hallway confirmed her initial observation. From its high curved ceiling, immense copies of Botticelli's *The Birth of Venus* and *Primavera* staggered first-time visitors. Along both walls were sculptures that imitated *Mercury* and *Abduction of a Sabine Woman,* by Giambologna, *Perseus* holding the severed head of Medusa, by Cellini, *David,* by Donatello and many more. She began to laugh as her friend approached.

"Hey, Bonnie. I guess if we can't go to Florence we can always come here. What do you think?"

"I think I need to persuade you not to see Gemelli."

Kate shook her head. "Let's go eat. We can talk about it over our early dinner. C'mon." The two women walked across the expansive lobby, filled with so many paintings and sculptures it looked more like a museum than the gateway to a hotel. Kate addressed the swank gentleman at the bronze door to the Duomo

Restaurant and Lounge. "Kate Temperance. We have reservations for three-thirty."

"Ladies, please follow me," he said. He brought them to an elevator, which they rode to the second floor. Then he escorted them to a granite-topped table on a balcony overlooking a vast inner courtyard open to the sky. Before them stretched a duplicate of the Piazza del Duomo, complete with a painstaking replica of the Santa Maria del Fiore Cathedral at one-fifth scale. Designer shops like Gucci, Luis Vuitton, and Versace surrounded the plaza on all four sides.

"Magdalena will be your server, and she will be with you shortly." Once he had left, Bonnie leaned over the table and whispered to her friend.

"Don't do this. Please. You're poking a hornets' nest. What do you possibly hope to accomplish by talking with..." She paused, as if looking for the right name. "Cruella de Vil?"

Kate laughed. "Cruella. I like it!" The humor left her face. "Sofia Gemelli knows things. I'm sure of it. My investigation into the disappearances has to start here. I'll be fine."

She and Bonnie had had each other's backs since high school, when Bonnie's bright red hair and freckles were like lightning rods for teasing by other girls. The same girls had teased Kate for her 4.0 GPA and for turning down the advances of the football team's quarterback. "The alpha dog," she had told Bonnie, "with the emphasis on *dog*." The two outcasts had been inseparable ever since, often calling each other "sis" in honor of their special bond. "We are family," they would sing along with Sister Sledge on karaoke night at Danny's Bar and Grill.

A young woman in a sleek black dress approached the table. "Would you like something to drink?"

Kate held up the wine list, a leather-bound book of ten pages. "We know we'll want a wine with dinner, but this is overwhelming. We don't know where to start."

"Let me take your orders, and I'll send Henri, our sommelier, to advise you."

In moments, a man in a black tuxedo was at the table, offering his advice. "Magdalena tells me you'd like wine with your dinner. Since you've both ordered salmon, may I recommend a Pinot Noir? It's very food-friendly. Medium-bodied, nice nose, floral and spice notes. Some dark cherry on the palate."

Bonnie expressed some doubts.

"Allow me to bring you samples, a taste or two of my current favorites," coaxed Henri.

Both agreed, and the sommelier returned with two small glasses of garnet-colored wine. "These are very special. The Duomo is the only restaurant in town that serves them, flown in from the Willamette Valley in Oregon especially for our owner, Ms. Gemelli." He placed them on the table and watched as the women tasted them.

Kate's eyes brightened. "I don't know much about wine, but both of these are excellent. What do you say, Bonnie?"

"I say we share a bottle of the first one."

When Kate nodded, Henri said, "Excellent choice, ladies. That's the Signature Cuvée from Enchanted Hill Vineyard. I'll bring a bottle to you."

When he arrived with the bottle, Kate took a picture of the label with her phone. "In case we ever make it out to Oregon," she told her friend.

Twenty minutes later, the two were enjoying cedar-planked salmon, enhanced by the Pinot Noir. As Kate filled their glasses again, she saw the worry in Bonnie's eyes. She reached across the table and touched her friend's hand.

"Relax, sis. I'll be fine."

Bonnie put her fork down and pursed her lips. "I won't relax until you call me after your meeting. Promise?"

"I promise. It'll be the first thing I do."

When they had finished dinner, they took the elevator back down and walked to the front entrance. Bonnie hugged her and stepped out to Valet Parking for her car. Kate stayed inside as her appointment time approached, trying to calm her rapid heart rate by taking slow, deep breaths. She hadn't let Bonnie know how truly nervous she was. She looked at her watch and waited.

Two large men in black suits came toward her, eyes alert, faces expressionless. Both were clean-shaven and looked as though they might burst the seams in their coats if they flexed their muscles. One had a small tattoo of a dragon just behind his left ear, the one with the listening device. The other held his right hand across his chest like a giant parody of Napoleon. She imagined that would give him quicker access to the pistol in his shoulder holster, but what did she know? Bonnie had told her she was in over her head, and her friend was right. Way over her head.

"Do you guys work as linebackers for the NFL on your days off?" she quipped, using humor to try to calm her racing heart.

Neither looked amused. The one on her left tapped his earpiece. "She's here." He nodded, then spoke to Kate. "Please come with us. She'll see you now."

Kate followed them into the gambling hall, an arena-sized chamber where scalloped crown molding, Tuscan columns, and elaborate crystal chandeliers continued the façade of Old World elegance. As with other casinos, there were no windows to the outside world, no clocks, no way for gamblers to orient themselves back to reality and away from the illusion that they would soon be rich.

She walked past rows of men and women sitting in cushioned chairs, worshiping at the enormous curved screens of next-generation digital slot machines. The acrid smoke of cigarettes stung her eyes, and she marveled again at how Nevada allowed indoor smoking throughout its casinos. *Anything to keep the players paying*, she thought. And of course, servers with trays full of cocktails and other beverages made it unnecessary to leave for a drink.

She heard the chatter of a roulette ball finding a pocket on its wheel and the rattle of dice from a nearby craps table. Then a shout of victory arose from the card parlor, where steel-eyed men and women in white shirts and black bowties were dealing Texas Hold 'Em and Black Jack to the devout. Finally, they reached the private elevator in the back of the hall. One of the men pressed his key card against the lock, and the doors opened. He used his card again to access the floor numbers.

"So, she's on the twentieth floor?" Kate said. When neither answered, she looked from one face to the other, then sighed. "Well, okay then."

The doors opened onto a paneled hallway hung with copies of paintings by Giorgio Vasari, Masaccio, Fra Angelico, and Giotto. At the far end was a carved oak door with a gold door knob. One of her escorts knocked.

"Enter," came a stern voice from within.

He opened the door and led Kate inside.

"You may leave us," said the woman standing behind the desk to her charges. With her piercing blue eyes and regal bearing, Sofia Gemelli was a commanding presence in the room. Hers was the beauty of the mature Hepburn and Loren and Bacall. Short silver-gray hair framed an aristocratic face without blemish. A stunning black dress flattered her tall, statuesque figure.

As the men turned to leave, Kate said, "So long, guys. It's been great talking to you."

The man with the earpiece frowned and closed the door. Kate swung toward the woman and extended her hand as she approached the desk. "I'm Kate Temperance, Ms. Gemelli. Thank you for seeing me."

Gemelli shook Kate's hand. "My pleasure. I have a few minutes before I meet with the mayor. Please sit." She motioned to a leather chair in front of the desk.

As Kate took her seat, she pointed to the paintings on the left wall. "You have some lovely pieces, Ms. Gemelli. Not copies, I presume?"

"Masters from Florence, Ms. Temperance. I've spent some time in Italy. I'm particularly fond of that one." She gestured toward a small Raphael.

"And I see that framed law degree from Harvard behind you. 1973? You must have been very young."

"High school and college were boring. I took accelerated classes throughout so I didn't waste my time."

Kate nodded her head. "If I may ask, what kind of law did you practice?"

Gemelli sighed. "I'm afraid I never got the opportunity. It was shortly after getting my degree that my father, Giancarlo, was killed and I had to assume control of the Florentine. It was a very sad and difficult time."

"I'm sorry for your loss. I can't imagine what that must have been like for you."

"Indeed. All my dreams shattered." She pursed her lips. "I think I dealt with my grief by throwing myself into the work here, enlarging the hotel, renovating the restaurants." She made a dismissive motion with her left hand. "But that's old news. How can I help you today? I understand you're an investigative reporter, but I must confess that sounds suspiciously like *paparazzi* to me."

Kate was quick to correct her. "You misunderstand, Ms. Gemelli. I don't write for the tabloids. I'm a serious journalist. You may have seen some of my pieces in *ProPublica*. And I was the main source for a recent *60 Minutes* story and the PBS documentary, *The Troubled Company We Keep*."

"Ah, yes, that documentary was impressive. But again, what brings you to my hotel and casino?"

"Actually, I'm looking into the very events you just mentioned. To this day, your father's murder has never been solved. His only son—your twin brother—vanished at the same time." She raised her eyebrows. "And there were several other disappearances back then as well."

"My brother Bobby—how I loved him! We were inseparable as children, as twins often are. For the first decade after his disappearance, I spent thousands of dollars on private detectives trying to find him, fearing the worst but hoping for the best." A shadow crossed her face. "I finally had to accept that the same people who killed my father must have caught up with him as well. Letting him go was the hardest thing I've ever done." She began to tap her long red fingernails on the desk. "We both know that Las

Vegas was a very different place in the 50s and 60s and 70s. There was a—shall we say 'shady' element operative at the time? It was not something my father condoned. The police said a 'gangland rival'—such a terrible term—killed him. But my father wasn't a gangster." She took a breath and continued. "Since then, we have cleansed our town of the taint, the infection, brought on by foreign interests. We are legitimate and family-friendly. I'm afraid your investigation would only open old wounds, frighten away the visitors and vacationers we depend upon for our livelihood. It would put a black mark on a city that has resurrected itself from the allegations of criminality and corruption."

Kate persisted. "I could really use your insights, and I promise I would keep our interviews brief. After all, the Florentine is one of the oldest and largest hotels on the Strip, and you've been at the helm for fifty years. No one knows the history of Las Vegas better than you do."

Gemelli stood up. "I have certainly seen things in this past half-century, Ms. Temperance, but nothing that would aid in an investigation like the one you describe. There are no skeletons left in the closet, no stones left unturned. It would be an exercise in futility. Please stop and pursue a different project instead, one more worthy of your talents." She shook her head back and forth. "I'm afraid I can't help you."

Unwilling to be put off, Kate stood and challenged her. "Can't or won't, Ms. Gemelli?" She saw a spark of anger ignite in the woman's eyes and realized she had gone too far.

Gemelli drew herself to her full height. "You are here to besmirch my father's reputation," she said, "and my casino's!"

"Not at all, Ms. Gemelli. I only want the truth."

"The truth? What is the *truth*, Ms. Temperance?" Gemelli put both palms on the desk. "For the last time, I insist you cease this witch hunt immediately. No good can come from it, only harm to our city and to my hotel." She paused as if for effect, then continued. "If you choose not to, I will be forced to use every means at my disposal to stop you."

Kate's eyes went wide, and she felt her heart skip a beat. "Are you threatening me, Ms. Gemelli?"

"Not at all, my dear woman. I'm only expressing my determination to protect my family and my father's legacy. I will simply not support the efforts of someone who seeks to advance her career at the expense of other people's lives." She reached under the edge of her desk. When the two men responded to her signal and opened the door, she said, "We have finished our interview. Please escort Ms. Temperance out." To Kate, she added, "Let's not meet again, shall we?"

Kate dropped her card on the desk. "Please call me if you change your mind, Ms. Gemelli. But do understand. I'm not quitting my investigation. I'll find the answers, with or without your help." She turned to the men, who had assumed positions on either side of her. "Hi, guys. Nice to see you again. Shall we?" She motioned with her right arm and walked out of the office toward the elevator.

In moments, she was on the ground floor. "I can find my way to the door, gentlemen. But we do have to stop meeting like this. My husband might get upset."

The men did an about-face and walked away.

Once she had left the casino and retrieved her car, she braved the traffic again on the Strip. As she inched south on the boulevard, she looked to her left, where the largest spherical building in the world, *Sphere*, was under construction and on-target to become the premier entertainment venue on the planet. Near it was what, until eclipsed by the Ain Dubai last year, had been the largest Ferris wheel on earth, the High Roller. *Only in Las Vegas,* she thought with a smirk. *I'm driving home past Roman statuary, an Eiffel Tower, a Statue of Liberty, and even a pyramid. Dear God, what a world!* At long last, she reached the on-ramp to I-15 South and sped out of town as fast as she could. She needed the emptiness of the desert to clear her head. As she had promised, she called Bonnie.

"Hey, Sweet Pea. I'll be at the Starr Avenue exit in about twenty. What's happening in Henderson? What's shaking?"

"You know I hate it when you call me that. And what's shaking is this body of mine, worried sick about you. How'd your meeting with Cruella de Vil go?"

"Not as well as I'd wished. She wants me to shut down my investigation completely."

"Well, do it then. You've got lots of other stories to write. Leave that one alone."

"You know I can't do that, Bon." She watched the sage and sand flash by as she accelerated and cranked up the air conditioning.

"I know it's costing you," Bonnie continued. "From what you've told me, Simon is none too happy with your 'obsession'."

Kate clucked her tongue. "My husband thinks it takes too much of my attention away from him. I don't think he understands that I have as much of a right to a career as he does."

"Let it go, Kate. You're messing with dangerous people."

"But the lady doth protest too much, methinks."

"What?"

"Shakespeare. *Hamlet*? Anyway, Gemelli insisted—very strongly, I might add—that her father was not a gangster, that I would 'besmirch' his reputation if I pursue this story."

The phone was silent for a minute. "Sounds fishy, Kate. In today's world, that would only make the Florentine more attractive, give it a lot of free advertising. You know, 'Let's go see where the Godfather lived.' They'd be booked out months in advance."

"Exactly. That's what I'm saying. She's making too big a deal of this thing." She could hear Bonnie exhale a deep breath on the other end.

"So, what's your conclusion, sis? What's that steel trap mind of yours saying?"

"That there's a lot more skeletons in Sofia Gemelli's closet, or at the bottom of that damn lake."

Bonnie coughed. "You've lost me."

"You heard they found another body at Lake Mead, didn't you?"

"What?"

"As the water level drops in this drought, they're finding bodies along the shore that used to be underwater. I think four or five so far. My guess is at least some of them are related to the disappearances I'm investigating." She paused to emphasize the importance of her next revelation. "They know one of the bodies was definitely a homicide—it was in a barrel and had a bullet hole in its skull. The clothing and sneakers survived, so they said it happened around the mid-70s."

"Like I said, dangerous!"

"But I can't quit now."

"I wonder if that's what the guy in the barrel thought before they killed him."

3. That 70s Place

Kate answered the call from Bonnie and looked at the time stamp on her computer screen. 11:37 AM. "What's up, sis? I thought you'd be at the bank."

"I'm taking today off. What are you up to?"

"Research, of course. Looking into the history of the Florentine."

"I swear, you're like a dog with a bone. Speaking of which, are you hungry? I could throw a salad together here, or I could meet you at Vincent's and split a nice Cobb or Caesar with you?"

"I need a break. Let's do Vincent's. That bartender makes a killer Old Fashioned."

Her friend groaned. "It's a little early in the day for me, but I guess that must be the kind of day you've had so far. I'll see you there in twenty."

In fifteen minutes, Kate was pulling into the parking lot of Vincent's, a hole-in-the-wall bar and grill favored by residents and unknown to visitors. The ancient neon sign had several letters out, so it read "Vi ce_." The customers knew Hal, the owner and official bartender, was not about to fix it, but joked with him about it anyway.

"Sign's still out, Hal," Kate said as she entered and addressed the man behind the bar with her standard greeting.

"Oh, is it? Thanks for bringing it to my attention, Kate. I'll get right on it. Meanwhile, are you here to eat or drink?"

"Both. And Bonnie will be joining me soon."

"Okay, then. At the bar or in the back booth?"

Kate nodded her head in the direction of the booth in the far corner.

"I'll bring you your regular in a minute."

As Kate walked past the bar and toward her accustomed seat, she couldn't help but smile. She remembered the song from *The Rocky Horror Picture Show* and whispered a line from it. "Let's do the time warp again."

The walls were festooned with icons of movies and musical groups from the 70s. One wall featured posters of *The Godfather*, *Star Wars*, *Alien*, and *Close Encounters of the Third Kind,* among others. She was especially fond of the austere picture from *The Exorcist*, portraying the priest in his overcoat and hat looking up toward the light from Regan's bedroom window. She also liked the one from *Jaws*, with the enormous, toothy shark swimming up to gobble the hapless girl at the surface.

The wall opposite the bar was decked out with covers from the vinyl of the top musical groups of the era. The Eagles and Fleetwood Mac were her favorites, while Aerosmith, Foreigner, Led Zeppelin, and Journey were also on display.

When Hal brought her the whiskey, she said, "They don't make music and movies like they used to, Hal, do they?"

"I don't know, hon. How would you know? Were you even born when these were popular?"

"My grandmother. I listened to her tunes growing up and watched her movies on VHS." She sighed. "Never knew my mother or my father. Grandma would plunk me down with the cassette player or the videotape machine and go cry her eyes out in the bedroom."

"Must have been tough."

"Thanks, Hal. It was. Oh, here comes Bonnie." She waved toward her friend at the door.

Bonnie whisked into the bench seat across from her. "Hal, would you bring me a Diet Coke please? And your sign's still out."

"You got it, Bonnie. And thanks for letting me know. Back in a minute."

Bonnie addressed her friend. "So, bring me up to date on all your sleuthing around. And please tell me you're done with the Florentine."

"No can do. Can't tell you I'm done with the Florentine and my new friend there."

Bonnie winced. "She's not your friend, by a long shot. I swear, you're gonna be the death of me. There's so many better stories you could be covering. That case is ice cold."

Kate took a sip of her Old Fashioned as Hal arrived with Bonnie's soft drink and two menus. "I'll come back in a few to take your orders," he said, as he returned to the bar.

Kate looked across the table at her friend, who was shaking her head back and forth. "There are too many missing persons, including Bobby, the son of the original owner, Giancarlo Gemelli—Sofia Gemelli's twin brother, no less. He disappeared right around the time his father was murdered. How can I walk away from all that?"

"Easy," Bonnie countered. "You say goodbye and start another story. Hell, we're talking what? Fifty years ago?"

"There's no statute of limitations on murder, Sweet Pea."

Bonnie grimaced. "I swear to God. You call me that one more time today and…and…"

"And what?"

"And I'll call you 'Blondie' and make you karaoke with me tonight at Danny's." Her smile melted Kate.

"I love you, sis. And I promise I'll be careful."

Bonnie raised the soda to her lips and took a drink. "I just don't want those to be famous last words. I have a bad feeling about this."

"Now you're sounding like Han Solo."

"Who?"

"You know. *Star Wars*?"

"Oh, right. How could I forget? You're all things 70s." Bonnie swept her arm in a broad arc. "Including this restaurant."

Kate motioned for Hal to return, and he took their orders to split a Cobb salad, with blue cheese dressing on the side.

"Refills on the drinks?"

Kate looked at Bonnie, who nodded as she lifted her glass again. "Sure, Hal. Another round for both of us."

Bonnie sighed and tucked a lock of her red hair behind her ear. Kate could hear resignation in her voice.

"Okay, like I said, bring me up to date. What have you got so far?"

Kate withdrew her phone from her purse and began to swipe through her notes. "There was a spate of disappearances during the early to mid-70s. At least six that I know of. I got into the morgues of several newspapers—"

Bonnie almost spit her soda at her. "Morgues? What are you talking about?"

Kate chuckled. "Not the kind for dead bodies. Morgues are private rooms where newspapers keep their back issues. I've researched archives on line, too, but they don't always have all of the stuff there. A lot of times smaller papers can't afford to digitize everything."

Hal approached the table with the drinks and their salads and set them down. "Can I get you ladies anything else?"

Kate picked up her fork. "Maybe a couple of waters?"

Bonnie nodded in agreement, and Hal turned to fetch a water pitcher and two glasses. "So, go on."

Kate finished her mouthful of salad. "Like I said, I've got the names of six so far. All guys. All involved in the casinos that were growing like mushrooms back then."

"But I thought the organized crime stuff was mostly before that—the 40s, 50s, and 60s."

"Sure. Once Howard Hughes bought the Desert Inn in 1966, the big corporations moved in and more or less shoved the mob out. But the dark side was still there, lurking in the shadows." She took another sip of her Old Fashioned and raised the glass to Hal at the bar in thanks for his bartending talent. He came over with their water.

"My guess," Kate continued, "is that the guy who was murdered, Giancarlo—Johnny— Gemelli, was trying to consolidate things, strengthen his hold on several of the casinos while he still had the muscle." She snorted and shook her head. "Hell, it could have been the corporate suits that whacked him."

Bonnie tapped her cheek with her hand. "Now you sound like the movies I watch late at night. Whacked him?"

They both began to laugh. "It's me being all tough and authentic." Kate grinned around another forkful of salad.

"But why, Kate? Why a cold case that isn't nearly as important as some of your other work?"

Kate closed her eyes and took a deep breath. She changed the subject. "How's your job going? I've been doing most of the talking."

"Well, I passed my real estate exam two weeks ago, and I've got my license. I've put in my notice at the bank. By the end of the month, Dan and I will be our own little business—Ballantine Realtors."

"That's got a nice ring to it."

"Yeah, we think so. He'll mentor me till I know my way around the block. Then the sky's the limit!" She finished the last of her Coke.

"How about the kids?"

"Jeremy is kicking butt in varsity football. He's a senior at Rosemount High. Susie is a freshman at Brown and doing okay as far as I know."

Kate put down her fork and dabbed her lips with a napkin. "Brown? All the way out in Rhode Island?"

"Yeah. I think she had to get away from nosy, prying Mommy. I miss her, but not our knock-down-drag-'em-out-fights. That girl has a temper, all right."

When Hal brought the checks, Kate insisted on treating her friend. "You get it next time. I'm going home to do more research."

She got to her car, what she called her 'entry-level Mercedes' with ten years and eighty thousand miles on it, and cursed. "Damn it! Hey, Bonnie, come over here and look at this. Somebody just keyed my car."

Bonnie approached and saw the deep scratch, like a white scar, along the whole length of the driver's side. "I didn't see anybody out here while we were eating."

"Neither did I. And who does this crap anymore? Shit!" She slapped her hand on the roof of the car. "And what the hell is this?" She stooped and picked up a matchbook from the pavement. The cover was emblazoned with a miniature image of Michelangelo's David.

Bonnie pursed her lips. "That's the logo of the Florentine. Could be a coincidence, but if it was me, I'd take it as a sign."

"A sign of what?"

"That nothing good comes from visits to that effin' place. Stay away."

4. Picture Perfect

Kate was sitting in her favorite coffee shop, The Real Bean, working on her third cup while continuing her internet research on her laptop. She had been here four afternoons this week after her lunch with Bonnie. It was a small shop, locally-owned, that ordered several varieties of green coffee beans from an outlet in Reno, roasted them, and ground its own proprietary blend. The walls were decorated with calendars from the 60s and 70s and 80s, a kind of silent protest against what it called the "corporate coffee" of the new millennium. REAL COFFEE FOR REAL PEOPLE was the slogan over the door. Kate loved it.

The young barista behind the counter was wiping down one of the machines as the last customer picked up her cappuccino and left the store. "You okay, Kate? Want me to top you off, give you a warmer-upper?"

"That'd be great, Jeannie. I get so wrapped up in this stuff, I drink half a cup, and the rest gets cold."

The server walked to the table. "Here you go. Nothing but the best for my favorite journalist." She filled the cup just short of the brim. "Mind if I ask what you're working on?"

"Researching the casinos for my next piece," Kate said, as she took a tentative sip of the steaming liquid.

"Can't wait to read it. Where will you publish it?"

"I'm actually hoping to get a TV gig for it."

"Ooh! Super! Well, don't let me distract you." She walked back to the counter to resume her cleaning activities.

Kate returned her attention to the screen and took another sip of coffee. As she found more bits of information about the six disappearances, she put them in a file she had labeled "Vanished." Bobby Gemelli was at the top of the list, followed by Tom Romano, part of the old man's team. Then there was Harry Costello, former owner of the Cactus Club. Francis Gianfrido had been a bookkeeper for Sun and Sand Casino, with an old warrant out for his arrest. The last two, Mickey Marchese and Sal Carminucci, had been accountants for the now-defunct Paradiso Hotel.

She looked at the list and let her mind wander. Were these people somehow related, other than for disappearing between 1968 and 1973? Was there another connection? And who had killed Giancarlo Gemelli?

Kate stood and stretched and cracked her knuckles. The fatigue of staring too long at a computer screen was beginning to settle in. "Jeannie, I think I have to head home. I'm wiped out." She left several dollars on the table for a tip and packed away her laptop and cords. As she turned toward the door, the barista called to her.

"I'm not working tomorrow, so I won't see you if you come in."

Kate waved in response and walked to her car. She was home in five minutes. She parked on the right side of the driveway, never bothering to open the garage door. Her husband Simon's Audi was only a few months old, so he had preferential parking rights inside. If Kate could just find the time and the energy to clean up her side of the garage, she might be able to park in there as well, but file cabinets, plastic bins full of paper, and countless books—the flotsam and jetsam of her writing career—were a daunting log jam preventing her access. She often considered renting a storage unit, and then promptly forgot about it when the phone rang or her computer beckoned. It never stayed on her radar long enough for her to do anything about it.

Once inside the house, she went to the bedroom to get into her cozies and a comfortable pair of slippers. Then she went to the liquor cabinet and withdrew the bottle of bourbon she had purchased yesterday. After pouring a shot into a Glencairn glass, she swirled the amber liquid, sniffed its aromas, and took a small sip. She smiled as flavors of toffee, sweet caramel, and vanilla greeted her tongue. Next, she added a small chip of ice to it in order to see what changes that might bring about in nose and palate. Pleased with herself, she poured a little more into the glass and walked into the kitchen.

The clock on the wall assured her that it would be at least an hour before Simon got home, plenty of time to bake two Yukon Gold potatoes and prepare asparagus for steaming later. Simon could grill the two small filet mignons outside on the patio, and, combined with the special Cabernet Sauvignon the wine steward at the store had recommended to her, they would have a lovely, if simple, dinner.

She furrowed her brow and hoped her attempt at a "make-up dinner" would ease the tension that had been brewing between her and Simon over the past few months. He was having a hard time with her being so busy with her career.

While the potatoes were roasting in the oven, she retired to the sofa in the living room, tucked her legs underneath her, and began scrolling through the evening news on her phone. She jumped when Simon walked in and slammed the door.

She stood up and turned to face him. "You scared the crap out of me! And you're early. What's your problem?"

"I thought I might catch you *in flagrante delicto*," he snarled.

"Quit the lawyer language. What are you talking about?"

He stormed into the living room and slapped a large manila envelope on the coffee table. His brown hair was disheveled, his blue tie loosened, and the top button of his white shirt undone. His jaw clenched as his eyes bored into her like lasers. Even from this distance, she could smell the alcohol on his breath.

"What the hell is this?" she said, opening the envelope. Four eight-by-ten photos slid out onto the coffee table.

"You tell me. Somebody left it at my office this afternoon. The note says, 'She's fucking my husband, and I thought you should know.'"

Her eyes went round and her jaw dropped. "That's not me, Simon."

"Oh? I recognize the face. The tits look like yours. And that sure as hell looks like Bonnie's husband Dan that you're riding."

Kate held her hand over her mouth and shook her head. "It's a fake. I swear. I'd never cheat on you. You know me better than that."

"I know you spend every spare minute obsessing about that damn casino. You haven't written another piece in how long? You're gone all hours. We haven't made love in weeks. Am I not good enough for you anymore? Or do you just need me for a paycheck while you whore around with Dan?"

"Stop it!" she shrieked. "I said that's not me. And it's not Dan. This is bullshit!"

"Sure." His lips drew up into a sneer. "I'm eating out tonight. Don't wait up for me. We can fight tomorrow, after I pay Dan a little visit tonight." With that, he spun around and strode out the door.

Kate collapsed onto the sofa, her whole body shaking as though caught in a cold wind. She swatted at the tears in her eyes. Although she knew that she had been inattentive the past few months and that Simon had been out of sorts with her for a while, she had never seen him angrier. It frightened her.

The photographs lay on the table, accusing her of a sin she did not commit. "Oh, Simon," she wailed. "I would never ever hurt you like this. Why can't you believe me?" She downed the rest of her bourbon in one swallow. She had to call Bonnie right away.

When her friend answered, the words rushed from Kate's mouth in a torrent.

"Honey, slow down," Bonnie cautioned. "I can't understand you. What happened?"

"Simon just walked out. Somebody gave him fake pictures of me fucking Dan."

Bonnie yelled so loudly that Kate pulled the phone away from her ear. "What the hell did you say?"

"I said somebody gave Simon fake pictures of me and Dan. *Fake pictures!* I'm not having an affair with your husband. Please believe me. I would never do that to you. But you'd better warn Dan. Simon said he was going to see him, and he's madder than hell."

"Oh, my God! My God! I gotta call him! I'll talk to you later." She ended the call.

Kate put her phone down on the sofa beside her, still trembling with the storm of emotions flooding her body. Who would do such a thing to her? Whose toes had she stepped on? She poured herself more whiskey and reviewed the stories she'd written over the past year. Judge Bandon and his tawdry adulteries and briberies. Diana Cambridge and her embezzlement of millions from tech giant Ladder. Clipper Ship's CEO Kevin Carlyle and his Medicare scam. No, those were old news, doing time in their respective penitentiaries. There was only one possibility—Sofia Gemelli. *Did you have some goon of yours do this? Were Bonnie and Dan just collateral damage?* She prayed that Bonnie was able to reach her husband before Simon did.

She went back to the living room to gather her thoughts. Was this an opening salvo in a campaign to make her back down and give up the story? She pounded her fist on the coffee table as her anguish morphed into rage. *That's not gonna work with me, bitch!*

She pulled the phone from her purse and tapped the number for Billie Newington, producer for KLKE-TV.

"You've reached Billie," came the recorded voice. "I'm away from my desk doing something that must be very important. Leave me a message, and I'll get back to you when I can."

"Hey, Billie, this is Kate. I've got a story idea I want to pitch to you—something for your true crime series. I should have it done in a couple months. Right now, I want to rattle some cages, and I'm wondering if we might make a trailer for it. You know, get the good guys salivating for a fun story and the bad guys shaking in their boots? Maybe get a little advance for me? What do you say?"

Ten minutes later, her phone buzzed. She touched her screen.

"Well, you've got my attention," said Billie. "You're the journalist who seems to know where all the bodies are buried. So, tell me about your project."

"It's about bodies, all right. Specifically, about a bunch that disappeared in the 70s. And the murder of Giancarlo Gemelli."

"Who?"

"The original owner of the Florentine. Assassinated. Nobody ever arrested for it."

"All cold case stuff?"

"I think there's some connection to the Florentine today." She heard Billie hesitate.

"Are we talking about Sofia Gemelli?"

"None other." Again, there was silence on the other end.

"Look, Kate, you know I love your work, but you heard we got sued last year? A reporter for our crime show got a little overzealous. Didn't have all her ducks in a row. We got slammed with a defamation lawsuit that cost us a mil."

"I hear you, Billie. My research isn't finished yet, but I would never compromise you or your company. I just need to shake things up. I won't name names or anything." She heard a deep exhalation on the other end."

"You'd give us exclusive rights to the story?"

"Absolutely."

"Okay. It's against my better judgment, but c'mon down to the station Friday morning, and we'll see if we can work something out."

"Thanks, Billie. I owe you."

"Indeed, you do, sister."

When she ended the call, her phone alerted her to a breaking news story. She opened it and read the headline: MORE HUMAN REMAINS FOUND AT LAKE MEAD.

"As the drought continues and the waters recede to their lowest levels ever, Lake Mead is giving up its dead. Yesterday two partial skeletons, both entangled in a heavy chain, were found along a shoreline that had formerly been under one hundred feet of water. As with the previous remains found, these will be subjected to an in-depth medical assessment, including autopsy, radiographs, and consultation with forensic dentists and anthropologists. Examiners will try to collect DNA as well. Authorities say that although it is often impossible to determine cause of death with only skeletal remains, they are labelling this a homicide since one end of the chain was clamped to a leg bone and the other to a cinderblock."

5. A Shard of Sky

When she got up the next morning, Kate found Simon asleep on the couch in the living room. She didn't bother to rouse him. Coffee first. As she suspected it might, the whine of the machine grinding the coffee beans awakened him. He staggered into the kitchen and glowered at her.

As the machine dripped coffee into her cup, Kate faced him. "Did you go see Dan last night?" She did her best to keep her voice calm.

He shook his head. "No, he called me. Said Bonnie warned him I might be coming. Swore on the Bible that he wasn't having an affair with you."

"Do you believe him?" Her voice was a whispered plea. "Do you believe me?"

"What I believe is how unhappy I am. Last night I was so pissed off I wanted to hit you." He took a deep breath and shook his head. "That's not who I am. I think I need some time away from you. Richard and I talked last night, and he's gonna let me stay with him for a while. Just till I figure things out."

"What things?" Kate immediately regretted asking the question.

He glared at her and clenched his jaw. "Whether I want to stay married to you or not."

She felt her heart sink. "You know those pictures aren't real. Is there anything I can say or do to make things better between us?"

He sighed. "We're past that, Kate. Seeing those pictures made me finally own up to how miserable I've been for a long time. I've been sweeping it under the rug, but it's like my shadow, always there when I stand in the light. Dogging my heels."

Tears began to course down her face. "Can I make it up to you somehow?"

A mirthless chuckle escaped his lips. "Can you even remember the last time we took a vacation together? The last time we snuggled on the couch watching a rom com? The last time we made love? We've been living separate lives already."

The truth of it was a knife to her heart. Her shoulders slumped. She picked up her coffee mug and left the kitchen.

Simon called to her as she was leaving. "And you know you drink too much, don't you?" When Kate didn't respond, he said, "I'll take a shower and pack some things. Probably call you in a couple of days."

A moment later, Kate was in her office. She set her coffee down on the corner of her desk and tried to catch her breath. After a few minutes, her heart rate slowed to a normal rhythm. Her three laptops were arranged in an arc around her workspace, each beckoning her to awaken them and lose herself in researching dead bodies, driving away any thought of the cliff that yawned before her marriage.

She swiveled her chair around to examine the office she inhabited. One picture graced the nearest wall, an old framed photograph of the Strip after dark, in all its gaudy splendor. It had been her grandmother's only decoration in the nursing home where she had lived her final days.

The bookshelves held her eclectic collection of literary classics. She smiled in spite of herself as she recalled that she re-read *A Christmas Carol* every December to get herself into a holiday mood. On that same shelf was *Moby Dick*, which she had read after a visit to the New Bedford Whaling Museum in Massachusetts five years ago. There was the shelf for what she called her "Russian period," displaying *The Brothers Karamazov*, *The Possessed*, *Anna Karenina*, and *War and Peace*. Her American shelf was home to *The Sun Also Rises*, *The Great Gatsby*, *The Scarlet Letter*, *East of Eden*, and many others. At some level, she knew her library was a fortress, a refuge from the private pain that had haunted her for as long as she could remember. Reading and writing were her anodynes.

Before long, she was imagining what she might include in her "preview of coming attractions" for Billie. Her prime purpose, of course, was to vent her rage at Gemelli, demonstrating that she would not be intimidated by Cruella de Vil's *mafioso* posturing. But it would not hurt to ignite some buzz for her piece and maybe glean an advance for herself. After all, she would have to convince the "powers that be" at KLKE that her story had legs, that it could generate income for the network and would be worth the investment it would take to produce. Studio execs were sometimes royal pains with their "bottom line" approach to everything. Show me the money, indeed. She remembered Billie's comment about her, that she was "the journalist who seems to know where all the bodies are buried." *But who are the bodies?* That was the real question.

Her reverie was interrupted by the sound of the front door opening and closing. Simon had left without saying goodbye. Tears flowed again. She stood and walked to the bedroom as if in a trance. Once there, she stripped off her pajamas and stepped into the shower, allowing her tears to mingle with the spray.

She lost track of how long she stood there. Finally, the water cooling seemed to rouse her. She turned off the shower, dried herself with a towel, and dressed in her favorite jeans and blouse.

"No time for self-pity," she chided herself. She decided to drive to Lake Mead for inspiration. She remembered flying over the lake years ago, struck by its sapphire iridescence, as though a shard of sky had fallen to earth and lay among the rock and sand of the treeless desert. That had begun her love affair with the largest reservoir in the country. Now the jewel was in jeopardy, its waters receding due to the relentless drought and leaving behind a giant white "bathtub ring" from the calcium carbonate in the Colorado River.

Her old Mercedes knew its way to Boulder City. Fifteen minutes later, Kate was driving under the arch into Historic Downtown and looking for the homey bronze sculptures that added to its "small-town charm." They reminded her of Norman Rockwell paintings. She especially liked the sculpture of the little girl holding tightly onto her brother's back as he pedaled his tricycle. Her other favorite was the statue of the woman holding her hat in an afternoon breeze. They never failed to relieve her tension and lighten her mood.

From there, she continued on to Hemenway Park to get her first glimpse of the water and possibly see a Desert Bighorn Sheep, down from the hills to munch clover and escape the sun's heat in the shade of one of the park's few trees. Her hope was rewarded when two sheep bounded away as she pulled into the small parking lot. She got out of the car and walked across the grass toward the covered tables. Beyond the tables was a trailhead that would bring her closer to the water, but she decided to return to her car and drive to the Lake Mead Overlook instead. She needed to see again the place where the first body, the one in the barrel, had been discovered.

The closer she got to the lake, the rougher the volcanic terrain became. She smiled when she recalled that she had told Bonnie once that it reminded her of large-curd cottage cheese gone bad—lumpy gray and brown.

Soon she was at the overlook, along with half a dozen other cars and two tour vans. As she stepped out of the car, the wind slapped her in the face and blew her hair into wild disarray. Thankfully, it tempered the heat of the blistering sun above. As she approached the stone wall bordering the overlook, she saw tourists posing for pictures with Boulder Basin behind them—the Boulder Beach Trailer Village and the Hemenway boat launch at the marina clearly visible. *Do any of you know you're being photographed with a crime scene for the backdrop?* she wondered. *That behind you they found a skeleton with a bullet hole in its skull?* She laughed in spite of herself.

She stood at the wall for several minutes, gazing into the basin. Where once had been azure depths were now sand bars and cracked mud drying in the sun. "You're giving up your ghosts one by one, aren't you?" she whispered to the lake. And an idea struck her. She leaped into her car and headed back toward Boulder City. As she drove, more images came to her in a flurry. Once back in town, she pulled the car to the side of the street and fetched her phone from her purse to record some notes. Her heart quickened. She forgot about her disintegrating marriage, her scratched car, the thinly veiled threats from Gemelli, and focused only on her creative process and *the story*. It was her counterfeit for joy, the closest she ever got to happiness.

She left the curb to head back to Henderson, her mind awhirl with new ideas. Once home she would begin the "simmering," during which she would write down what thoughts came to her and let them "cook slowly," returning periodically to "stir the pot," making additions and corrections, adding "seasoning." By the time of her meeting with Billie on Friday, she would have something worthwhile to present to her.

She was so engaged in plotting her project that it took several moments to register that there was a police car following her with its lights flashing. As she pulled her Mercedes to the curb, her elation quickly morphed to dread. Had she been so distracted she drove through a stop sign or traffic light? Was she speeding? She watched in her rearview mirror as the police officer parked behind her, got out, and strode toward her vehicle. The officer was a tall woman wearing dark sunglasses that accented the scowl on her face. Kate rolled down her window.

"License and registration," the officer growled. "And proof of insurance."

"Yes, Ma'am." Kate handed her the documents. She wanted to ask what she had done wrong but thought better of it. There was no friendliness or compassion on the other woman's face.

"Put your hands back on the steering wheel where I can see them."

Kate's fear grew. Why was the officer snarling at her like that?

"Do you know how fast you were driving?"

She couldn't see the eyes behind the sunglasses, but the frown on the officer's face was chilling. "I'm sure I was driving within the speed limit."

"That's not what my radar indicated." The officer began making checkmarks on a form. "Speeding through a work zone carries a fine of $410. But we can't stop there."

Kate felt her heart pounding and her breath come in short gasps. What was happening?

"I've been following you ever since you parked illegally back there."

"Illegally?"

"Too far from the curb. That's a fine of $35. But we can't stop there."

Kate's throat was so dry she could barely swallow. "Please, Officer. I had no idea."

"Ignorance is no excuse for breaking the law. Speaking of which, your left brake light is out." Her lips curled into a humorless smile. "I'll give you a pass on that until you can get it fixed."

"Thank you, but—"

"But we can't stop there. Your unlawful U-turn is going to cost you $230."

"Now just a minute!" Kate could feel her fear transforming into anger. "I didn't—"

"All right, get out of the car!"

"Wait a minute! Hold on!" Her world was spinning out of control.

The officer shouted, "Out of the car! Now! If I have to say it again, I'll charge you with disobeying a traffic officer and slap you with another $305 fine."

Kate leaped from the car. "Please, please! I'm obeying! I'll do whatever you say. I just didn't expect to be getting $1000 in traffic fines on my way home."

The officer's expression might have been carved from stone. "Stop talking and stand against the car." She returned to her cruiser and marched back with a small device in her hand. "This is a breathalyzer. You can refuse to take the test, but if you do, I'll take your driver's license."

Kate's stomach turned and her knees wobbled. It felt as though she had been swept into an alternate reality where nothing made any sense. Could she really lose her license like that? She didn't know, but she hadn't been drinking, so why refuse? She couldn't hide the tremor in her voice. "Of course, I'll take a breathalyzer test."

It was over shortly. The officer tore the ticket from her pad and handed it to Kate, along with the documents she had confiscated.

"Have a good day, Ms. Temperance." She strode back to her car and appeared to be busy entering information into her computer.

Kate stood there, stunned, every muscle in her body shaking uncontrollably. She leaned against the Mercedes for balance. She struggled to catch her breath. When her stomach flip-flopped again, she ran around the car and vomited into the gutter. As she wiped her mouth with the back of her hand and turned to get into her car, the police officer pulled alongside her vehicle and rolled down her window.

"Ms. Temperance?" she said.

"Yes, Officer?"

"Ms. Gemelli sends her regards."

6. Visiting Cruella

She wasn't sure how she got home. Her mind was clouded by a storm of rage and terror. What had she gotten herself into? Cruella de Vil's claws reached from the casino to the internet and the police department. This was harassment, pure and simple, but there was an edge to it that frightened her. How far was Gemelli willing to go to make Kate drop her investigation? And why?

As she pulled into the driveway, her eyes misted over again. *Not much point to parking outside if Simon isn't here*, she thought. She tapped the garage door opener and drove inside. A part of her wanted to pour a tumbler full of whiskey and drink herself into a stupor, but reason prevailed, and she went into her office to log on to her array of computers. She would lose herself in work rather than alcohol. Time for bourbon later.

She listened to the notes she had recorded on her phone and began to create a scenario for previewing her story that would engage audiences and producers alike. She let Lake Mead inspire her, let its mystery percolate and its ghosts arise, then quickly entered whatever occurred to her. Editing would come later.

She smiled as the title popped into her mind, springing from the fertile ground of murder and the missing. "This is going to work," she told herself aloud. Like the breathless growth of a newly fertilized egg, the concepts expanded to fill her consciousness and banish her pain. She typed furiously, trapping all the ideas on her screen and then printing them out for review.

An hour later, she stood and stretched. She would let the ideas simmer overnight and reread them over morning coffee. Now she would get into her cozies and pour herself that drink. She had no desire to cook a meal, so she phoned in an order for a home-delivery pizza, knowing that whatever she didn't eat tonight would be tomorrow's breakfast.

As she awaited her pizza and sipped her bourbon, the alcohol enhanced her anger. Should she confront Gemelli? Wouldn't Cruella de Vil simply deny Kate's allegations? Cruella de Vil. Bonnie had coined the term and it fit perfectly. Despite the dread that had taken up permanent residence in her heart, the name brought a smile to her lips. Her old defense mechanism—using humor to fight fear. She hoped it would keep working.

Another thought occurred to her. *I wonder what Simon is doing?* Her smile was gone in an instant. *Is our marriage really over?* Despite her determination not to cry, several tears coursed down her cheeks before she could stop them. "Damn it!" she said aloud. The doorbell announcing the arrival of the pizza rescued her.

"That was fast. Thank you so much." She handed the young man a tip while she took the box from him.

"Enjoy!" he said as he ran back to his car.

Kate locked the door and returned to the kitchen with her prize. Lifting a cheese-engulfed piece from the box, she proclaimed, "I'm coming for you, Cruella."

#

The next day, she showered and dressed early, after deciding against cold pizza. Instead, she would treat herself to breakfast at Dido's, another of her favorite coffee shops. When she opened the door to the garage, a blast of hot air from the day before buffeted her. *Nevada*, she thought. *I wish my story took me somewhere cooler.* She walked to the driver side of the car, running her finger along the deep scratch. The keyed car, the photographs, the traffic stop—Gemelli had it in for her all right. But why?

She was at Dido's in minutes. The shop's décor was art deco, with glass lamps on all the tables and posters of stylized paintings from the early 1900s adorning the walls.

"Hi, Kate. Nice to see you again." Dido looked to be in her mid-30s, with an impish grin to accompany her sometimes caustic wit. Her short black hair framed a face whose only wrinkles, Kate knew, were born of frequent laughter.

"Good morning, Dido. I'd like a 'Brooklyn' on a sesame seed bagel and a twelve-ounce coffee, no room for cream."

The barista rang up the charges on Kate's card and handed it back to her. "I'll have your order out in just a bit. You can take your coffee now."

Kate sat in a brightly upholstered chair by the front window, seeing traffic go by but lost in thought. She liked the hot astringency of the coffee on her tongue as she took a sip. She was hungry when her breakfast arrived.

"Here you go, darlin'. Lox and cream cheese on a toasted bagel, with thinly sliced red onion and capers. *Buon appetito!*"

It was perfect, a symphony of flavors and textures and aromas that hit all the right notes. Kate regarded it as food for the soul as well as the body. As she finished the last delicious mouthful, she was more determined than ever to confront Gemelli.

She waved goodbye to Dido and returned to her car. As she drove north to Vegas and the Florentine, she wondered if Gemelli would see her without an appointment. She also wondered what exactly she hoped to accomplish.

Forty minutes later, after slogging along the Strip for what seemed an eternity, she dropped her car at Valet Parking and entered the ornate casino. The lavish furnishings no longer charmed her. They were the web of a deadly spider, one bent on making her one of its meals.

With the clear purpose in mind of getting Gemelli's attention, she walked briskly past the slot machines and poker tables to the rear elevator. As she had expected, the two men in black who had accompanied her on her previous visit accosted her again.

"You can't be back here," the taller one said. "This is a private elevator."

"I know. Would you please tell Ms. Gemelli that Kate Temperance would like to see her again?"

"She's busy."

"I'm sure she is. Harassing other journalists, no doubt. Please give her my message."

The man turned and walked a few paces away while his partner stood facing Kate without saying a word.

"I like your suit," she said. "Looks just like the one you were wearing the other day. Is it like a uniform?"

The man's lips curled into a frown and his brows knit. "Don't talk."

"Wow. You can even make simple words like 'Don't talk' sound terrifying. I'll bet you had to practice that in front of a mirror." When the man's face grew even darker, Kate decided not to push her luck. She waited in silence until the other man returned.

"Ms. Gemelli said she'll see you for one minute only. Come with us." He applied his key card to the elevator pad, and the two men escorted her inside when the doors opened. In moments, they were at the penthouse office of Sofia Gemelli.

The silver-haired lady looked up from behind her desk. "Please wait outside the door, gentlemen. This won't take long." To Kate, she said, "I have no interest in meeting with you, Ms. Temperance. I told you that last time. I'm extending this courtesy to you today, but I will not do it again."

On the way up in the elevator, Kate had decided she would jump in with both feet. "What are you afraid of, Ms. Gemelli? What don't you want me to find out?"

The other woman stood and pounded her fist on the desk. "That's preposterous! I'm afraid of nothing! Now get out and don't come back!"

The two men hurried in. Each grabbed one of Kate's elbows and pivoted her toward the door.

Kate shouted over her shoulder. "Vandalizing my car! Sending fake photographs to my husband! Using the police to harass me! Stop it! Stop all of it, you witch!"

"That's enough." Gemelli's calm voice barely hid the menace just under the surface. "You'll be hearing from my lawyer shortly. Consider a 'No Trespass' order to be in effect immediately. If you venture onto these premises again, I will have you arrested."

The men took her back downstairs and out the main entrance. Kate couldn't resist taunting them again.

"Can I give you guys a breath mint before I leave?" She was rewarded by seeing both of them clench their fists. "No, huh? Oh, well, maybe next time."

Once back in her car, it was ten minutes before her pounding heart resumed a normal rhythm. "Girl, what are you doing?" she said aloud. "That was a little like playing Russian roulette." She took a deep breath. "I'm just glad the hammer fell on an empty chamber. I may not be so lucky next time."

7. All the Bodies Do

She was early for her appointment with Billie. The network's local headquarters, at the northern end of the Strip, occupied the top three floors of the thirty-story San Franciscan Hotel. The lobby contained a potpourri of modern art, with large abstract paintings in strident colors on the neutral walls and oddly shaped metal sculptures punctuating the open spaces. Kate sat in a chair that had been designed for looks but not for comfort. She scrolled through news headlines while she awaited her friend.

"Kate!" Billie gushed as she strode across the room. "I've missed you!" Her brown hair was styled in a flawless pixie cut that lent authority to her intense dark eyes and prominent jawline. "You haven't gifted me with a story in far too long, but you'll have to do a better job of pitching this Florentine idea." She embraced Kate, then stood back and grasped her by the shoulders. "Let's get coffee and go back to my office."

In moments they were ensconced in Billie's suite, luxuriating in overstuffed chairs, coffee mugs in hand.

"Ever get tired of this view?" Kate asked, pointing to the glass that looked south over Las Vegas Boulevard in all its over-the-top splendor.

"Not tired of it, exactly, but 'used to it.' Know what I mean? I can spend whole days and not notice it—not see it. Then, one day I walk in and get blown away, especially if it's dusk, with all the lights like galaxies of stars. I guess there's part of me that's still that wide-eyed little girl from Kansas."

The two were silent for a minute, sipping coffee. Billie filled the void. "So, all right. Pitch me."

Kate cleared her throat. "I have to be honest with you, Billie. Sofia Gemelli is gunning for me."

"Ouch! You're not here to spread some of her bullets around, I hope. Because I'm definitely not interested in that."

"No, no, not like that. Let me start again." She fortified herself with another sip of coffee. "I'm investigating disappearances here in town back in the 70s. The last one, Bobby Gemelli, happened on the day his father was gunned down in what they think was a mob hit."

"Whoa, slow down, Kate. I thought Vegas was pretty much cleaned up by then."

"It was. This was like the gangs' last gasp. Six disappearances in two or three years. No bodies ever found. Until now."

Billie sat up in her chair. "Now?"

"You've heard about the bodies they're finding as Lake Mead dries up? They know the one in the barrel was a homicide. Had a bullet hole in its skull."

"Yeah, but didn't they ID another as a swimmer who drowned twenty years ago?"

"Uh huh. I'm not saying all the bodies wound up in the lake, but I'll bet a bunch did. Just the other day, they found two skeletons tangled up in an anchor chain with a cinder block attached to one of them."

Billie was shaking her head. "Where are you going with this? And how does it involve Gemelli?"

"Gemelli took over the Florentine after her father's death. I went to talk to her about it." Kate's lips curled into a frown and she exhaled a deep breath. "She reamed me a new one just for asking."

"Doesn't want the past dug up?"

"And how! Stuff has been happening. First, my car got keyed. Then somebody sends my husband fake pictures of me screwing somebody else. Most recently, I got pulled over and royally harassed by a police officer who said Gemelli sent me her regards."

Billie stood up and walked to the glass. "I'm asking you again. Where are you going with this?"

Kate pulled her phone from her purse and opened the notes she had written. "Gemelli is hiding something. She's way too set on intimidating me to drop the story. And I won't be scared off."

"You mean 'freedom of the press' and all that bullshit?"

"Something like that." Kate lowered her gaze.

Billie turned to her. "What aren't you telling me? It sounds personal. What's your stake in this?"

Kate was quiet for a minute, then pivoted. "I just want to get to the bottom of it. I'm guessing the medical examination of those remains from the lake will come up with some of those missing persons. And maybe what Gemelli has to do with them. She would have been around twenty or so at the time they vanished."

Billie looked thoughtful. "And the purpose of this 'preview' we do for your story?"

"To shake things up. Maybe get Gemelli to tip her hand." Then she smiled. "And, of course, to make you and me a lot of money with a show people will be dying to see."

Billie grimaced. "Poor choice of words, Kate." She continued, "So walk me through it."

Kate got up from her chair and swept her left arm in a broad arc. "Okay. In the background, we hear 'Gimme Shelter' by the Rolling Stones. The camera walks down to the lake at Boulder Basin, pans around, shows the marina and the bathtub ring on the hills, then focuses on the drying lake bed. Maybe there's a boat, encrusted with rust and dried algae, sunk twenty years ago, a derelict on the cracked mud. Maybe an old junk car, windows gone, rotting away. The voice over is this guy who sounds like Darth Vader, explaining how Lake Mead is at its lowest level ever because of the drought. Then he says something like, 'It's not just sunken boats and old trash that are being found.' The camera zooms in to the dilapidated barrel they found by the Hemenway boat launch, the one the body was in. 'This was the final resting place of a man murdered fifty years ago. His body, once under one hundred feet of water, has surfaced.'"

Kate could see she was weaving a spell, drawing Billie in. Her friend was staring at her, leaning forward. Kate read notes from her phone. "All the bodies do. They appear, they're discovered, they give up the ghosts they've been hiding for decades. Family secrets long buried—the affairs and adulteries, the lies and the scandals, even the murders—are one day revealed. No sins can remain covered forever. They all rise to the surface. All the bodies do."

Billie exhaled noisily. "That's quite a hook. I like it. And I think I can sell it to the execs. Maybe get you a nice advance."

Kate rushed to her and embraced her warmly. "Thank you, Billie. You won't regret it. We'll snag you an Emmy."

"An Emmy, huh? Well, I gotta love your confidence." Her eyes took on a far-away look. "Mm hm. I've got a place for that little statue right there on my desk. Just the decoration it needs." She gazed back at her friend. "Now get out there and finish your story!"

"Aye, aye, cap'n." She turned toward the door. "I'll show myself out."

"I'll be in touch soon, Kate. I've got a meeting with the bosses this afternoon. Fingers crossed."

"You bet."

8. Spoofed

Still glowing with the success of her pitch to Billie, Kate rushed home to continue her research. *I still know how to tell a story*, she thought. *How to hook people into wanting more*. She felt rejuvenated, pushing the troubles of the last few days to the back of her mind as she devoted herself again to her project. *I'm a journalist, an investigative reporter, and a good one. And I'm sitting on a prize-winning story.*

She had her computers up and running in no time. As she had been doing, she called up the names of the six missing men and went burrowing through internet archives, digging up any facts she could about them and their potential connection to the Florentine. Two had direct connections—Bobby Gemelli, the owner's son, and Tom Romano, who seemed to be bouncer in the gaming rooms and bodyguard for Bobby's father. *So where were you when he was murdered, Tommy-Boy? Asleep at the switch, or were you already gone?*

It was hard to determine the exact date of the disappearances, since they often weren't reported on the day they happened. The exception was the young Gemelli, who went missing right after his father was killed, according to newspaper articles she had read. Another detail she uncovered—two of the names on her "Most Wanted" list, Tom Romano and Harry Costello, dropped out of sight right around the same time as each other, but they had worked for two different casinos. Was there a link she hadn't found yet?

As she continued her digging, her phone rang. She let it go to voicemail. Ten minutes later, when she stood up to stretch, she listened to the recording.

"This is Phillip Carver at the Henderson Credit Union, Kate. Would you please give me a call back at your earliest convenience? Many thanks."

What now? she thought. She called the number.

"Thanks, Kate. We just wanted to double check with you about your recent transaction. A bigger bank wouldn't bother, but we're a small community operation, and we value our customers, especially one like you who has been with us for so many years."

"Okay, Phil. So what transaction are you talking about?"

"We noted this morning that you requested us to withdraw all the money from your savings account and transfer the funds to a bank in Reno. That's perfectly fine, of course, but it does mean we'll have to start charging you a maintenance fee for the savings account since you won't have the required minimum deposit of one thousand dollars. Would you prefer that we close that account, or would you rather leave a thousand behind to keep it open without any fee?"

Kate furrowed her brow. "Hold on, Phil. I didn't request any transfer."

She heard him take a deep breath. "Kate, our records have you initiating that telephone transaction at ten-thirty-six this morning."

She could feel her panic rising. "That's impossible. I was meeting with a friend this morning at that time."

"Oh, dear." The line was silent for a moment. "Tell me, Kate, have you used any unsecured wifi networks for your computer activity recently? You know, public wifi—in the airport, in a store or coffee shop?"

"I've spent several days doing my computer research at a café in town. Why do you ask?"

"I'm afraid you've been spoofed."

"Spoofed?"

"Your identity's been stolen. Thieves must've hacked into your computer, tracking your keystrokes, logins. Someone called the credit union this morning with all the information they needed to convince us it was you."

Kate sat down hard and expelled a breath. "Oh, dear God. What can I do?" Her mind was reeling.

"Well, thankfully, your money is still safe. We hadn't made the transfer yet until I talked with you. But I suggest you take your computer into a shop to make sure it's clean of any malware. Then immediately change all your passwords."

Kate tried to process this. "I'm so grateful you called, Phil," she managed to say. Then another thought occurred to her. "Hey, would you please give me the name of the owner of that account in Reno, the name of the bank, and the account number? I'd like to see if I can track down what happened."

He hesitated. "Usually that information is kept confidential. I have to file a report with our Fraud and BSA Department."

"BSA?"

"Yeah. The Bank Secrecy Act—the Federal regulations for all this stuff. But I have to be honest with you. These crimes are hard to prove and even harder to prosecute." He paused again. "Let me put you on hold for a second."

Kate tried to catch her breath as an inane elevator version of "Hey, Jude" filled her ears.

Carver came back on the line. "You didn't hear it from me, but that account is owned by Cana and Company Bridal Boutique."

"Is that some kind of joke?"

"Nope. That's the account owner at the New Bristol Credit Union in Reno. And here's the number. But like I said, you didn't hear it from me."

Kate jotted down the information on a scrap of paper. "I can't thank you enough, Phil! If I was in your office, I'd be giving you a big hug right about now. You really saved my bacon."

"Well, Kate, I'll take a rain check on the hug. We try to take care of our own. Have a good day."

Kate sat back and took several deep breaths. Then she quickly shut down all three of her laptops. Once that was accomplished, she let out a scream of rage that echoed through the empty house.

She poured a glass of water in the kitchen and chugged half of it. "What else can possibly go wrong?" she said aloud. Her face contorted in a grimace as she looked at the ceiling. "Hold on, Universe. I withdraw the question. No sense jinxing myself."

Returning to her desk, she picked up her phone and Googled Cana and Company Bridal Boutique. She found a listing in Reno on North Virginia Street featuring a cute storefront with white-gowned mannequins in the window. She tapped the number. An automated voice responded.

"The number you are calling has been disconnected or is no longer in service."

"Damn!" she shouted. *This has Gemelli's fingerprints all over it. Or am I losing my shit? Is this how paranoia starts?*

She called Bonnie to hear a voice of reason. Instead, she heard her friend unraveling, out of breath.

"I can't talk now, sis. We're at the vet's. Our dog Toby got real sick all of a sudden. The vet thinks he may have been poisoned. I'll call you back as soon as I can." The call ended.

Kate exhaled. *Just put one foot in front of the other*, she counseled herself. *Do what you have to do first and ignore the rest for now.*

With that, she picked up her computers and stowed them in a large shopping bag. She ran a comb through her hair, applied a bit of lip gloss, and took the bag out to her car. "Welcome to the Hotel California," sang the Eagles, as she sped off to Laptop Emergency Department.

Traffic was light. In ten minutes, she was parking under a sign that proclaimed CYBERNETIC CARE FOR ALL YOUR CYBERNETIC NEEDS.

"How can LED help you?" said the scruffy twenty-something in the War on Drugs T-shirt. He was hunched over a computer on a glass countertop, surrounded by a half-dozen other laptops with their insides exposed, reminding her of organ pictures she'd seen in an anatomy textbook.

She was mesmerized by the sleeves of tattoos that covered both his arms. "The guy at the bank said my accounts have been spoofed, and I may have malware on my machines."

The young man pushed the glasses back up on the bridge of his nose. "That's bad, but we can fix it."

"How long will it take? These machines are my livelihood. I'm a journalist."

He tilted his head and pursed his lips. "Normally, I would say next week. But we could put a rush on the job. Get 'em back to you late tomorrow. It'll cost you more, though."

"Let's do it that way. I need them back as soon as you can."

He tagged and catalogued each machine and took down all her necessary information. "Gardner's coming in at four, and he'll get started right away. Don't worry. We'll be in touch."

She left the shop feeling reassured. As she eased out into traffic, her phone rang. "Bonnie, I'm so glad you called. Is Toby all right?"

"The vet says he's stable, but she wants to keep him overnight just to be safe."

"I'm so relieved. I know how much you love that dog. Does the vet know what Toby got into?"

"She's not sure. She's sending some stuff off to a lab for analysis. It's a puzzle. We never let him off his leash except when he's in his own backyard, and that's fenced in."

A chill crept over Kate despite the Nevada sun through the windshield. "You think it was intentional? Like someone threw some tainted meat over the fence?"

"I hate to think that. Our neighbors love us and Toby. It just doesn't make sense."

"Well, I've got a lot to tell you. Can I interest you in cocktails by the pool at my place?"

"Yeah, I could use a drink and a swim. Half an hour?"

"Perfect. See you then."

#

The two women climbed out of the pool and wrapped long white towels around themselves. They walked to a table under an umbrella, where Kate poured two margaritas from a tall, ice-filled pitcher. "Here's to us," she said, as they raised their glasses and stretched out in two chaise lounges.

"To us," echoed Bonnie.

Kate could hear a slight hitch in her voice. "You almost lost Toby," Kate said, as she reached over and stroked her friend's arm.

"I love that dog. He's been part of the family for ten years. As sweet as dogs get."

Kate sighed. "I'm glad he'll be all right. And I'm so glad you headed off that disaster between Simon and Dan. That really freaked me out."

"You think you were freaked out? Let me tell you…" Her voice trailed off. "Show me the pictures?"

"Sure. I'll go get 'em." She walked into the house and came back with the manila envelope. "Here you go."

Bonnie pulled out the pictures and grimaced. "Ugh! Sure looks like you and Dan. I can't blame Simon for losing it."

"They're incredible fakes all right. I'm just so glad you believe me. I hate to think what would have happened if Simon got hold of Dan before you did."

"Could the police do anything with these? Track down who made them?"

"I doubt it. I'll bet whoever did this didn't use any local photo shop. No public footprint."

Bonnie took another drink. "It's a new age, huh? We'll never again be able to tell what's real and what's not. Crap!"

Kate reached for the pitcher and topped off their glasses. "Now can I tell you what happened to me today?"

As Bonnie listened to Kate and the story of her almost stolen savings, she shook her head back and forth. "You think it was Gemelli, don't you? Not just some random bad-luck-of-the-draw?"

"I know identity theft happens all the time, and from the way the bank talked about it, it's an everyday thing. But I'm not very big on coincidences, especially after that cop pulled me over and told me Gemelli sends her regards."

Bonnie licked some salt from the rim of her glass and took a generous swallow of the limey cocktail. It made her lips pucker. "These are really good, by the way. You've got the recipe down."

After another sip, she said, "For what it's worth, I think it was Cruella, too."

Kate could sense there was something Bonnie wasn't saying, something even Kate was afraid to speak aloud. Then Bonnie took the risk.

"Do you think that bitch had somebody poison my dog?" The quiet comment was as deafening as a thunderclap.

Kate sat without saying a word. It had been a fear she wouldn't allow to surface, an ache in a tooth she pretended wasn't there. Was she being reckless to pursue her investigation? It was one thing to risk her own wellbeing, but the thought that her work might endanger her friend…? As if reading her mind, Bonnie spoke again.

"I have to be honest—that possibility terrifies me. What if Gemelli goes on some kind of rampage, attacking anyone or anything with any connection to you? A dog is one thing, but what about my kids? What about me and my husband and our new real estate business?" Her hands were trembling as she put her drink down on the small table by her side.

Kate was at a loss for words. What defense did they have against something like that? Some old saying she hadn't heard in years was tickling the back of her consciousness. What was it? Where had she heard it? Then it whispered to her. *The best defense is a good offense.* But what did that mean? She took another sip of her margarita and leveled her gaze at Bonnie.

"We can't just sit back passively and wait till Gemelli strikes again," she announced. "We have to fight back. We have to attack."

Bonnie sat up as though the back of her lounge had grown suddenly hot. "Are you out of your mind? How do you attack somebody with the resources she has? What could we possibly do?"

"I don't know. I haven't figured that part out yet. But we have to do something."

Bonnie stood up. Her expression darkened as her lips curled into a frown. "Are you willing to sacrifice our friendship to your crusade?"

Kate's eyes went wide. "What?"

"Does our relationship mean that little to you? We're talking about the possibility that the bitch you crossed is engaging in a campaign against you—and now maybe against me, too. Your car, the pictures, the police, the bank—my dog?" She clenched both fists. "Attack her? Where will it end? Does somebody have to get physically hurt before you call it off, before you stop your damn investigation? Who cares about a fifty-year-old case, anyway?"

Kate leaped to her feet. "I do! Because—" She stopped what she was about to say. "I have my reasons. Please believe me, Bon."

"Oh, I believe you. A Pulitzer Prize in journalism? Some TV exposé with an Emmy nomination? Another notch in your career?"

"It's not like that. Really." Kate hung her head. "Please, Bonnie."

Her friend wagged a finger at her. "I have a career, too, you know. A new one I'm about to launch. Isn't that important to you?" She was shaking her head and breathing heavily. "What if Gemelli tries to torpedo our real estate business before it even gets off the ground? Fake reviews on *Yelp*, maybe? Complaints to the Better Business Bureau? Get my license revoked? Who knows what she could do?"

"What can I say, Bonnie? You're my best friend in the whole world. I don't want to hurt you."

"Just say you'll call it off."

Kate stared at her friend, unable to speak a word, while tears clouded her vision.

"Your silence says it all." Bonnie spoke slowly, without any discernable emotion, as though stifling all her feelings. "Thanks for the drink. I'll show myself out."

As Bonnie walked back into the house where she had left her clothes and her purse, Kate wept. Why wasn't she prepared to tell her friend the whole truth? Could the wound still be so raw after all these years? The question she couldn't voice aloud echoed in her brain.

Can I live with myself if Gemelli hurts Bonnie or her family?

9. Close Encounters of the Mob Kind

Bonnie stood in her newly remodeled kitchen, leaning on the table as if she might fall to the tiled floor without its support. The centerpiece of bright, fresh-cut flowers contradicted her mood. The speckled granite countertop, the buffed steel appliances—all the things that had given her such pleasure two weeks ago mocked the sadness she felt inside. She heard Dan come in through the garage door.

"What's the matter, honey? Have you been crying?" He put his briefcase on the floor by the counter and put his hand on Bonnie's shoulder. "What's happened? Can I help?"

Bonnie buried her face in his chest and sobbed. "Kate and I had a fight," she managed, as her whole body shook.

"Come sit by me on the couch and tell me all about it."

They walked into the living room and relaxed on the plush sofa. Bonnie spewed the words at him, the worry and fear and anger she had bottled up since leaving Kate. "And there's something else—something Kate's not telling me. Some reason she won't give up her investigation." Bonnie looked into her husband's face, hoping he would understand.

He stared back at her, furrowing his brow and pursing his lips. "But you have no proof for any of this?"

"Proof?" Her mood curdled into rage, and she shouted at him. "Our dog almost died! Isn't that proof enough for you?"

"I mean, there's nothing we can go to the police with. No evidence that ties Gemelli to any of this. Is it possible that it's not all connected like Kate thinks it is?"

"Men!" she yelled as she leaped up from the couch. She started to leave, but he stood and took her hand.

"Honey, honey. I'm sorry. I'm just thinking out loud, weighing our options. What do you think we can do?"

She turned and fell into his arms. "I don't know. Gemelli is a spider with webs everywhere. Is she having Kate followed? Is that how that cop found her coming home from the lake?"

"I don't know, darling. That takes a lot of manpower—a lot of hours. It'd be easier to just stick a tracker on her car."

Her eyes went wide. "Oh, shit! I never thought of that. That's how they found us at Vincent's! Now they've seen us together, and they targeted Toby!"

"Honey, please, that's still a stretch. We don't know what Toby got into. Let's see if the vet and the lab come up with anything."

Just then the front door swung open, and Jeremy strode in with his gym bag and his back pack. He had his mother's red hair, but the tall, lanky build of his father.

Dan raised his hand in greeting. "You're home early, son."

"They canceled practice. The coaches are sick. Got anything to eat?" He walked into the kitchen and opened the refrigerator.

"Why don't you have an apple for now?" said Bonnie. "I'll start supper in a minute." She turned back to Dan. "We'll talk more later."

Jeremy called from the kitchen. "I don't want an apple. They're soft. I'll just have a can of soda."

They heard the hiss as Jeremy opened the can and drank half of it without taking a breath.

"Funniest thing on the way home from school. I was walking with Kaiden, you know? He spotted this black car with real dark windows about half a block behind us. It was driving real slow. Followed us all the way here and then turned down Milton." He took another big swallow. "People can be so friggin' weird, you know? Somebody called in a bomb threat around lunch time, and we had to evacuate the school for like forty-five minutes till they checked everything out. False alarm. People, right?"

Bonnie grabbed Dan by the shoulders and looked into his eyes without saying a word.

#

She was in no mood to cook, so she put a pot of water on the stove to boil for pasta, took a jar of tomato sauce from the cupboard, and retrieved a bag of meatballs from the freezer. A spaghetti dinner was ready in fifteen minutes, and no one complained.

After gobbling two helpings of pasta and five meatballs, Jeremy removed his plate to the kitchen sink. "I'm going over to Kaiden's. Back by nine."

Bonnie looked at Dan with an expression that asked, "Should we let him go?" When Dan nodded, she said, "Be careful, honey, and stay away from any strange cars."

Once he was out the door, she said, "Do you think he's safe?"

Dan studied his wife and sighed. "We have to be careful, sure, but we can't let ourselves get caught up in Kate's paranoia."

"I don't think she's being paranoid. I think Gemelli is really dangerous."

"So, we stop living our lives? Lock ourselves inside?"

"C'mon, you know I'm not saying that. But it feels like Kate's got us involved in this thing now, too. That was your face in the pictures."

Dan smirked at her. "I haven't seen the pics. Would I like 'em?" He made an obscene gesture.

She punched him playfully in the arm. "I'm being serious and you're carrying on like a twelve-year-old." She took a deep breath. "Did you hear any more from Simon today?"

"Not a word. Heard plenty last night, though, before I calmed him down." He shook his head back and forth. "Yowza! If you hadn't given me that heads-up, we'd be having a very different conversation right now, probably from a hospital room."

"But that's what I'm talking about. And what if it gets worse?"

He reached over and stroked her cheek. "Let's not go there now. Let me help you clean up the kitchen. Then we can sit out back and start planning our marketing strategies for Ballantine Realtors."

#

Even though dusk was approaching, the heat stored in the subdivision's streets after a day of Nevada sunshine radiated from the asphalt like an enormous toaster oven. Jeremy was on his phone as he walked down Cornwall toward his friend's house. "I think I can borrow my dad's car Friday night. Up for a movie?" He paused. "Well, think about it. I'm on my way to Kaiden's right now. I'll call you later."

He wondered what was going on with Angie. She had been avoiding him ever since the party three weeks ago. She always had other plans, other places she had to be. It bothered him.

As he slipped his phone back into his pocket, he noticed a black SUV with dark windows stopped at the intersection with Almeida Street ahead. Was it the same car as before? He kept walking. When he was a half-block past the intersection, the car turned out onto Cornwall and drove slowly behind him, careful to maintain the same distance. Jeremy looked over his shoulder and scowled. An aggressive football player, always ready to plunge through a defensive line, he whirled around and ran toward the vehicle. The car stopped abruptly, and he slapped the hood with palm of his hand. The driver's window rolled down.

"You're the Ballantines' kid, right?" came a gravelly voice from inside.

"Who's asking?" Jeremy countered with a snarl. "And why the hell are you following me?" He tried to make out the faces of the two men in the front seat.

"Aw, that's not very neighborly. We're friends of your mom and dad. Just wanted to get a message to 'em is all."

Jeremy clenched and unclenched his fists. "Oh, yeah?" he said through gritted teeth. "What message?"

"Tell 'em they shouldn't be hangin' around with that Temperance chick. She's nothin' but trouble. Like that COVID bug a while back. Know what I mean? Get everybody sick." The window rolled up, and the car sped away.

"Assholes!" Jeremy shouted, waving his fist in the air. He immediately called his mother and told her what had happened.

"Come home, Jeremy," she replied. He could hear the anxiety in her voice.

"Mom, they're gone. I'm not in any danger. I gotta see Kaiden. Like I said, I'll be home by nine." He ended the call and put the phone back in his pocket.

A week later, neighbors saw Bonnie put a sign in her front yard.

FOR SALE
BALLANTINE REALTORS

10. The Cicada

Kate tapped the red "end" button on her phone and laid it down. She replayed Simon's call in her mind.

"I don't want to gouge you. I want us to play fair. We both have good careers, so let's go fifty-fifty and call it square."
Her voice was mechanical. "Anything you say, Simon."

She sat at the kitchen table, staring at her coffee cup as though she didn't recognize what it was. How could they be getting divorced? It didn't make sense. She loved Simon, and she thought he loved her.

And what about Bonnie? How could her best friend have put her house on the market and plan to move away?

"I'm scared, Kate," Bonnie said, after describing Jeremy's encounter with the men in the black SUV. "They told me and Dan not to hang around with you—that you were like COVID and would get everybody sick. I've got too much at stake. I can't risk it. I'm sorry."

Once her brain stopped spinning, she felt empty, as though drained of some essential life-force. That feeling triggered a memory from her tenth birthday.

"Can I have a birthday party, Grandma?" Kate didn't know whom she'd invite. Tennyson Elementary was the third school she'd been in this year, and she hadn't made many friends yet. She didn't know why she and Grandma kept moving.

"You've asked me that every day for a week, and my answer is still no. Grandma is too busy and too tired to have kids here. Besides, look at our place. There's only room for you and me."

In fact, each move had taken them to a smaller apartment. This one had a tiny kitchen with a four-burner stove, an ancient white refrigerator, and a table with two wooden chairs. A stained couch in the living room was the only furniture, aside from the shelves which held a 25-inch color television, a VCR, a phonograph, and a collection of records. No pictures relieved the barrenness of the beige-colored walls except an enlarged photograph of Las Vegas at night. According to Grandma, that picture had originally belonged to Kate's mother.

"Did Mommy love me, Grandma?" It was a question Kate had been asking ever since she had learned to talk.

"Of course, she did, Katie. Your mother loved you more than anything in the world. You were Samantha's daughter, and Samantha was my daughter. And I loved her more than anything, too."

"What happened to her, Grandma?" She already knew the answer.

"God wanted her to be in heaven with Him. That's where she is."

The next question also got the same answer every time. "Do you think Daddy will send me a birthday present this year?"

"Honey, I've told you a hundred times. Your daddy left your mommy before you were born. I don't know where he went. He probably doesn't even know about you."

"But what was his name?"

"Okay, darling, that's enough. I have to go lie down. You can either listen to music or go outside and play."

So, she went out into the small yard behind the apartment complex. She sat on the swings and scuffed her shoes in the dirt. Then she noticed movement on one of the poles that supported the swing set. It was a fat brown insect a little more than an inch long. As she watched, mesmerized, a transformation took place. Its back began to break open, and another insect emerged from the skin and unfurled its wings. It flew away, leaving behind the brown shell, like an empty husk.

"That's me," she thought. "Empty like that bug."

At school the next day, she learned that the insect was a cicada, shedding its nymph form to become an adult. She also *discovered that the nymph could stay underground, all by itself, all alone, for ten years or more.*

She nodded her head in recognition. "I'm a cicada, too."

She hoped she would become an adult soon.

She shivered at the recollection, feeling the ache of that little girl who wanted so desperately to grow up and flee the aloneness that was her constant companion. This wasn't the adulthood her younger self had imagined. Her life was whirling out of control, getting worse the longer she pursued the disappearances. Instead of cementing her relationships, she was losing them—first her husband and now her best friend. Was her search worth the cost?

But she knew the answer to that. Whatever the cost, she had to pay it. After all, it's what had driven her into investigative journalism in the first place—the quest to discover how her mother had died when Kate was less than a year old. Was it suicide? Her gut told her it had something to do with Kate's father, whoever he was, abandoning her mother.

Her phone interrupted her train of thought. When she saw it was Bonnie, she immediately answered. "Hi, Sweet P—" She stopped herself. "Hi, Bon. It's good to hear from you."

After a brief hesitation, her friend said, "I've already received six offers on the house in a week, four over asking price, and two are cash with no contingency. I've got to take one of them."

Kate was silent for several breaths. "I'm not sure what to say. I mean, I'm happy for you, but I don't know what life will be like without you right down the street, five minutes away." She could feel tears begin to flow, but tried to keep any sound of them out of her voice. She dabbed at her eyes with a napkin.

"Maybe when this whole thing blows over you can come and visit, wherever me and Dan wind up. We're checking out Carson City and Reno right now."

Kate's voice was matter-of-fact. "Those are pretty far away."

"Yeah. Maybe we'll find something a little closer. Not sure yet. Oh, before I forget to tell you again. When I told Dan about all that's happened to you, he wondered if Gemelli had somebody put a tracker on your car. Sorry it slipped my mind before, but with all that's been going on, I'd forget my head if it wasn't attached."

"Duh! I should've thought of that. Thanks, Bon."

"Well, I gotta run, sis. Talk soon." She ended the call.

Kate stood and stretched. A part of her wanted to go back to bed and sleep for days. Another part wanted to start drinking. The best part of her wanted to resume her research, and that's the part she obeyed, after one more phone call.

"Connor Mercedes," came the voice. "How may I direct your call?"

"Service, please," said Kate. She heard the click as the call was transferred.

"This is Mike in service. How can I help you?"

"Mike, this is Kate Temperance."

"Oh, hi, Kate. No trouble with that brake job, I hope?"

"No, no, Mike. I'm wondering if somebody put a tracking device somewhere on my car. If they did, is that something you could find and remove?"

"Sure, no problem. You got a stalker?"

"I think I may have."

"Well, bring it in anytime, and I'll take a look at it. Shouldn't take long."

"Thanks. Maybe tomorrow morning early."

"You got it, Kate. I'll be here."

With that taken care of, she went to her desk and logged on to her computers, again thankful that LED was able to clean them of any malware and get them right back to her. For the time being, she had narrowed her search to the three names most closely related to the Florentine—Bobby Gemelli, Tom Romano, and Harry Costello. Even though Harry was the owner of the Cactus Club and wasn't directly connected to the Gemelli casino, she included him in that group since he had disappeared at the same time as Tom Romano, who had definitely worked for Bobby's father.

She had to ask herself, *"Was Bobby killed, too?"* After all, he was the heir apparent to the Florentine. And he had disappeared on the day of his father's murder. If someone went to the trouble of murdering Giancarlo, would they have eliminated his son as well, never imagining Sofia would assume the throne? Or could Bobby have escaped and gone into hiding?

If they were gunning for his father, Bobby would have had to get out of Dodge, and fast. McCarran International Airport, now Harry Reid International, was only a few miles away. That would have been the way out.

Kate tried to find out if there were Passenger Name Records data from back then, but trying to track down PNRs on her laptop was opening a rabbit hole, with every site saying something different. After an hour of fruitless searching, she tried another approach—accessing archived newspapers.

Two hours later, still with no results, she needed to rest her eyes from staring at computer screens. She made herself a cup of coffee and sat back at her desk, swiveling her chair around away from the laptops. Her relaxation technique was to let her eyes go out of focus looking at her grandmother's Las Vegas picture and get lost imagining herself walking the Strip back in the 70s, when the iconic Sands Hotel still dominated the landscape. Six months after her twenty-third birthday in 1996, it had been imploded so the larger Venetian could usurp its place. *Just what Vegas needed*, she thought, *canals and gondolas.*

As she was about to get herself another cup of coffee, her phone rang.

"Billie! I'm so glad you called. I was beginning to get worried when I didn't hear from you. Did my idea not fly with the higher ups?"

"Well, Kate, it's a little more complicated than that. It was an uphill battle, but we finally reached a compromise, and I did get you a nice advance."

"Thanks, but what's the compromise?"

"One of our executive producers, Tom Nolan, has bad blood with Sofia Gemelli and would like to see her taken down. At the same time, he knows how deep her pockets are and how connected she is all over town."

"And so?"

"And so he wants to protect our investment. He's assigning one of our staff to…" She hesitated as if looking for the right word. "…assist you in your investigation."

"Assist me?" She almost shouted at her friend. "I don't need any assistance. I work alone. You know that. Doesn't Nolan trust me?"

"Kate, we got burned in that last lawsuit, and he doesn't want that to happen again."

"So, he's assigning me a babysitter?"

"No, no. Think of him as an extra pair of hands. He's a good reporter, and he has other skills as well."

"Such as?"

"He's good in a fight, and he has a concealed carry permit."

Kate almost dropped her phone. "Shit, Billie! Nolan thinks I'm a damsel in distress? What the hell!"

"Calm down, Kate. It's not about you, it's about Gemelli. Nolan has a history with her. She and her goons got real nasty with him. He wants you to be safe if you go around messing with her organization. He thinks you need backup."

"No way." She ended the call, and let out a shout that echoed in the empty house. "Hell with the coffee," she said aloud. "It's time for bourbon." She stomped to her liquor cabinet just as the phone rang again. "Look, Billie, my elementary school teacher always gave me 1s and 2s—Ds and Fs—on my report card because she said I didn't play nice with others. That's still true. I can't work with some testosterone junkie ready to karate-chop or shoot his way out of uncomfortable interviews."

"Kate, it's not optional. If you want us to produce your story—and to hand over this nice fat advance I'm holding in my hand—you have to work with Nolan's guy." She paused. Kate said nothing. Finally, Billie said, "At least come and meet him before you run off and peddle your story elsewhere. My office tomorrow at eleven sharp." She terminated the call.

Kate grabbed her bottle and a glass and retreated to her favorite recliner in the living room. Once she had poured a generous amount, she swirled it around and inhaled its sweet aromas. The burn on her tongue soon settled her nerves.

#

At ten forty-five the next morning, she was pacing the lobby of the television station, winding her way through the metal sculptures and glancing at the paintings on the wall. Her brain was on overload. The adrenaline in her bloodstream fanned her temper and fast-forwarded scenarios of how she could defy the network's demand that she accept an "extra pair of hands." *Hell with that!* she thought. *Who exactly is coming to my rescue?*

Billie entered the lobby and approached her as she would a dog who might bite her. "Hello, Kate," came her soft greeting.

Kate whirled toward her. "Hi, Billie." She pursed her lips. "Let's get this over with. Who is it by the way?"

"Come and see."

The women entered Billie's office. A slender man stood looking out the window with his back toward them.

As the man turned around, Billie said, "Kate, I'd like you to meet Jay Scott."

Instead of extending her hand, she brought it to her mouth in shock.

"Yeah, I get that a lot from first-timers," he said.

"I-I read about you a few years back. You were assaulted. Please forgive me for my reaction." She offered him her hand.

He shook it warmly. "No judgment. It's natural. One of my subjects didn't like the piece I did on him. Thought I needed an acid cocktail one afternoon at happy hour. But I got off easy. Missed my eyes, so I can still see. Got my right ear pretty good though—not much of it left."

The right side of the man's face was a mass of scar tissue. Like the magnetism of a traffic accident, it drew Kate's eyes so she couldn't look away. "Surgery?" she managed.

"Lost count how many. My kids got tired of the teasing and name-calling, so when they're in school, they call me Two-Face or

PO." He paused. "That's some kind of defense mechanism, I think. What do the shrinks call it? Identifying with the aggressor?"

Kate shook her head in bewilderment. "I'm afraid I don't understand."

"Two-Face was a Batman villain. Harvey Dent. A famous district attorney in Gotham City until a mob boss threw acid on him. PO is my kids' abbreviation for Phantom of the Opera."

Kate was reeling, all of her objections to having a partner lost in her confusion. "I-I'm sorry. I don't know what to say."

"Don't be sorry. My family's joke is that I don't have to wear a mask at Halloween."

She felt dizzy and sat down. Billie and Jay followed suit.

"So, Kate, as I've explained, Tom Nolan wants Jay to assist you in your investigation. I think the deeper you get into it, the more you'll appreciate his being around."

Jay swiveled his chair toward her. "I love your stuff by the way. I think I've read everything you've written." He clucked his tongue. "I gotta confess, you've been kind of a role model for me. That last piece you did in *ProPublica* really knocked me out."

Kate let out a deep breath. "So how exactly would this work?"

The unscarred portion of his mouth curled upward in a smile. "You do all the writing in your office at home. When you leave your house to pursue a lead or interview somebody, I go with you. I promise I won't get in your way."

"You're my babysitter?" Her skepticism stained every word.

"Hell, no!" he laughed. "I'm your gunslinger. Nolan thinks you'll be in danger, a danger that'll get worse the closer you get to whatever Gemelli is hiding."

She looked at Billie. "Can I think about this overnight?"

Billie walked to her desk and removed an envelope from the middle drawer. "Of course. This advance will be waiting for you right here. May I suggest you two get to know each other before you decide?"

Jay turned toward Kate. "Can I treat you to lunch? Any place you want."

She hesitated for a moment, but then relented. "Sure. I'm kind of partial to Vincent's, down in Henderson."

"Cool! Me and Hal go back a long way."

Kate looked incredulous. "A long way? You've gotta be twenty years younger than me."

"I'm getting close to thirty-one to be exact, so you're right. You've got twenty on me. Is there a problem with that? I know it's usually the older guy with the young chick, but I'm okay being seen with an older woman."

Billie winced and Kate gritted her teeth.

"Hey, I'm sorry. That was my pathetic attempt at humor. Vincent's it is. Want me to drive?"

"I'll meet you there." Kate scowled at Billie and strode out of the office.

Billie caught Jay by the shoulder. "Stay for a sec." She waved at Kate. "I won't keep him long. He'll see you at Vincent's."

Kate didn't return the wave. She retrieved her car from Valet Parking, got in, and sat for a moment. Was it worth it, getting chained to a scary-looking thirty-something? Or was that simply prejudice rearing its ugly head? Would she be feeling this way if Jay were as handsome and dashing as some of the men wowing their dates at the poker tables across town? "Shit!" she exclaimed, slamming her fist on the steering wheel.

She started the Mercedes and was greeted by a blast of stale air from the A/C. It soon cooled, and she began to feel more herself. "I'll give him a chance," she announced to the empty car as she pulled out into traffic. "But if lunch is a bust, I'm outta here. Billie can keep her advance. I'll sell my story somewhere else." Another thought occurred to her. On impulse, she tapped the phone button. "Call Billie Newington," she said.

After two rings, a familiar voice. "Well, hello, Kate. I didn't expect to hear from you so soon. Have you made up your mind even before lunch?"

"Billie, what happened that Tom Nolan thinks I'm stepping on a rattlesnake?"

There was a moment of silence. "I thought you knew. He was doing a piece on Gemelli and the Florentine and things started happening. Nothing he could ever prove or connect with her, but he was convinced she was behind it."

Kate was holding her breath as Billie continued.

"Car got keyed when it was parked in the garage. A couple flat tires the next week. Got pulled over for a bogus traffic stop and fined a thousand bucks."

Kate felt her heart rate increase. "What else?"

"House got broken into and the only thing that was stolen was his Emmy Award."

Kate heard a silence that only heightened her dread. "What aren't you telling me?" The words were almost a shout.

"Two weeks before his story was to go live, his daughter Layla was kidnapped. She was out at UC Berkeley doing an MBA. A few days after she went missing, he gets this package in the mail." Billie paused. "Her finger, with the ring he had given her as a birthday present."

"Oh, shit! Did they kill her?"

"No. Tom yanked the Florentine story. Next day, cops found Layla wandering around campus, bloody rag wrapped around her hand. Pretty drugged up. Kept repeating, 'I was alone in the dark. All alone. Underground. In the dark.'"

Kate was gasping for breath.

"Anyway, no witnesses, no leads, no evidence but the 'coincidence' of her release when he buried the story. Tom's sure it was Gemelli's doing, but no proof."

Kate lowered the window and inhaled the fresh air as though she were a swimmer rising from a great depth, demanding oxygen.

"You still there, Kate? Did I lose you?"

"I'm here. Is Layla okay now?"

"Not sure that's the word I'd use. She never was able to go back to school. Works at the Goodwill in Boulder City now. Seems to like her therapist."

The two women were silent for a long minute. Finally, Billie said, "And that's why Tom thinks you're stepping on a rattlesnake.

But understand. He wants you to take that snake out. Chop its damn head off."

Kate stared down Las Vegas Boulevard, realizing that the garish displays concealed a soul-eating darkness. "Thanks, Billie. Gotta go." She ended the call and continued south toward the highway.

Maybe she needed a gunslinger after all.

11. Dancing in the Dark

Kate sat in the corner at Vincent's, looking toward the door, her mind whirling. Aromas of grilling steaks and burgers made her hungry. She saw Jay walk in.

"Hi, Hal," he called. "Light's out."

"Thanks, Jay. I'll get right to it."

Kate watched as he approached the bartender and asked him something she couldn't hear. Then Hal reached under the bar and withdrew a bottle she recognized instantly. Her eyes went wide as she saw Hal pour two glasses and return the bottle to its hiding place.

Jay turned and walked toward her, glasses in hand. "May I join you?" he asked coyly, setting the drinks down.

"Are you kidding? Oh, my God! Pappy Van Winkle's? What did you say to Hal and how can you afford that?"

"I asked Hal what you like to drink. When he said bourbon, I knew I had to have him pour us the Pappy's."

Kate stared at the amber liquid. "I've never tasted this before. What kind of budget are you on anyway?"

He gave her his half-smile. "Before you get the wrong idea, there's no way I can afford a $2500 bottle of bourbon. I won it in a lottery. I also knew that if I brought it home, I'd have it gone inside a week. So, Hal holds it for me. I come in for a bit of it once or twice a month." He raised his glass. "A toast?"

Kate picked up her drink. "You're one surprise after another, Jay. Cheers." She clinked her glass to his, inhaled its aromas, and took a sip. She moaned in pleasure. "Okay. If God drinks bourbon, he drinks Pappy's. Wow, that's good!"

Jay appeared to chew his mouthful before swallowing it. "I must agree with the journalist's assessment." He put his glass down and looked at Kate. "I really do hope you'll let me work with you."

"Well, you do know how to bribe a girl. I'll give you that."

"In all seriousness, it would be an honor."

Kate took another sip and looked over her glass at him. "Tell me about yourself."

Jay cleared this throat. "Let's see. Married to the same woman for fourteen years. Sharon's been a real trouper through all of this." He pointed to his face. "She teaches at JFK Community College. We've got two kids. Mark's in fifth grade. Kind of a nerdy wiseass. A real *Star Wars* junkie, if you can believe that. Dana is in fourth grade, and she's my sports fanatic." His eyes seemed to glow. "We watch football and basketball together every chance we get. She's taking SCUBA lessons now and has visions of diving off the California coast. I'm betting she winds up studying marine biology." He sat back in his chair. "All I know about you is what I read in your bio, which isn't much."

Kate motioned with her hand toward the bar. "Hal, may we have a couple of menus?" She turned back to Jay. "I was orphaned when I was a year old. That's the hardest part. Apparently, my father left my mother before I was born. He may not have even known she was pregnant." She sighed. "I think my mother got so depressed, she killed herself, but I don't know for sure." She took another sip of her whiskey. "My grandmother took over and raised me. I think she knew my father's name, but she would never tell me. The only clue I've got is this picture of the Strip in the 70s. It was originally my mother's. My grandmother hung it on the wall in every apartment we lived in, and we moved around a lot."

Hal arrived with the menus. "I'll give you two a couple of minutes and then come back and take your orders."

Jay picked up a menu and glanced at it, then back at Kate. "So, you never knew who your father was?"

"Nope. My birth certificate identifies him as 'Max,' but my grandmother told me that was the name of my mother's dog when she was a kid. I think my father had something to do with Vegas and the casinos. Wanting to find out who he was and how my mother died is what drove me into investigative journalism." She looked at the menu as she saw Hal approach.

"You two decide what you want to eat?"

She handed him her menu and smiled. "The smells in here are making my mouth water. Let me have a burger, but no fries. A small house salad instead." As an afterthought, she added, "And an iced tea with lemon."

"You got it, Kate. And you, Jay?"

"I'll do the burger, too, but I'll take the fries with mine. And the iced tea."

After Hal left with their orders, Kate continued, a sheepish grin spreading across her face. "When I was fifteen, I took out a personal ad in every paper within a fifty-mile radius. 'Hey, Dad, whoever you are. It's me, Kate Temperance, Samantha's teenage daughter. Call me.'" She chuckled. "I listed my grandmother's telephone number, and for about a week, the phone rang off the wall. All these weirdos wanting to connect with their long-lost little girl. My grandmother never let me hear the end of it. She was pissed!"

Jay laughed and drank the last of his whiskey. As Kate finished hers, she furrowed her brow.

"This is going to sound like a real stretch, but I'm sure my grandmother knew a lot more than she was letting on—not only my father's name, but what happened to him. I don't know why I'm telling you this—I've never said it to anybody before, even my best friend—but my gut tells me my father is at the bottom of Lake Mead."

Jay's mouth opened in surprise. "Wow. I didn't see that coming. That's what's driving you?"

"I shouldn't have said anything." She shook her head back and forth. "Now you think I'm crazy."

"Not at all, Kate, not at all. You've got the best 'gut' in the business. Now please let me help you dig up your father. And while we're doing that, let's put the hurt on Sofia Gemelli."

Kate frowned. "She's already doing that to me."

"What?"

"It started with small stuff, like Nolan had to deal with. Somebody keyed my car in the parking lot here at Vincent's. I even got a bunch of bogus traffic tickets like he did. Hell, this morning my mechanic removed a tracker from my car."

"Holy shit! You think it was Gemelli?"

"Had to be. Of course, I can't prove it. But that's not the worst of it. Not only have I won her undying love, but I've lost my husband and my best friend in the bargain."

Jay leaned forward in his chair. "Oh, my God. How did that happen?"

"Simon received an anonymous envelope full of pictures showing me screwing my best friend's husband. I'm not sure if he ever really believed they were fakes, but he decided he'd had enough of my obsession with Gemelli and the Florentine. Anyway, he says I drink too much, and we both know I'm a workaholic. He's serving me papers. Twenty-five years of marriage down the tubes."

Jay reached across the table and touched the back of her hand. "I'm sorry. That's terrible. And what happened to your best friend?"

"Scared her off. She thinks her family is in danger if she hangs around with me. She's selling her house and moving away." Kate looked up as Hal brought over two large glasses of iced tea.

"Burgers will be out in a minute."

After Hal left, Jay looked into Kate's eyes, which had misted over with her revelations. "It must feel like you've been orphaned all over again."

"I hadn't thought of it like that, but yeah, you're right. It does." She took a long draft of her cold drink. "Thanks again for the Pappy's by the way. That was above and beyond."

"My pleasure." He reached into his pocket. "I've got something else for you." He put a flash drive down on the table and pushed it to her.

"What's this?"

"That's all of Tom Nolan's research for his story on Gemelli and the Florentine. He yanked the story, but he kept a copy of his notes. I thought you might be interested."

"Oh, my God! Interested?" In her sudden surprise, she almost knocked over her glass of iced tea. "That's gotta be the damn Rosetta Stone for this case!"

He raised his hands as though motioning her to slow down. "Look, just don't tell Billie you've got it. Okay? I didn't exactly get

Nolan's permission to give it to you, and I don't know how she'd react."

Kate laughed. "What kids used to call a 'five-finger-discount' when they grabbed a candy bar they didn't pay for, huh?"

"Something like that."

"Deal." She picked up the drive and stowed it in her purse. Then she extended her hand. "Okay. I guess there's no avoiding it. We're partners now. For better or worse."

"For better or worse," Jay echoed.

Their lunches arrived, and both ate with gusto. As Jay rubbed his last French fry into what remained of the catsup on his plate, he looked up. "You haven't said anything about kids. Got any?"

"No." That word brought a flood of emotions that made her tremble momentarily.

Jay rushed to respond. "I'm sorry. I don't mean to pry."

Kate pursed her lips. "That's okay. Just haven't thought about that in a long time." She took a final bite of her salad and chewed it slowly. "It was cancer. Doctors got it all. No recurrence, but no babies either. Simon wasn't interested in adoption, so we both dove into our careers." She harrumphed. "And here I am." She dabbed at her lips with her napkin. "So, changing the subject, tell me more about yourself. Billie says you're good in a fight."

Jay chuckled. "Well, I had taken martial arts for years when I was younger. Got pretty good at it—aikido, karate, jiu jitsu—but I got lazy and let it all slide in college." His eyes took on a faraway look. "The assault changed me. I decided I was going to protect myself better, so I got back into martial arts with a vengeance. Now I work out three times a week."

"And guns?"

"Yeah, that, too. I go to the range at least twice a month. I'm a pretty good shot."

She took another swallow of her drink and looked at him with a curious expression.

"What?" he asked.

"Teach me?"

"To shoot?"

"Mm hm. I've always been afraid of guns. I don't want to be afraid of anything anymore."

His half-smile beamed at her. "This gun's for hire."

She laughed as she completed the Springsteen lyric, "Even if we're just dancing in the dark."

12. Of Moles and Men

Jay drove home from Vincent's in the BMW that had been gifted to him three weeks before. He turned into the Paradise Hills Community and paused as the steel gate slowly creaked open. At Pharaoh Place, he turned left, touched the button on his rearview mirror, and pulled into his driveway as the garage door slid upward to admit him. In moments, the door closed behind him, and he was hidden away from any curious neighbors.

The house was anything but modest. Its four thousand square feet were appointed with impeccable taste. The vast kitchen featured the latest in stainless steel appliances, along with countertops of Brazilian granite and a center island with an additional sink. The living room was a feast for the senses, with brilliant works of abstract expressionism on the walls, plush seating, and an unparalleled sound system. The theater room on the lower level rivaled any cinema in town. The bedrooms upstairs were a nod to hedonism at its most pretentious.

As he removed his tie, the phone in his pocket buzzed. He had been expecting the call. "Hi, boss. How's the weather in Oregon?"

"Hello, Jay. It's perfect here. Cool nights, warm sunny days without too much heat. The grapes are loving it. Should be a fine harvest this year." He paused. "So, tell me. Apparently, Temperance has decided to pursue her investigation, despite our best efforts to dissuade her. How did your meeting with her go?"

"Just as you predicted. That bottle of Pappy's you sent me was a stroke of genius. That's what got her to let down her guard. You must have a hell of an *investigative* team backing you up."

"We have our ways of finding out things. That whiskey would get any bourbon-lover salivating. I'm glad she took the bait."

"But isn't giving her Sofia's copy of Nolan's files a little too much? Isn't that taking an enormous risk?"

"A calculated risk, my boy. You go to Vegas. You know you have to gamble big to win big. I wanted to make sure she would let you in. I guessed those files would seal her partnership with you and persuade her not to sell her story to another network. Sofia agreed."

"Sure, it worked. But what if she tracks you to Oregon?" He couldn't keep the worry out of his voice.

"In that case, you'll be here with her—our first line of defense. Just like you were with Nolan and his story."

"Well, I want to go on record as being real nervous about all this. It could come crashing down on us in a heartbeat."

"Trust me, Jay. You can't stuff a T-shirt into a hole in the bottom of a sinking boat."

"What?"

"Let her show us where all the holes are. Where our vulnerabilities lie. Then she can have an unfortunate accident before the story goes public, and we can put the boat in dry dock once and for all."

Jay sighed. "I'm not sure I follow your metaphors, but I trust you." He took a deep breath. "You know, you and Sofia are like the parents I never had."

"And you're like..." The voice hesitated a moment, as if the words were hard to say. "...a son to me."

"I mean it, boss. When I exhausted my health insurance on this face, you guys came to my rescue—you even helped me get off the oxy. When my wife divorced me and took the kids to Connecticut, you had Sofia take me under her wing. When my job went belly up, you two were behind the scenes, calling in favors, pulling strings, getting me hired at the network." He stood up and swept his right arm in a broad arc that only he could see. "This house. My new car. It's all you."

"We saw untapped potential in you, Jay, and you're the best investment we've ever made. The particular services you provide—your expertise. You're the crown prince, and don't you ever forget it."

"Thank you...Dad—if I can call you that."

"Please do."

Jay cleared this throat. "Let me put you on speaker while I get myself a glass of water." He took a tumbler from the cupboard and brought it to the refrigerator to fill.

The voice followed him. "What do you plan to do next with Temperance?"

Jay took a big swallow of cold water. "Would you believe she wants me to teach her how to shoot?" He heard laughter on the other end.

"My, my. She's a feisty one, all right. Keep a close eye on her. She's a much better investigative journalist than Nolan ever was. Don't underestimate her."

"You got it. Anything else?"

"I shipped you a case of the 2018 Reserve Pinot yesterday. It should be there in a few days."

"Super! I'll keep you and Sofia updated on any changes at this end."

"I knew you would. We'll talk again soon."

Jay took his water into the living room, put it down on an end table, and sat in the tan leather recliner. His mood darkened. He could maintain his bravado with his boss over the phone, but couldn't when he was alone. In spite of his gratitude for the luxuries showered upon him by his benefactors, his duties exacted a corrosive cost.

"I think I was a good man once," he lamented to the empty house. His eyes grew heavy.

Initially, his job had been mostly minor operations—bribing a police officer to look the other way or to make trouble for someone who had provoked Sofia, keying someone's car or flattening a tire to express Sofia's displeasure with them, making sure no regulations that would negatively impact the Florentine ever made it through the city council or the mayor's office. All the while, he was maintaining a job as a journalist at the network, submitting just enough stories to keep him on the payroll, reporting only to Tom Nolan, who regarded Jay as his "charity case." But then his real job turned a corner, and nothing was the same again.

"PTSD," his therapist said. "You've got all the symptoms—nightmares, flashbacks, exaggerated startle response. And that sense that somebody is in your room when you're dropping off to sleep? They call that false proximal awareness. That and hearing voices can make you think you're going crazy. But you're not. It's just your brain trying to deal with some very tough shit. Weekly therapy sessions and medication should help. You up for it?"

He was. Of course, he had never told her what he had actually done.

He closed his eyes, the big lunch and the whiskey finally taking their toll. His last thought before drifting off to sleep elicited a quiet moan.

Kidnapping Layla Nolan and cutting off her finger broke something inside me.

13. Home on the Range

As soon as she got home from her lunch with Jay, Kate rushed into her office and booted up her computers. She had to look at the flash drive! She plugged it into a USB port in the middle laptop and drummed her fingers on the desk while it loaded. In moments, the screen opened on Nolan's work. She marveled at his meticulous organization. *It takes an obsessive to know an obsessive*, she thought with a smile. He had been looking into the disappearances of fifty years ago as well, and had devoted individual files to each of the missing. She smiled again. *The dramatis personae of our little soap opera.* She opened them one at a time and read their contents, cuing in on facts she hadn't known about the vanished. *Wow!* she thought. *What a gift! Thank you, Jay!*

After three hours of examining the data Nolan had uncovered, she stood and stretched. She wanted to look at one more file before calling it quits and making herself a light supper. It was labeled, *Quirks*, and she clicked on it.

Mickey Marchese—probably cooked the books for the Paradiso. Had a thing for S&M and liked to be the one whipped. Went to St. John's Catholic Church every Sunday in a shirt and tie, all nice and proper.

Francis Gianfrido—afraid to come out as gay. Spent weekends with a lover in Boulder City. Somebody found out and was blackmailing him. Not sure who. Yet.

Bobby Gemelli—last seen at McCarran. A guy named Larry Hogan from Indiana insisted he saw Bobby at the airport waiting to board a plane for Paris. Who or what's in Paris? Can't confirm the details. Yet.

Harry Costello—was poised to expand his Cactus Club to rival the Sands and the Florentine. Said his lucky charm never failed him—a Super Bowl ring he always wore around his neck.

Tom Romano—rumor has it he was the collections guy for Johnny. Real sadistic streak in him. Like the song says, "dirty deeds, done dirt cheap."

Sal Carminucci—word was he was into child porn and cocaine. Deathly afraid of any Friday the 13th—never left his penthouse on one of them.

The file went on for another page, documenting the sins and superstitions of the vanished. *The devil is in the details*, she thought. *Where did Nolan find all this?*

She was especially interested in the notes on Gemelli and Costello. *Bobby Gemelli must still be alive*, she thought. She echoed Nolan's sentiment—*Who or what's in Paris?* And the note about Costello and the ring was tickling something in the back of her brain.

She turned to another of her laptops. Her fingers flashed over the keyboard as she accessed her own files cataloguing information into the disappearances that most piqued her interest. She found herself muttering a line from the *Lord of the Rings*. "…one ring to find them…" She was certain she had read something about a Super Bowl ring.

Thirty minutes later, she found the old Sunday Supplement article from June 21, 1970.

"Harry Costello, owner of the Cactus Club, says he won't go anywhere without his lucky charm. In this case, it's not a rabbit's foot, but a New York Jets Super Bowl III ring that he insists he won fairly in a private game of Poker with a player he refuses to name. 'The Jets have always been my team,' he says, 'and Joe Namath is my go-to quarterback. They inspire me to make my casino the best on the Strip.'"

"Okay, Tom, we're on the same wavelength," she said aloud. She closed her laptops and headed toward the kitchen. "Enough excitement for one day," she muttered.

Once at the refrigerator, she decided to have breakfast for supper—two slices of avocado toast on sourdough bread. Her version included mayo, a slice of tomato, thinly sliced red onion, and capers, in addition to the avocado that she crushed into paste with a fork. *A little salt and pepper, and this'll work just fine*, she thought.

She finished her light supper and decided to sip a little bourbon while she watched the evening news. The vase of fresh flowers on the coffee table lent their light fragrance to the hint of burnt toast that still lingered in the air.

Despite her preconceptions and misgivings, Jay had won her over. He was young, smart, and generous, and he had a face that could stop a clock. The files he had given her on that flash drive would save her many hours, if not days, of work. Once she had a chance to examine them more closely, what other clues would she find?

The world news began, but she was too preoccupied to watch and listen. She still could not believe she had asked Jay to teach her how to use a gun. He was so eager to do it, he had arranged to pick her up tomorrow morning at ten o'clock for her first lesson at the shooting range. *In for a penny, in for a pound*, she thought.

#

At ten o'clock, she was standing outside waiting. Jay arrived in his BMW five minutes later.

"All set?" he asked as he opened the passenger door for her.

"As ready as I'll ever be."

"On the way to the range, I'm going to give you some safety instructions. That's the most important piece of today's lessons."

"I'm all ears, professor."

As they left the subdivision behind, the drive through the desert's almost lunar landscape revealed a stark beauty that always captivated her. She thought of the desert as an experiment in minimalism—terrain reduced to its barest essentials. It was a haiku by Basho, rather than an epic by Milton. And the plants that grew in such a harsh environment—like sage and creosote bush, Apache plume and globemallow—inspired her. Like them, she persisted. She was a survivor, too.

Twenty minutes later, with Kate feeling versed in the necessities of gun safety, they pulled into the parking lot of a long brick building with a sign proclaiming:

**THE FIRING LINE
YOUR HOME ON THE RANGE**

"That building is for indoor shooting," Jay explained, as he pointed to a long structure adjoining the office. "Police do a lot of training here. We have to go inside first and register." He kept talking as he got out and opened the trunk. "I've been a member for years. We can go in there to shoot when it gets too warm, but for now we'll use their outdoor setup behind the building. Help me carry this stuff."

He hoisted a backpack from the trunk and handed it to her. "Careful. It's heavy."

"Oof! You got cinder blocks in here or what?"

"That's three pistols in their holsters. Let me slide the backpack straps over your shoulders. I've got the ammo in this duffel, along with a pair of binoculars, a pad of targets, and hearing protection for both of us. I brought some water, too." He slammed the trunk and touched the lock on the driver's door handle. "Follow me."

"Hello, Jay!" said the pink-haired young woman behind the counter inside. Her black T-shirt said SWIFT 89. "Back so soon?"

"Couldn't stay away, Ariana. This is my guest, Kate Temperance."

Kate extended her hand. The office reminded her of the nondescript mobile office at a construction site she had investigated for a story three years ago. "May I ask what your shirt means? A favorite athlete?"

The woman smiled. "Taylor Swift was born in 1989. I guess you don't get out much."

Kate's face glowed red. "Please forgive me. I guess that's my prejudice showing. I never expected to meet a Taylor Swift fan in—" She swiveled her head around. "a place like this."

"You were thinking more along the lines of 'Give me the second amendment or give me death'? Or maybe 'They'll have to pry my gun from my cold dead hands'?"

"Yeah, I guess I was. My bad." She heard gunfire coming from behind a door to the right and from behind the building.

Ariana leaned over the counter and, in a conspiratorial whisper, said, "Just between you and me and that hole in the wall, I'm not big on assault rifles. There's too many whackos in the jungle out there. Like hand grenades and rocket launchers, only the armies should have combat weapons. But don't tell my boss that!" She straightened up and gave the sign-in book to Jay. Then she turned back to Kate. "I'll need to take a picture of your driver's license, please."

When they were all squared away, Jay led Kate out the rear door. "There's ten separate areas, kind of like car ports, each with its own table for holding our gear. We'll be shooting into sandbanks, so there's no bullets flying around."

The first two stations were occupied. Kate jumped when she heard seven shots in rapid succession as they walked by. Jay claimed the third station and laid their bags on the table.

"Now remember the safety stuff we talked about in the car. Safety always comes first." Kate nodded, and he continued. "I'll show you all about these pistols." He took the guns from the backpack one at a time and put them in a row on the table. "This one is a Glock 19 in 9mm. This one here is a SIG Sauer P365, also in 9mm. That pretty one in stainless steel is a .45 Colt 1911."

"Are they very loud?"

"Yep. While we shoot, we'll be wearing these hearing protection ear muffs. They deaden the sound of the gunshots, but we'll still be able to hear each other talk."

Kate listened intently to her mentor and took time with the hands-on part of his tutorial. As she became familiar with the operation of each firearm, her fear of them left her. When she began shooting and started hitting targets, she was surprised at how thoroughly she was enjoying herself.

Once each gun was empty, Kate went back to the table to reload the magazines. A deep sigh escaped her lips.

"Something the matter?" Jay asked.

"I wish my friend could be here with me right now. This would be a fun experience to share with her."

Jay put a hand on her shoulder. "I'm sorry Bonnie was scared away. You must miss her terribly."

That comment jarred her, but she tried not to let it show. "I do miss her. I should call her tonight."

Seventy-five rounds of ammunition later, Kate had had enough for one day. "Maybe we can come back another time for the indoor range? I'm pretty tired."

"Sure thing. Are you hungry? Can I take you out to lunch?"

"Not today, thanks. I'll make myself a salad at home. Then I want to do more work on that flash drive you gave me."

On the ride back to her house, Kate was quiet. Finally, Jay broke the silence.

"So, what do you think? Do you like shooting?"

"A lot more than I thought I was going to. Thank you." She volunteered nothing further. When she got out of the car in her driveway, Jay reminded her of their agreement.

"If you decide to go out and interview somebody or do some other research out and about, please call me, and I'll come right by. Safety first?"

"Safety first. Thanks again."

She was relieved to get into her house and lock the door behind her. Before she did anything else, she walked into the living room, sat in her favorite chair, and closed her eyes. What had just happened? Why had things gone so terribly wrong? Her mood had plummeted from her original excitement with her new adventure to a dark foreboding that churned in the pit of her stomach.

It was Jay's offhand comment at the shooting range.

She had never told him Bonnie's name.

14. Taking Down Empires

"Hi, Kate. I didn't expect you to call." The voice paused. "I know I've really upset you, but can you understand?"

"Yeah, Bon. I understand. You're probably doing the right thing." She let out her breath in a drawn-out sigh. "It's dangerous to be around me. But I needed to hear your voice tonight."

"I think I needed to hear yours, too. I miss you so bad." The voice choked on the words. "But I can't put my family at risk. Gemelli's gang knows all of us and where we live. I'm hoping once we're out of town they'll leave us alone."

"That's my hope, too. And you were right about my car. My Mercedes guy found a tracker on it. Gemelli probably had someone put it there. I'm beginning to think she has more tentacles than an octopus."

"So let her know you're quitting the story. Take back your life."

Another sigh. "I can't, sis. I have to be honest with you. I never told you before, but I think I'm an orphan because of Gemelli's father. That's my personal stake in this story."

"What?"

"I think her old man had my father killed. My guess is my father had something to do with the casinos. And I think his body is at the bottom of Lake Mead."

"Oh, my God!"

"It gets worse. I don't know exactly how my mother died—my grandmother would never tell me—but I think she committed suicide after my father was murdered."

The phone was silent for a long, breathing minute. Finally, Bonnie said, "So you think Gemelli wants you to drop your story because you'll find out her father is a murderer? Does that make any sense? Why would that be such a big deal to her fifty years after his death?"

"I don't know, Bon. There's no statute of limitations on murder. Suppose she's involved somehow? She would have been fresh out of law school around that time."

"I don't know, honey. All I know is you're swimming with the damn sharks, and I just wish you would climb out on dry land while you still have all your arms and legs."

Kate chuckled, then became somber again. "There's one more thing."

"One more thing! Are you kidding me?"

"My friend at the network that's doing my story assigned me a bodyguard."

"Well, that's an improvement, isn't it?"

"Except I think he may be playing both sides of the fence. He might be Gemelli's spy. He knew your name before I ever mentioned it to him." She could hear a quiet intake of breath on the other end of the call.

The voice was struggling to speak. "Kate, you know I love you. Is there anything I can do?"

"Yeah, if you're willing. I was thinking that in the next couple of weeks I'll copy all of my research, including this other flash drive I have, and send it to you. If anything happens to me, you can bring it to the police. Maybe they can do something with it."

Silence. Then a soft voice. "That wasn't what I expected to hear. But okay. If we move before then, I'll send you our new address."

"Thanks, sis. I appreciate that. Now let's talk about something else besides my untimely demise. Have you found any new shows on Netflix?"

#

She went back to studying Nolan's files, but she was distracted. Was Jay really Gemelli's *fixer*? Would he keep tabs on everything Kate was doing until Gemelli thought she was getting too close to the truth and decided to pull the plug? And what would be Kate's punishment? After all, she didn't have any kids that could be kidnapped. Would Gemelli go after her soon-to-be ex-husband? She decided it would be a good idea to give Simon a heads-up just in case. Hopefully, Bonnie and her family would be out of harm's way soon.

Just then, the doorbell rang. She went to the door and wasn't surprised to see a process server. Just as he offered her the envelope, she said, "I know the drill. I've been served. Good timing, by the way. I was just thinking about him."

The man nodded his head. "Have a good day, ma'am." He turned and walked down the sidewalk to his car.

Kate closed and locked the door. She walked into her office and opened the envelope of divorce papers. "So it begins. Let's keep it friendly, Simon." She picked up her phone and called him.

"Sorry I can't take your call right now," came the recorded voice of the man she loved. "Please leave a message after the beep."

"Hey, Simon. I just got the papers. If we're careful, we can do this without hating each other." She paused to collect her thoughts. "One more thing. It looks like my current investigation is poking a hornets' nest. I don't think they'll try to hurt me by going after you, but just in case, stay alert. I wouldn't want anything to happen to you. Talk to you later."

She had barely ended the call before her phone rang.

"Kate!" Simon shouted. "What the hell are you talking about? Hornets' nest! What kind of bullshit is that?"

"Easy, Simon. Calm down. I'm not trying to be alarmist or anything, but Gemelli's goons scared Bonnie—told her not to be hanging around me. She and Dan are selling their house and moving away." She did not mention the kidnapping of Nolan's daughter.

"So, you think they might try something with me? What about you, for God's sake? What kind of danger are you in?"

She took a deep breath. "I'll be okay. The station has bought the rights to my story and assigned me a bodyguard."

There was a slight pause on the other end. "Does he tuck you in at night?"

"No, and that's a cheap shot, Simon."

"It was. I'm sorry. You're really okay?"

"Yep. No sweat." She wished she felt as brave as she sounded. "I'll keep you posted if there are any changes."

"Please do."

She ended the call and put the phone down on her desk. "I'm fine," she told the empty house.

#

The next day, after showering, dressing, and pouring her first cup of coffee, she sat in her office, staring at her computer screens. "This is obviously not going to work," she said aloud. Unplugging her phone from its charger, she called Jay. "Buy me breakfast at Dido's. I'll meet you there in an hour." She terminated the call without waiting for his response. *I'll get it out of you, you sonofabitch,* she thought.

She was there in thirty minutes. As she walked through the door, she was greeted by the welcoming aromas of coffee and the faintest hints of toast and cinnamon pastries.

"Good morning, Dido."

"Hi, Kate. Nice to see you again. Your usual?"

"Yes, please, but this guy Jay will be here in a bit, and he'll pick up the tab."

Dido raised her eyebrows in a playful smirk.

"No, no, not like that," Kate responded. "This is strictly business."

"Got it. Here's your coffee. I'll have your bagel out in a few."

She took a seat by the window and stared at the lamp on the table, its globe like a spherical stained glass window. The brilliant colors reminded her of the kaleidoscope she played with as a child.

The bell over the door announced Jay's entrance. He walked toward her. "Hi, Kate. May I sit?"

She pointed to the counter. "Go pay Dido for my breakfast first."

He turned to the register and took a credit card from his wallet.

"Would you like anything before I run this?" Dido asked.

"No, thank you. Just hers."

"Here you go," she said, handing back his card. "Sign the top copy, please."

With his task accomplished, he returned to the table. "You don't look very happy, Kate. What's up?"

Before she could answer, Dido brought her bagel to the table.

"I'm going to eat this first while it's still warm. Then we'll talk."

Jay squirmed in his chair, as though uncertain what to do and uncomfortable watching Kate eat. Finally, he said, "I'll go get myself a cup of coffee." Five minutes later, with something to occupy his hands and his eyes, he seemed to settle down.

Kate took her time eating, enjoying the spectacle of Jay's discomfort. When she finished, she dabbed her lips with a napkin and riveted her gaze on him. Without any preamble, she said, "Are you working for Sofia Gemelli?" Was that a flicker of fear she saw in his eyes? A *gotcha*?

"Wh-what are you talking about? I work for the station—for Billie and Tom and the rest of the crew."

She made her hand into the shape of a gun and aimed it at him. "But are you on her payroll, too, working both sides of the fence?" she hissed through clenched teeth.

"Absolutely not! How can you say such a thing? If I was working for Gemelli would I be giving you all the dirt Nolan dug up?"

She lowered her hand and expelled a deep breath. *Why indeed?* "Then how come you knew my friend Bonnie's name before I ever told you?"

"Jeez, Kate, I'm an investigative reporter, too. Remember? I figured if I'm going to keep you safe, I'd better find out everything I can about you—who your friends are, where you go out to eat and shop, your daily routine and other habits."

"You know all that stuff?"

"I know your other favorite coffee shop is The Real Bean, and you like to work there on your laptop. You shop at Mardi's when you get an advance on a story. When you're feeling up to it, you exercise at Schirle's Gym." Jay seemed to be on a roll, talking faster and faster. "You take your car to the Mercedes dealership over on Grand, and they just pulled a tracker off it. Your husband just served you with divorce papers. Want me to go on?"

"Shit."

"Hey, easy. I'm on your side. We're in this together, Kate. We're going to nail Gemelli and her whole slimy operation."

She felt her eyes glaze with tears. Jay stood and walked to her side of the table. Leaning over her, he wrapped his arms around her shoulders. "You're a helluva journalist, Kate. Taking down empires is hard, dangerous work, but I know you can do it."

She arose and embraced him. "Thanks, Jay. I needed that. I've been feeling so alone, like I'm sitting out on the end of this big branch all by myself while someone's sawing it off."

"You're not alone, Kate. Not so long as I'm here."

15. The Silver Fox

Sofia Gemelli's bright hair and keen intellect had earned her the nickname "Silver Fox" from her friends. Sitting at her desk, she looked over her shoulder at the Harvard Law Degree hanging on the wall behind her and sighed. She regretted that she had never had the opportunity to practice the corporate law she had studied so diligently. After graduation, she had assumed control of the Florentine, a job that demanded all of her business savvy. Not only that, she had sacrificed her personal life as well. There was never enough time for long-term commitments, for marriage or children. The only things she lacked were those that money could not buy. In stressful times like these, she wondered what other path she might have chosen all those decades ago.

She stood and walked to the bookcase that held her favorite volumes, the ones she re-read time and time again. Her pace was slowed by the arthritis that had begun to afflict her back and her right knee. She drew *The Little Prince* from the shelf. It was a birthday gift from her brother long ago. The paper had yellowed with age and the binding had cracked, leaving some pages loose within the covers. She opened it to a dog-eared page where, as a young woman, she had made notations in the margin. She read aloud the text she had underlined.

"Where are the people?" resumed the little prince at last. "It's a little lonely in the desert..."
"It is lonely when you're among people, too," said the snake.

She returned to her desk and wiped at her eyes. *There's no time for loneliness either*, she thought bitterly. Leaning back in her chair, she surveyed her paneled office as a queen might examine her throne room. Here were original paintings by Florentine masters to relieve the tedium of oak and mahogany. Her prize possession was a small Madonna by Raphael, but she also had a Masolino and a Filippo Lippi. Fresh-cut flowers in the vase on her desk added floral perfume to the smells of leather and fine wood. The small bar to the right of the desk held crystal decanters of Scotch and bourbon and a pitcher of ice water. She clenched her teeth at the thought that the empire she had built over a fifty-year span might be toppled by a nosy journalist. At that thought, she took her phone from her purse and tapped a number.

"Hello, Sofia. We're on the same wavelength. I was going to call you today."

She acknowledged his comment with a click of her tongue. "So tell me, Jay, what have you learned?"

"Well, I think I've figured out why my earlier attempts to make Kate quit her snooping around didn't work."

"Oh?"

"She thinks her father is on the bottom of Lake Mead."

Sofia caught her breath. The silence lasted almost a minute. "That's not good." Another pause. "And what does she think about her mother?"

"She thinks her mother committed suicide."

She exhaled. "Well, that's a relief, at least. It's not a total disaster. Does she know anything about Bobby?"

"Not yet, but I'm guessing it's only a matter of time. She's really sharp. If she finds out about Oregon, what do you want me to do?"

"Go with her. Stay close. If she needs to have an accident, I'll let you know."

"You got it. I'll keep you posted."

Sofia terminated the call. She drummed her long red fingernails on the desk. The decades of hard work, the extraordinary personal sacrifices, now threatened by a brash reporter who wouldn't take "no" for an answer. *Does she have a price? Can I buy her off?* But she immediately dismissed those ideas as absurd. *No, this journalist will not be bribed.*

She walked to the mini-bar and poured herself a glass of ice water. *How long before that wretched newswoman finds out about Bobby? Or identifies her father? Will her father's remains appear on the shore along with those others that I've heard about on the news?* She uttered a curse to the drought that was drying up Lake

Mead and laying bare the crimes of two generations. Then another thought occurred to her. *The empire falls if she discovers what happened to her mother.*

She couldn't let herself dwell on worst-case scenarios like that. Over the course of her tenure at the Florentine, Sofia had provided jobs for many hundreds of people—people raising families who needed decent housing, health care, money for their kids' college educations. She had entertained myriads of visitors and guests, rescuing them from their drab lives with the dream of untold wealth and the best shows the world had to offer. She had donated millions to charities all over the globe. She was a force for good on the planet.

She picked up her phone again and called her brother.

"Hello, dear one," came the voice on the other end. "How's my sister on this fine day?"

"Worried. You know the latest about Kate Temperance?"

"Yes. I speak with Jay regularly. I think we can contain her."

"What if she comes looking for you in Oregon?"

"I'm sure I can manage an uppity reporter."

"It's no joke, brother-of-mine. She thinks her father is in Lake Mead." She paused when she heard the silence on the phone. "You never told me that whole story."

"Don't trouble yourself, Sofia. You mind your shop, and I'll mind the vineyard. We'll be fine."

"If you say so. I miss you, by the way. Maybe I'll have to get out of this desert heat and come visit you."

"That would be nice. The weather's perfect this time of year. The spare bedroom is there for you. Love you, Sof."

"Love you, too."

As she returned the phone to her purse, she smiled. Her brother always made her feel better. She was reminded of the games they played as children. Their favorite was "Us Against the World." By strategically positioning blankets over the backs of chairs, they made elaborate forts in the living room. Sometimes they were camping in tents on the savannas of Africa. Other times they were on the ice fields of Antarctica or the mountains of Peru. Always it was the two of them against all adversaries. Of course, the meanest adversary was their father.

She shivered at the unbidden recollection. Their father demanding they take down their tents immediately. Their father insisting they eat every last bite of supper before they could leave the table. Their father physically punishing them in ways that would not leave any marks for school teachers to notice. Their father slipping into her bedroom at night when she was a young adolescent…

"No!" she shouted aloud to drive the memory away. But it would not be banished.

#

It was eleven o'clock in the morning, but her bedroom was dark, the curtains drawn tightly over the windows. She heard a soft knock on the door.

"Sis? Can I come in?"

"No. Go away."

"You missed breakfast again. Are you sick? It's our fourteenth birthday. You can't be sick on our birthday. Twins stick together."

"Please, Bobby. Just leave me alone."

He opened the door, walked in, and closed the door behind him. "Why is it so dark in here? And it smells funny." He pulled the curtains back and leveled the venetian blinds. The morning sun streamed through the windows. "You've been crying." He sat on the edge of her bed. "Are you okay?"

"No." She buried her face in the pillow. Her shoulders heaved.

"Talk to me, Sof. Please. What happened?"

She raised her head and turned to him, tears streaming down her face. "Is Daddy still home?"

"Yeah. They had another fight. He threw his plate against the wall."

She fell back into the pillow. "It's all my fault," she wailed.

"No, it's not. How can their fighting be your fault?"

She lifted her face and tried to control the hitching in her voice. "Daddy says I'm too sexy. He says I'm to blame."

Bobby leaped from the bed. "What are you talking about?"

Sofia pulled herself up into a sitting position. "Just go. Please."

"No. I'm not leaving until you tell me what's going on."

She could hear the stubbornness in his tone, his growing impatience, and knew he would not relent. "You'll hate me if I tell you. I couldn't bear that."

Bobby began to pace the room. He took a deep breath and let it out slowly. "I won't hate you, sis. I promise. Just talk to me."

She hesitated a moment longer, then got out of bed and stood facing him. She could see the look of surprise on his face.

"You've got all your clothes on! When did you get dressed?"

"Last night...after Daddy left." She saw her brother's look of surprise change to one of confusion as her cheeks burned with shame. "He comes into my room at night after he's been drinking." Her breathing came in short gasps. Tears fell again. "He touches me...down there...and he makes me touch him."

Bobby clamped his hands over his ears and ran to the window. His body was trembling. "What are you saying?"

Sofia wiped her eyes with the corner of the bed sheet. "I don't blame you for hating me. I feel so dirty."

Bobby wheeled around and grasped her by the shoulders. "I don't hate you, Sof. I hate him. I hate myself for not doing anything to help you or Mom." She saw him clench his jaw. "Well, that's all going to change right now."

Just then, the bedroom door burst open and slammed against the wall. The sound made them both jump. Their father stood in the doorway, face contorted with rage, both hands knotted into tight fists. "What's gonna change?" he yelled.

Bobby drew his sister behind him and faced his father. In a calm voice that sent chills through Sofia's body, he said, "You're going to leave my mother and my sister alone. If you touch either one of them again, or me, I'll kill you."

At first, Giancarlo looked astonished. Then he started laughing. "Oh, yeah? You and what army? I could beat the shit out of you one-handed, you little snot. In fact, I think I'll do that right now." He stepped into the room.

Bobby extended his right arm, pointed his finger at his father, and nodded his head. His voice was ice and fire. "I know you can beat me up, Dad. I'm only fourteen and you're bigger than me. But you have to sleep sometime. And when you do, I'll tiptoe into your bedroom with my baseball bat. And I will fucking kill you."

All color drained from the man's face. His brows knit and his lips curled downward. He stood as though carved from stone. A minute passed. Without saying another word, he left the room.

Bobby turned to his sister, and she embraced him. She cried into his chest. "Thank you," she managed. "I think he believed you."

"He'd better. It's true. I'll never let him hurt us again."

16. One Ring to Find Them

A week passed without any new breakthroughs. Kate burrowed in "like a tick on my dog Toby," as Bonnie would say. She examined the files, going over each in minute detail, trying to connect her own research with Tom Nolan's, looking for clues to the identities of the missing men. *What's in Paris?* and *Where's Bobby now?* she asked herself again and again. The longer it took, the more she feared she might never solve the puzzles, that her story on the network would leave unsatisfied viewers with more questions than answers. Every day she became more dispirited.

Jay called often. "Nothing new to report," was her tiresome refrain. In desperation, she called Bonnie again.

"Hi, sis. Sorry for calling again so soon, but I feel like I'm at a dead end. I'm intellectually constipated."

"Ooh. That sounds serious. What are you stuck on?"

"Trying to figure out where Bobby Gemelli is now and why he went to France in the first place."

"Well, I can remember your telling me that when nothing is moving, you 'free associate.' That's your mental laxative. You jot down a list of anything at all that comes to mind and sort it out later. So free associate to 'What's in France?'"

"Okay. Here goes. Let me get a piece of paper." She sat at her desk, pen in hand, blank page before her. "Paris. The Louvre. Mona Lisa. La Rive Gauche. Notre Dame. Versailles. Champs Elysées. Champagne. Wine." She wrote the words as quickly as she could.

Bonnie clicked her tongue. "Hmm. I've actually been reading a little about wine since our jaunt to Cruella's. In France, they name wines by where the grape grows, while here we name them after the grape itself. So a Burgundy there is a Pinot Noir here."

Kate sat up straight. "What did you say?"

"I said their Burgundy is our Pinot Noir."

She couldn't suppress her excitement. "Is it possible?"

"Is what possible?"

"That wine we drank at the restaurant in the Florentine. It was a Pinot Noir—"

Bonnie interrupted her. "That the wine guy said was exclusive to their restaurant—a special order to Gemelli herself. And only to Gemelli."

"Okay. Okay. Is it possible that Bobby goes to France, studies winemaking in Burgundy, and comes back to start his own vineyard here in the States? That he sends his twin sister the best Pinot Noir he has to offer?"

"Kate that sounds every bit as possible as dead bodies showing up on the shores of Lake Mead."

"I love you, Bonnie! Now I gotta run!"

"Love you, too, sis. Have a glass for me. Bye."

Kate sat back in her chair. *It's a stretch*, she thought, *but my gut says to go with it. What have I got to lose, except maybe a plane ticket to Oregon? And it'll get me out of this damned heat.* She took out her phone and pulled up the picture of the wine label she had taken in the restaurant.

2018
Enchanted Hill Vineyards
Signature Cuvée
Pinot Noir
Willamette Valley * Oregon

She Googled the winery. The home page featured an eye-popping view of green slopes covered with grapevines, shining in a late afternoon sun. Near the top was a chateau-like tasting room with a tower and a large outdoor patio hosting an array of umbrella-covered tables. At the summit was a house, presumably the owner's, partially hidden by tall fir trees. Written across the blue sky was the inscription:

Wines to rival France,
sustainably grown,
harvested with care,

produced with love.
--Gavin Hartford, Co-Founder/Winemaker

Buy me a ticket, she thought. She scrolled through the various menus, fascinated by how the winery paid attention to environmental concerns, including its use of water, corks, recycling. Pictures of the employees and their bios were featured on another drop-down menu. Immediately after Hartford's was a Bobby Amato, an elderly gentleman who looked about the same age as Hartford. *Did you change your last name, Bobby? Have I found you at last?* There was a blog, information on joining a wine club and purchasing stock, specifics on each available wine. "Trained in Burgundy," she read aloud, "Gavin Hartford and his partner, Bobby Amato, brought back French clones to the perfect climate of the Willamette Valley. After completing their quarantine at Oregon State University, these vines were propagated for use in Oregon, and their Pinot Noirs are now the crowning achievement of Enchanted Hill Vineyards."

Is it crazy to take this leap of faith—to let myself believe, on the flimsiest evidence, that I've tracked down someone whose trail has been ice-cold for decades? She raised her eyes to the ceiling and spoke aloud. "Okay. If anybody is listening, would you show me a sign, give me some proof that I'm not off my rocker and about to waste my hard-earned cash—or the network's—on a trip to Oregon?" She waited. After a few minutes, she said, "Not this time, huh? Well, you can't blame a girl for trying."

She looked at her watch. Time for the evening news. She stood and stretched and walked into the kitchen. Quickly scrubbing a small potato, she put it into the oven to bake. She removed a pork chop from the refrigerator to let it warm up on the counter before grilling it. Then she rinsed the broccoli she had picked up at the grocery store yesterday and put it in a sauce pan with some water. Once preparations were complete, she poured a small glass of bourbon and turned on the television.

A dark-haired woman looked earnestly into the camera while a light breeze blew errant locks of hair into her eyes. "Noreen, we have breaking news in Nevada in a case that simply gets curiouser and curiouser by the hour. Here we are, back on the sad, drying shoreline of Lake Mead, where a startling discovery was made earlier today by two young boys with their metal detectors. Searching in the mud and sand not far from where two partial skeletons and chains were found recently..." *She pointed to a place behind her.* "...they unearthed a ring. Once they brought it home and cleaned it up, doing research on the internet in true detective fashion, they determined it was a New York Jets Super Bowl III ring, from a game that was played in January of 1969. Unfortunately for them, when they proudly posted pictures of their incredible treasure on Tik Tok and Facebook, the police immediately confiscated it as evidence in their ongoing investigations into the Lake Mead mysteries. The plot thickens, Noreen! Now back to you."

Kate leaped from her chair. "I found you, Harry!" she shouted. "Harry Costello, that's your lucky ring. Touchdown!" She did a little happy dance around the living room before becoming thoughtful again. "I guess it wasn't lucky for you that day." She sat back down and took a sip of bourbon. Raising her eyes to the ceiling, she whispered, "Sign accepted. Thank you."

Her mind was working at light-speed. There were two partial skeletons on that beach, one chained to a cinder block. Most of the other missing men were administrative types, accountants and bookkeepers. Except one. What had Nolan's notes said about Tom Romano? Something about being "the collections guy for Johnny?" Was that mob talk for "enforcer" or "muscle?"

"I'll take HIT MEN for $600, Alex," she announced to the empty house. Then she imagined she was playing Texas Hold 'Em. "I'm all in, Tommy boy. Giancarlo's plan to have you whack Harry went terribly wrong. You and Harry both wound up at the bottom of the lake."

Pieces of the puzzle were falling into place. Her original idea that Giancarlo Gemelli was trying to consolidate his hold on the casinos of Las Vegas no longer seemed like such a flight of fancy. Could he have orchestrated all the disappearances using Tom Romano? And how much did Bobby know about what his father was up to? *Is that what Sofia is trying to prevent me from exposing?* "Dirty deeds, done dirt cheap?"

When it was finally time to remove her potato from the oven, cook her broccoli, and throw her pork chop on the grill, she did so with a profound sense of self-satisfaction. *I've got this*, she thought, grinning from ear to ear. *Get the Emmy Award ready! Hell! Pull out the Pulitzer!*

After supper, she called Jay. "Hey, book us airline tickets to Portland, Oregon. Make it tomorrow, if any seats are available. Charge it to the network. I'll tell you all about it in the morning."

17. The Gentleman Winemaker

Gavin Hartford smiled over his second cup of coffee. This year promised to be a wonderful vintage. After the wet spring that he knew would delay the autumn harvest, the cool nights, and the dry, rainless summer were a perfect formula for Pinot Noir, Oregon's premier grape, and the jewel of the Willamette Valley. Although there were fewer bunches of fruit to harvest, the juices in them were wonderfully concentrated, and he was sure the resulting wine would garner accolades from *Wine Enthusiast Magazine* and *Wine Spectator*. He expected scores higher than 93 for his estate wines and over 95 for his Signature Cuvée. There was even a chance to have a wine of his ranked number one for the year. If that happened, the vineyard's entire inventory would sell out in a matter of days, and his fame as winemaker might put a rock star to shame. It could be a very good year indeed.

From where he sat at his kitchen table, the bay window commanded a breath-taking view of the west-facing slope, its green vines heavy with dark fruit. Harvest was fast-approaching. The weather report continued to be favorable, not predicting any rain for the foreseeable future. This late in the game, rain was the real enemy. If thirsty grapes drank a day or two of heavy rain, their skins might burst, their juices might be diluted, disease might strike, and the wine they would produce would plummet from spectacular to less than ordinary. As co-owner and chief winemaker, it was Gavin's duty to proclaim exactly when that harvest would begin. He would be on the slopes today, checking grapes for the perfect degree Brix, the measure of sugar content that would assure optimum fermentation once the grapes had been picked and pressed. At his word, the staff and seasonal workers at the winery would spring into a frenzy of activity, gathering his "babies" to begin their transformation into the nectar of the gods.

He smiled at those thoughts. Although Enchanted Hill Vineyards cultivated some Chardonnay and Pinot Gris, Pinot Noir was the undisputed Queen of the winery. She was a demanding mistress, thin-skinned, susceptible to rot, pests, and mutation, influenced by the slightest changes in soil composition. At her best, she defined elegance in wine, with her medium body, garnet-red clarity, smooth tannins, and flavors of cherry, strawberry, blackberry, floral hints of rose petal and hibiscus, sometimes cinnamon and cloves, and, with aging, earthy notes of forest floor and truffle. Gavin was in thrall to her.

After his last sip of coffee, he stood and walked into the bathroom for a final check in the mirror. He wore his seventy years well, thanks to regular exercise and healthy eating habits. A shock of white hair adorned his head and complemented his regal bearing. His brilliant blue eyes called to mind Paul Newman in his early films, when the young actor could enrapture his co-star and his audience with a single glance. Always clean-shaven, Gavin had the square-jawed intensity of a politician or a priest. Whenever staff would ask him why he always wore a shirt and tie to work, his response was, "I am in service to the Queen," leaving them all with knowing smiles, nodding their heads. His dress had earned him the moniker, "The Gentleman Winemaker," or "GW" for short.

In other ways, the years had not been kind to him. His wife Guinevere had committed suicide twenty-five years ago, two weeks after the overdose death of their teenage son, Jonas, their only child and the light of their lives. Gavin had drunk himself into a stupor and had driven their BMW into an oak tree. Three weeks in the hospital and a month at a rehab facility had restored him to a semblance of life. A therapist might try to persuade him to look at how he handled his grief, at how his obsessively ordered life might be an attempt to keep his inner demons at bay. But Gavin never went to therapists. He grew grapes and made wine.

With the last adjustment of his tie complete, he stepped out his front door and walked down the hill to the winery's large tasting room. He preferred to start his workday there, checking in with all the staff, convincing himself that everything was as it should be for the influx of customers expected when the winery opened at eleven o'clock.

The large oak and glass doors gave entrance to the central seating area, filled with polished mahogany tables, each decorated with a crystal vase of freshly cut flowers. A granite-topped bar ran the length of the right wall, facing its smaller counterpart on the opposite side. The doors behind the lesser bar opened into the kitchen, where the chef and his assistants were already preparing for luncheon guests. Behind and above the tasting bar on the right were racks of Riedel glasses, a different shape for each wine varietal. Lights behind the glasses made them sparkle like a diamond tennis bracelet for a giant. In the middle of the room was an open gas firepit whose tall flames would be lit once the cold rains of autumn and winter had begun.

"Good morning, my dear friends and fellow servants of the Queen!" Gavin announced. It was a greeting he made every day without fail, a kind of structure that could be relied upon no matter the weather, the stresses personal, business, and otherwise. Its regularity was comforting. Although it sometimes left new employees scratching their heads, those who had been there a while basked in his acknowledgement of their presence and loved him for it. They stopped their bustling around, turned toward him with a smile and a slight bow of the head, and responded, "And to you, GW."

The ritual complete, he walked down the stairs into the cellar to test the progress of previous vintages, maturing in barrels of French oak. The barrels lay on their side, many long rows that filled the basement. He thought of them as "sleeping" in the cool cavern, though he knew that at a molecular level they were anything but asleep, more active than children on a playground. Smells of wine and dampness relaxed him as surely as any soporific. He was at home and at peace.

After picking up his thief, a clear pipette for sampling the wine, and a glass he kept on a small shelf, he walked halfway down the central path between the barrels. He pulled the bung, the silicone stopper, from the bunghole of a barrel on the right, inserted the thief, and withdrew an ounce of wine. He poured the wine into the glass, observing its color. Then he held it to his nose, inhaling its subtle aromas. Finally, he lifted it to his lips and sloshed the wine around in his mouth before spitting it into the cellar's spit bucket. Then he repeated the whole routine with four more barrels.

Almost ready for bottling, he thought. The Pinot Noir rested here for twelve to eighteen months, maturing, drawing flavors from the oak, and accentuating its own delicate complexity. The bottling process would be a shock to the Queen, would "bruise" her dignity and actually change her taste, so she would remain in the bottle for another three to six months to recover and regain her poise. Gavin smiled and walked back toward the stairs. Time to walk the slopes of the vineyard and check the latest iteration.

Outside, the sun had crested the house behind him and was shining obliquely down the hillside upon the rows of lush green vines, their leaves shielding tight bunches of black berries. He peeled back the leaf canopy on the first vine and saw several empty stems. Pulling the phone from his pocket, he called the foreman.

"We need the bird bangers out here, José. Start on the west slope, the Sunset Block. Better get to it right away."

"Gotcha, GW. On it."

The reports of the propane cannons, sounding like random blasts of a shotgun, would scare the pests away from the grapes until his staff could harvest the succulent clusters. It was another of the myriad variables Gavin had to manage.

He restored the phone to his pocket and walked farther down the slope. As he turned into another row of vines, he withdrew a device that looked like a spotting scope from his jacket. The black eight-inch tube had a prism at one end and an eyepiece at the other. A sad smile curled his lips as he recalled four-year-old Jonas, who loved to accompany him on his forays through the vineyard.

"What is that, Daddy?" the little boy said.

"It's a refractometer, son. It tells me how much sugar is in our grapes. That way I know when they're ready to be picked."

"How does it do that?"

"Let me show you." Gavin plucked a berry and squeezed a drop of its juice onto the prism. "See? Now I close the lens cover,

hold it up to the light, and look in this end. It gives me a number called the degree Brix."

"Bricks like the toys I build houses with?"

"No, Brix with an 'x.' Here. You look inside."

"I see a bunch of numbers like on a ruler and a blue line."

"That line points to the number we're looking for. We want it to be between a little more than 23 and a little less than 25."

"Hmmm. It's closer to 20."

"So, we have to let our grapes grow some more before we pick them. They're not ready yet."

The boy handed the device back to his father. "How come you're so smart, Daddy?"

"Because I studied for many years in France, learning all I could about how to grow grapes and make the best wine from them."

A tear welled in the corner of his eye. But he hadn't been smart enough to see the signs of depression and drug use in his sixteen-year-old son. And his own grief had blinded him to his wife's catastrophic heartache.

He shook his head as if to dislodge the offending thoughts. "I have work to do today," he scolded himself aloud. "No time to be maudlin."

Picking a grape from the nearest vine, he squeezed some juice onto the lens, popped the crushed berry into his mouth, and looked through the eyepiece. "Almost," he whispered aloud as he smacked his lips. It was also a signal for him to begin a more careful examination of his Queen. Before the morning was over, he would gather grapes randomly from different clusters in several blocks, keeping each block's fruit in a separate plastic bag. Back in the basement laboratory at the winery, he would extract a cupful of juice to represent each block and subject it to analysis by one of his more accurate digital refractometers. In addition, he would use his pH meter to determine the juice's general acidity and later, he would calculate its titratable acidity. Due to its exposure, the Sunset Block usually matured first, so harvesting most often began there, leaving the Cascade Block for the very end. His measurements would determine if this year continued to follow the pattern.

When his phone rang, he pulled it from his pocket.

"Hi, GW. This is Alyson in the office. I have a Kate Temperance calling for you. Says she's a freelance writer for several of the wine magazines and wants to know if she can interview you for an upcoming issue of *Wine Spectator*. You on board with that?"

He smiled. "Absolutely. Tell her I'm happy to make time for her this week or next. The closer we get to harvest, of course, the harder it will be to get away."

"You bet, GW. Will do."

He returned the phone to his pocket and exhaled a satisfied breath. *It's begun*, he thought.

#

At midday, he and co-owner Bobby Amato held a staff meeting with the chiefs of their crew in the private banquet room downstairs. Per their custom, Gavin chaired the gathering. A large koa table, an extravagance Gavin had imported from Hawaii, dominated the chamber. The opalescent grain of the wood invited a reverent stroke from anyone who sat there. Three of the room's walls were enormous wine racks filled with bottles designated as the vineyard's "library collection," its oldest wines from its finest vintages. The fourth wall was glass, with a sliding door out onto a patio overlooking a steep, vine-covered slope. The foothills of the Coast Range were purple in the distance.

"Cannons are up and running, boss," José said. As if on cue, a loud bang echoed up the hill.

"Indeed," Gavin said with a grin. "Other news?"

A young woman in jeans and a red blouse lifted her head. "Most of the clones we planted in the Brookside Block are doing well. We'll keep the grow tubes on them for now." Carol smiled at Gavin and the five others seated around the table. "Lots of rabbits on that hill, and we don't want them nibbling into our profits!"

When the chuckling subsided, Gavin said, "Looks like it will be a good year. And thank you, Carol, for spotting that powdery mildew in the North Block early. We stopped it before it got very far."

"Speaking of all things fungus, can I give you the latest on our very own *Avenger*, GW?" Darren was the resident geek, fresh out of college, and interested in all things high-tech. His scruffy, five-day beard and roadie T-shirt belied a brilliant intelligence. Gavin motioned for him to continue.

Darren stood and addressed the group with the flourish of a professor. "So, you know we've entered into a research partnership with Oregon State University, and the robots are among us!" His colleagues laughed. "If you've been here after dark, you've probably seen the *Thorvald*. I call him *Thor*, for short. It's that big white arch that straddles the vines and rolls up and down the rows at night, glowing. Thor uses ultraviolet light to kill powdery mildew by altering its DNA. No chemicals! It has to be done at night because blue light in sunshine—"

Carol closed her eyes and pretended to snore. José chuckled.

"The short version, Darren?" said Gavin.

"Bottom line—Thor works great. OSU is publishing a big study. The Saga Robotics firm in Norway is over the moon with how this will promote their baby to wineries all over the globe, and Enchanted Hill Vineyards will get three more of the critters for our trouble."

The group clapped as Darren took a bow and sat back down.

Roberta, a woman in her early fifties with piercing blue eyes and a razor-sharp wit said, "The God of Thunder scores again! Congrats, Darren. Meanwhile, at Bobby's direction, I've gone ahead and hired a new chef. He's putting the finishing touches on a new menu that we'll launch this weekend."

Gavin nodded in approval and gave a thumbs-up sign to Bobby. "Specialties?"

"He's dynamite with seafood. I've sampled his steelhead fillet and his Oysters Rockefeller, and they're to die for. Soups are another of his things, but I haven't tried any of those yet."

"Very good." Gavin looked toward a woman at the far end of the table. "Let's hear from our Wine Ambassador. Cherise, what have you got for us?"

The blonde-haired woman surveyed the room as a politician might, gauging her connection with her audience. Her stunning good looks were surpassed only by the clarity of her booming voice and the self-confidence she exuded from every pore.

"Club membership is up twenty percent from the last quarter. Restaurants in town are clamoring for the Estate Pinot we just released. And I'm planning our next wine-pairing dinner event, when our new Chef Girard can showcase his stuff. So, it's all good, GW."

Gavin nodded. "And last but not least, though certainly the *elder* statesman among us, I understand our supervisor of all things EHV has a birthday coming up. Bobby, what do you have to say for yourself?"

All eyes turned toward the gray-haired man, who stood and smiled. "Watch the 'elder statesman' crap, GW. I'm only two months older than you, remember? And I can still duke it out with the best of them." He flexed his muscles, and laughter filled the room. "Anyway, as Roberta said, we've got a new chef for our expanded tasting room. I've hired four more servers, and I've already heard good reviews of them from our regulars."

"Thank you, Bobby." Gavin withdrew an envelope from his jacket pocket. "Here's a little something we all chipped in on to help you celebrate your birthday."

Bobby took the envelope and shook his head. "You guys! I could say you shouldn't have, but what I really want to say is how much you make me feel like part of a family. I can't thank you enough."

Gavin took a deep breath. "And we all thank you, Bobby, for your years of dedication to our vineyard—this grand project of ours—and the decades of friendship you and I share." He surveyed the room again. "We are a family, everyone. With our combined efforts, we're on track for having a record year." He smiled again. "Vintage, as they might say." He stood and the others followed suit.

"Thank you all. I have a feeling Enchanted Hill Vineyards will be making headlines very soon."

18. It's Willamette Dammit!

In all her years of investigative reporting, Kate had decided that nothing really surpassed living in the place of her story—engaging all her senses to see and hear and taste and smell what her characters did. That gave her the *feel* of her story. Not that she didn't spend days and weeks and sometimes months doing research online, but there was no substitute for getting into the *skin* of her protagonists. It lent the signature authenticity to the work that her publishers loved so much. Rather than spend money on hotels that made her feel claustrophobic after a week, she would rent or lease a house.

Before the plane had taxied to a stop in Portland, Kate had already used her phone to find a property manager in Salem. Once she and Jay had secured a rental car, she called Alla Georgiou of HomeFinders Lease and Rental and introduced herself.

"Welcome to our beautiful valley, Kate," came the jaunty response, "nestled in between the Coast Range on the West and the Cascade Range on the East. Everything's green here! We grow grapes, grass seed, Christmas trees, hazel nuts, and lots and lots of cannabis!" She paused for a moment and then began to spell a word. "Just so you know—W-i-l-l-a-m-e-t-t-e rhymes with 'dammit.' It's Willamette dammit!"

Kate wasn't sure what to think, but she chuckled at the woman's enthusiasm. "Jay and I will need a two-bedroom, two bath rental home in Salem. Do you have listings for anything like that?"

"Sure do. If you're leaving Portland now, you can be at my office in about an hour. Just come straight down I-5 and take the Kuebler Boulevard exit. I'll pull up everything I've got so I'll be ready when you and your husband walk through the door."

"Oh, Jay and I aren't married."

"Hey, no harm, no foul Kate. We're pretty liberal here, except for that gang over on the far eastern side that wants to leave Oregon and become part of Idaho. See you soon."

Kate ended the call and turned to Jay. "Fingers crossed, man. She sounded a little strange."

"Maybe into the weed already?"

She laughed. "Maybe."

#

Three days later, sitting at the kitchen table in the small house Alla had found for them, Kate finished entering the appointment in her phone's calendar. Rather than begin by confronting Bobby Amato—Bobby Gemelli?—immediately, she decided to chat with Gavin Hartford first and "legitimize" her poking around the winery.

The sliding glass door at the back of the kitchen afforded her a view of the Douglas firs and oak trees that marked the boundary of the back yard. As she looked over the table and out the door, she saw two blacktail does, ears twitching, eyes scanning for danger, emerge timidly from the forest. A moment later, they were joined by three fawns, already grown enough to have lost their protective spots. She knew that, barring a fright from a passing car, they would make their way between the houses to her neighbor's pond across the street for their morning refreshment.

"I love it here," she whispered aloud, relishing the cool temperatures after the stifling heat of the desert and awed by the deep green surrounding her. She watched the deer disappear from view.

She stood and walked to her bedroom to retrieve a light sweater, still surprised at how chilly she got after sitting still before her computer for a few hours. There was her grandmother's photograph of 70s Las Vegas hanging on the wall above her bed. Kate had brought it as a kind of connection back to the life she knew and the best friend she treasured. She decided she wanted it by her computer to keep her inspired. Taking the picture down and returning to the kitchen with it, she laid the framed photo on the table and poured herself a third cup of coffee from the pot on the counter. "But I do miss my coffee machine!" That thought reminded her of Bonnie, complaining about the "fancy pants" machine Kate had purchased last year.

"What? No cappuccino? No latte? You buy a machine that does everything but sing the national anthem, and all you make is a boring cup of black coffee?"

"Yes, a boring cup of coffee is all I need. And this makes a great one."

She could still hear Bonnie's laughter. *I miss you so much, sister. I hope Gemelli never bothers your family again.* She clicked her tongue. *And now I have to get back to work.*

Having never written an article about the wine industry before, despite what she had told the receptionist at Enchanted Hill Vineyards, she thought she had better educate herself before her interview with Hartford next week. Internet research was her stock-in-trade, of course, and she found it an enjoyable way to spend an afternoon. Before long, she was fully immersed in her study, learning about Brix, the intricacies of fermentation, and something called "carbonic maceration." She chuckled. *This is making me thirsty!*

By four-thirty, she had had enough for one day. Withdrawing her phone from her purse, she called Bonnie, but the call went immediately to voicemail. "Hey, girl," she recorded. "Nothing important. Just checking in. Love you." When she ended the call, she felt and heard her stomach rumble. On impulse, she tapped another number.

"Hi, Jay. Where are you? Are you hungry? Up for going out to dinner? Give me a call."

Ten minutes later, he responded. "I'm starving, and I have just the place in mind. I'll be there in a few minutes."

Kate returned the phone to her purse next to the extra set of car keys and wondered again if they should rent a second car. Jay had insisted he wanted to be with her whenever she went out, but that meant she was without transportation if he left. She chafed at his overprotectiveness and determined to use a Lyft or an Uber if she wanted to be off on her own. *Stuff it, Jay.*

She changed her blouse, ran a brush through her hair, and freshened her lipstick. Just as she heard Jay at the door, her phone signaled an incoming text message. "It's from Billie. They've finished the promo for my story."

"I know. She sent it to me ten minutes ago. You'd better look at it."

Kate clicked on the link and was taken to an aerial view of Lake Mead, the so-called "bathtub ring" clearly visible. As though previewing a new horror movie, a deep, Darth-Vader-type voice asked, "Do you know what the drought exposed last summer as the waters receded?" The camera zoomed in to the now-infamous barrel, lying in the mud near the Hemenway boat launch. The image inside the drum was blurry, but the voice seemed to relish saying, "There was a bullet hole in his skull." Next the camera flew to the coastline along Boulder Beach and Swim Beach, and the voice described the skeletal remains found there. In a flash, the scene changed to the Las Vegas Strip, but instead of giving glimpses of all the big hotels, the focus was on the Florentine. The camera flew through the front doors and into the gaming rooms. Color leached from the picture, turning it to gray and white, as the voice boomed out the "hook" Kate had devised for Billie. The screen turned black. Large white letters scrolled across it, spelling out the narrator's final funereal message, "All the bodies do."

Kate put her hand to her mouth. "Oh, my God! Talk about rubbing it in Gemelli's face."

Jay nodded his head. "My thoughts exactly. When it airs next week and she sees it, she'll have a shit-fit. Who knows what she'll do?"

"I'm so glad she doesn't know where we are."

Jay turned to the small kitchen sink and poured himself a glass of water. "You and me both."

Once her phone was back in her purse, Kate said, "So what eatery did you have in mind?"

"Ancora Vineyards, about a twenty-minute drive southwest of here. I saw it online. Supposedly, they make a killer wood-fired pizza."

"I'm all for that. Let's go."

In minutes, they had left the urban boundary and were driving along forested country roads. Emerging from the oaks and Douglas firs, Kate had yet to grow accustomed to the sprawling vistas of green, rolling hills that nurtured hundreds of vineyards. "It massages the eyes, doesn't it?"

Jay kept his hands on the steering wheel but turned briefly to her. "What?"

"This countryside. This Oregon landscape. It's so beautiful."

"Better than sagebrush and succulents, huh?"

"Mm hmm. Maybe I'll never go back to the desert. You can plant me here."

Jay did not respond.

19. The Invisible Man

A thousand miles away, Sofia Gemelli snarled in displeasure. "All the bodies do, indeed, Ms. Temperance." She had just watched the promotional video, the link to which Jay had sent her a few minutes earlier. Lifting her phone from her purse, she called her brother in Oregon. "Did you get that infernal video from Jay?"

"Well, hello, Sofia, and yes, I did. I haven't had an opportunity to watch it yet."

"I'm beginning to regret we didn't dispatch that little tart while she was here in Las Vegas." She heard her brother clear his throat.

"All is not lost, dear sister. As we had planned, she will show us all the places where our alibi is the weakest. We'll patch the holes and then arrange for her unfortunate demise."

Sofia tapped her long fingernails on the desk. "I'm having misgivings about assigning Jay to this job. He's young, emotional. You don't think he's growing too fond of her, do you?"

"Hardly. He owes us, after all."

"But does the heart really know such things? Does love trump loyalty?"

The voice was silent, as though its author was considering her questions. "A conundrum, no doubt. I'll keep a close eye on both of them when they come to the winery next week. Will that make you happy?"

"I'll be happy when we're finally rid of her, and not until then."

"I'll keep you informed. Goodbye for now."

Sofia frowned. She remained unconvinced that they should wait before doing something definitive about Kate Temperance. Jay had been good about keeping her informed, but she sensed something in his voice. Her intuition told her he was developing feelings for the reporter, admiring her thoroughness, persistence, and her integrity. Would that cloud his judgment at a critical moment?

Against her brother's wishes, she decided to take matters into her own hands. Just as her father had had a favorite man in collections, so did she. Over recent years, James Ward had distinguished himself as someone more than capable of managing unpleasant business. He was detail-oriented, efficient, and discreet. More than that, there was nothing particularly notable about his appearance. He was a kind of dark-haired, clean-shaven "everyman" who easily disappeared into a crowd. No scars, no tattoos, no features to make him stand out in a police lineup. She called him her "invisible man." He answered her call on the first ring.

"Hi, Sofia. What a nice surprise! Would you like me to come by your office?"

"Yes, James, please do. Today, if you're available."

"I'm always available for you. You know that. I can be there in an hour, if that's convenient."

"Perfect. I'll see you then."

#

Always prompt to a fault, Ward showed up at her office sixty minutes later. He was dressed in black jeans and a light-blue polo shirt, and he looked like an ordinary tourist about to spend the afternoon working the slot machines in the gaming rooms downstairs. Once her men had escorted him in and left, she pointed to the chair in front of her desk. "Please have a seat, James. It's good to see you. May I get you something?"

"A Scotch would be nice. Neat, please."

She walked to the mini-bar and half-filled two crystal glasses with the honey-colored whiskey.

"That's a very generous pour," he said. "I still have to drive, remember."

She laughed. "We'll take our time. We have a lot to discuss." She handed one glass to him and raised hers in a toast. "To old friends and good times."

"Hear, hear," he responded, extending his glass toward her, then lifting it to his lips. "Ah! That's an incredible Scotch. You serve nothing but the best." He took another sip. "Please tell me how I can help you."

She smiled at the flattery and got right down to business. "There's an investigative journalist attempting to do a defamatory piece on the Florentine. All my efforts to dissuade her have failed. She needs to be stopped."

"I understand. Tell me more."

#

Now she could relax properly, knowing that the thorn would be removed from her paw soon. James had called her back shortly after leaving her office to say he had booked a flight to Portland tomorrow morning. He expected his task to be completed within a week.

Still feeling the effects of the Scotch, she recalled a bad joke her brother had told her years ago that concluded with the punchline, "Necessity is the mother of murder." It still made her groan, though she had to admit the truth of it. *The visitors to my casino, the guests in my hotel rooms have little appreciation for what it takes to run an empire like mine, catering to their every whim. Difficult decisions, hard choices sometimes have to be made. If the Florentine were to collapse, an economic earthquake would rattle all of Nevada. My business supports the mayor, the governor, the taxpayers. I can't let any harm befall them.*

She looked toward the bottle of Scotch, but decided to eat something before drinking any more alcohol.

#

Portland International Airport was undergoing extensive renovation and expansion. Posters along some of the corridors proclaimed the improvements visitors could expect in the coming months. James Ward was certain that the word "expansion" was correct. All airport upgrades meant that the walk from "Point A" to "Point B" would be exponentially longer.

Although he knew it was permissible to carry a firearm in checked baggage, he rarely did so, since he didn't like having to declare the gun to security and draw attention to himself. Instead, it was always his preference to bring only a carry-on bag and get a firearm once he had arrived at his destination. With that in mind, he took the escalator down to BAGGAGE CLAIM AND GROUND TRANSPORTATION, where he spotted a young man dressed in a Coldplay T-shirt and holding a cardboard sign with the letters J. W. scrawled in magic marker.

"Mr. James Ward from Las Vegas?" the sign-holder said.

"That's me. You must be Chiang." He offered his hand, but the man only nodded.

"There's a gray Honda Accord waiting for you in Economy Parking. Take the shuttle to the Blue Lot, Bus Shelter P. Here's the key fob and the ticket to get out of the gate. Your package is in the trunk." He handed Ward the items, then turned and walked away.

The exchange took only a few seconds, just the way Ward liked it. He stepped outside, pleasantly surprised by the cool air of Portland after the heat of Las Vegas. The shuttle arrived at the curb a few minutes later, and he was at the parking lot in less than ten minutes. Once he got off the bus at Shelter P, he had to laugh as he looked at rows and rows of almost identical automobiles. *Hell*, he thought. *I can't find my own car at an airport when I've parked it myself!*

Finally, after several minutes of frustration, he located the Honda and popped the trunk to look at his package. The pistol was a favorite of his, a 9 mm. SIG Sauer P320 with a titanium suppressor. Satisfied, he closed the hatch and got into the driver's seat. After starting the car and checking the gauges and mirrors, he input the address of the new Wine Country Hotel in Salem into the GPS. "Houston, we are go for launch," he said aloud. "At last."

An hour later, he checked into his suite, then went to the Grapevine Restaurant on the first floor for a late lunch. Pictures of vineyards from up and down the valley splashed color on the walls. Labels under the paintings and photographs identified wineries in the Yamhill-Carlton District, McMinnville, the Dundee Hills and many others. One showed empty grapevines laden with winter snow. Another saw the sun cresting over a slope where small green buds announced the arrival of spring. In several, row upon row of vines were heavy with dark fruit hanging in cone-shaped clusters. He especially liked a large painting entitled, "Harvesting the Valley's Black Gold."

Once he had taken a seat at a small table away from the door, a server in a white shirt and tie greeted him. "May I get you something to drink?"

"I've never been to Oregon before, but I've heard a lot about Enchanted Hill Winery. Would you have one of their Pinot Noirs?"

"We have several, sir. May I recommend a favorite?"

"By all means."

Soon he was sipping a glass of wine while he awaited a fillet of fresh salmon. *When in Rome...* he thought. Fine dining always slowed him down so he could plan his strategy. Jay had given Sofia the address of the house he and Temperance were renting, and Ward would go there first. Sofia had insisted that Ward not harm Jay. She also said that she would not be informing Jay about Ward's presence in Oregon. *Ah, the technicalities make the job more interesting.*

He hadn't yet decided the *how* of his assignment. Of course, he could use the gun and then do enough damage in the house to lead authorities to presume a botched robbery. That was the simplest way. Strangling was a possibility, but depending on the woman's size and athletic ability, the attempt could go south quickly, and he risked being injured. He had a hypodermic with a fast-acting sedative with him. Could he knock her out and make it look as though she had fallen in the bathtub and drowned? Again, complicated.

As his plate of salmon, baby red potatoes, and mixed seasonal vegetables arrived, he smiled at the thought of his old tried-and-true axiom, what he called his "Occam's Razor of Murder."

Usually, the simplest way was best.

20. Flowers for Kate

Two days later, Kate was showered and dressed and sitting in the kitchen, sipping her first cup of coffee. The back slider was open, and the perfume of something blooming outside wafted through the screen. She could hear robins chirping and a crow cawing in the distance.

Jay walked into the kitchen and announced, "I'm going out for breakfast. Want to come?"

"No, thanks. I've got more to do before our meeting with Hartford the day after tomorrow."

"So, you're staying in while I'm gone?"

"Of course...Daddy! I swear, you're getting on my nerves."

"I'm just doing what I've been told to do—nothing more, nothing less."

"Well, it's beginning to piss me off."

He pursed his lips and sighed. "Hey, stay safe. See you in a bit."

After he had gone, Kate plugged a new flash drive into her computer. With the deft moves of long experience, she copied her own research files as well as Nolan's onto it. *If I'm marching into the lion's den*, she thought, *it's time to send a copy of this to Bonnie, just like I told her I would.*

Kate opened the Lyft app on her phone. She input the address of a mail depot called Packages Plus. An icon of a black BMW X3 bore the caption "3 minutes" and she selected it. Andreas would be her driver.

She put the phone and the drive into the back pocket of her jeans and walked into the bathroom to check her hair. She was surprised when the doorbell rang a minute later. *Drivers don't leave their cars*, she thought.

At the front door, she looked through the peephole and saw a dark-haired man holding an enormous bouquet of red and blue and white flowers.

"Are those for me?" she asked when she opened the door. A broad smile spread across her face.

The man made a show of reading the envelope attached to the flowers. "If you're Ms. Kate Temperance they are. Here you go." He extended the bouquet to her, and she grasped it in both hands. "Now back into the house and don't make a sound."

"What?"

"Get into the house and shut up." He aimed a gun at her chest.

Kate dropped the flowers and backed up. Her stomach went into freefall. Her heart pounded as she struggled to catch her breath. She reached a hand behind her, afraid she might stumble into something. "I-I don't understand."

"I said shut up." With a quick glance over his shoulder, he slammed the front door and locked it, never moving the gun from its target. He followed her as she continued backwards into the kitchen.

Kate bumped into the counter. She raised her hands in front of her. "Please don't. I don't know you. I can't identify you. Take anything you want and just go."

"Sorry, lady. What I have to take is you." He raised the gun to her head.

Just then a loud automobile horn blared out front. Startled, the man glanced toward the sound. Kate spun around. She grabbed the coffee pot and hurled it at the man's head. The pot shattered, spewing scalding coffee everywhere. The man howled in pain, rubbing the burning liquid from his face and eyes. Kate bolted for the screen door. She threw it wide and sprinted toward the trees. She heard *Pop! Pop! Pop!* behind her as she ducked under the low-hanging branches and out of sight.

Kate had never ventured into these woods before. She kept running, heart pounding, breath rasping in her chest. She yelped in pain when she stumbled into a blackberry tangle. The thorns tore at her arms and pricked through her jeans. She pulled herself from the needle-sharp canes and charged ahead.

Behind her, she could hear her assailant crashing through the brush. A shriek of pain told her he had also blundered into the blackberries. *Thank you, God, for small favors*, she thought. Then another favor. *A trail! This must be how the deer come and go!* She raced forward without looking back.

Fifty yards down the trail, she stopped to catch her breath. She took the phone from her pocket and silenced it. Then she texted 911. "Man with gun. Kate Temperance hiding in woods behind 6151 Rose Tree Court Salem." She copied that message and sent it to Jay as well. In moments, she was running again.

#

Jay had just finished breakfast at Bacon and Eggs, a small grill in South Salem, when his phone pinged with the message. He leaped to his feet, threw a twenty-dollar bill on the table, and ran out the door.

"What the hell?" he shouted. He got into the car and texted Kate. "U OK?" When he got no immediate response, he rammed the car into gear and sped out of the parking lot.

His brain was going in a hundred directions at once. *Is this random—a case of being in the wrong place at the wrong time? Would Sofia send somebody after Kate without telling me? Don't they trust me anymore?*

Minutes later, he was back at the house. If Kate had contacted the police, he had beaten them there. The front door was open. He drew his gun and cautiously entered. A bouquet of flowers lay strewn across the entry way. He walked toward the kitchen, feet crunching on shards of glass. Coffee covered everything, even Kate's photo of the Strip, whose shattered frame lay on the floor. Her computer was gone.

He stalked to her bedroom, gently pushing the door open with his left hand, pistol at the ready in his right. All the clothing had been pulled from the bureau drawers, and the mattress had been overturned. Everything in the closet had been dumped in a heap on the floor. *Robbery?* he thought. Just as he turned to leave and check his own bedroom, he heard a shout from the front door.

"Police!" A heartbeat later, "Gun! Gun!"

The muzzle flashes were the last thing he saw.

21. Vigil

Kate sat in an uncomfortable chair in the corner of the room, looking out the window over the parking lot to the trees beyond, as the last bright sliver of sun disappeared beneath the horizon. Had two days gone by already? It was all a blur. She turned her gaze back to the white-draped form of Jay, lying motionless in the bed. Two IVs hung from poles near his head and dripped into his arms. One held blood, the other, a clear liquid. A bag hanging at the side of the bed was collecting pink-stained urine. Another tube was draining red fluid from his chest. Kate's breathing fell into time with the hiss of his ventilator.

She stood up and walked to the bed. Grasping his right hand in both of hers, she said, "I don't know if you can hear me, Jay, but I have to say this out loud again. Please forgive me for texting you. I know you came flying home to save me, but if you hadn't, you wouldn't be lying here, all shot up. The police would have rescued me, and we'd both be drinking a bourbon right now to celebrate our lives." She bent over and kissed his forehead.

"There's another thing. An important thing. I haven't cleaned up the mess at home yet, but it wasn't a robbery." She paused as a tear trickled down her cheek. "He knew my name! He told me he was there to kill me!" She choked back a sob. "Nolan's notes said Gemelli's father had 'a man in collections'. I think that's mob-speak for 'hit-man.' My guess is she has a hired gun, too, and somehow, she found out where we are. I'm not sure what to do next. You've got to wake up and tell me." She exhaled a long breath. "You've got to."

She released his hand and went back to the chair. Her mind was reeling. She looked again at the man with the ruined face, the man who had run into danger to save her life, and was now barely clinging to his own. Her heart went out to him, and her eyes filled with tears. "Please don't die, Jay," she whispered.

The phone buzzed in her purse. She retrieved it and swiped the screen. "Hi, Billie."

"You're in Oregon, Kate? Admin here says they paid for two plane tickets to Portland. What the hell is going on? You were supposed to keep me in the loop. Remember? Now I get a phone call from the police asking me to verify who you and Jay are, and they tell me Jay's been shot. What the fuck!"

Kate spoke with as much calm as she could manage. "Take it easy, Billie. Jay's out of surgery. The doctor said his condition is critical but stable, whatever that means. He's in a coma, and they don't know when he'll come out of it. I'm staying here with him."

"The police said it was a robbery?"

"No, Billie. I told them somebody tried to kill me, and he's still out there somewhere, for all I know. I'm afraid I wasn't much help trying to give a description of him to the police. Everything happened so fast."

"You think Gemelli's behind it?"

"Who else? No proof, of course."

"Well, that settles it. Let's scuttle the story, and I'll tell her to call off her dogs."

"No, way, Billie. I'm taking that bitch down."

"At what cost?"

Kate was silent for a moment, again painfully aware that she was risking other people's lives as well as her own. "This is something I have to do. That's all there is to it." She heard Billie click her tongue.

"And what are you doing in Oregon, for God's sake?"

"I've found Bobby Gemelli. At least, I think I have. He's going by the name Bobby Amato now."

"Holy shit! You are unbelievable, Kate."

"So they tell me. Just keep that corner of your desk dusted off for the Emmy Award."

"You're also impossible. Call me every day with updates. Every damn day. Got it?"

"Got it."

"And stay safe."

When the call ended, she wondered what she could do to stay safe. Then she decided her "safe days" were behind her.

#

Kate was startled awake by a nurse coming in to check on Jay.

"Sorry. I didn't see you sitting there." She logged onto the computer perched on the tall tray. "You Mr. Scott's wife?"

Kate yawned and stood up. "No, I'm Kate Temperance. We're…partners." Saying that made something tug at her heart.

"I'm Nurse Holliday. My shift is ending. Terry Martin will be coming on board when I leave." She looked at the array of machines monitoring her patient. "Vitals look okay. I'll swap out that empty IV and be on my way."

Dawn was beginning to brighten the horizon. Kate wrinkled her nose. "Well, I stink after the past couple of days. I think I'll go home and shower and get something to eat. Then I'll come back."

"Sure thing."

Once outside, she took great breaths of cool, sweet air untainted by the smells of alcohol and Betadine. She stopped suddenly. Was her killer lurking nearby? She turned in a slow circle, peering into the shadows, willing the daylight to brighten. *It's one thing to be cautious*, she thought, *but I can't make myself crazy about it.* Satisfied she was alone, she made her way to her car in the parking garage. Hearing the engine start and the radio come on relaxed her. She was at the house in twenty minutes when she remembered. *Oh, crap! I haven't cleaned up the place yet!*

She decided to do a quick pick-up now and a deeper clean later. Taking care to lock the door behind her, she picked up the flowers and brought them to the waste basket in the kitchen. Then she grabbed a broom to sweep up the pieces of coffee pot. As she was emptying the dustpan, she noticed her prize picture in its broken frame lying in a pool of coffee on the floor.

"Oh, no!" She dropped the broom and dustpan and picked up her picture as she might an injured animal. "Grandma. Momma." She tilted the picture to let the coffee drain from it. The paper covering the back of the frame had completely disintegrated. She carefully extricated the photograph from the shards of glass. Laying it on the table, she began to tap it dry with paper towels, hoping the image was salvageable. She turned it over to dab at the back as well. And there it was.

A message written in pencil, addressed to her mother, faint but still legible.

> Hey, Sam
> Imagine this pic a few years from now, when the Cactus is the biggest club on the Strip. Then we'll have the kind of wedding you deserve.
> XXX
> H

Kate felt her knees buckle, and she grabbed the table to keep from falling. A soft moan escaped her lips. All of her research, all her efforts to track the man down, now lay exposed for all to see on the drying shores of Lake Mead.

Harry Costello, the man chained to a cinder block, was her father.

22. Cracks in the Foundation

Sofia sat in her penthouse suite, sipping a second cup of coffee before going to her office to begin the work day. The bright kitchen, perfumed with bouquets of fresh-cut flowers, hung with priceless works of art, and looking out on stunning views of Las Vegas and the desert beyond, usually brought such joy to her. But not today. James Ward had called her late last night with the terrible news. Just the thought of it brought tears to her eyes again. Jay, dear Jay, lay in critical condition in an Oregon hospital, while Temperance still roamed free. How could it all have gone so frightfully wrong? And how long before Bobby found out?

As if in answer to her question, her phone rang.

Bobby's voice was a feral snarl. "Tell me that was a botched robbery and you didn't hire somebody to take Temperance out."

"Bobby...I..."

"How could you?" he shouted. "The man I consider a son is dying because you couldn't listen to reason?" He began to sob. "My boy is dying because of you."

"Our boy, Bobby, our boy. I love Jay, too. That was not supposed to happen. The damn police! But Temperance is a threat to both of us. Now she's knocking on your door, for God's sake. She'll never stop until she ruins everything we've worked for."

"I'll be the judge of that, damn you. Is your gun still out here? Do I know him?"

She took a deep breath and wiped the tears from her eyes before continuing. "You've never met him. He's good."

"Good? Recent events would seem to contradict that. Call him off."

Sofia spoke a single definitive word, without nuance or appeal. "No."

Bobby was silent for a moment. "What did you say?"

"I said no. Your judgment is compromised. She needs to be eliminated now."

Neither spoke. Then Sofia saw that Bobby had ended the call. She sat back in her chair and exhaled. She had never defied her brother like that before, but it had to be done. He wasn't thinking clearly, not appreciating the gravity of the situation. As she raised her coffee cup to her lips, she allowed herself to utter what had been troubling her about recent interactions with him. "Is Bobby going senile? Can I trust him?"

Just then her phone rang again. It was Lydia Bloomfield, her Chief Financial Officer.

"Good morning, Ms. Gemelli. I just wanted to remind you that we have a meeting with the mayor in twenty minutes. That big donation you're making to the city."

"Oh, yes, Lydia. Thank you. I'll be right there."

Time for the Silver Fox to make another of her civic-minded appearances, she thought. She stood and walked into the bathroom to brush her hair and freshen her lipstick. Before leaving the suite, she took her phone and tapped Ward's number.

"James, my brother is very angry, so be careful."

"He doesn't know me, Sofia."

"But he knows you're there. He may put some kind of watch on Temperance, for all I know. I'm not sure what he's capable of anymore."

"Did I tell you last night that I had Temperance's computer?"

"No. She probably has copies of everything she needs, but that may slow her down a bit. Overnight it to me so I can have someone hack into it and find out what she has."

"Will do. And again, I'm so sorry for what happened."

"Make it right, James."

She ended the call and left to meet her public.

#

That evening, as she relaxed with a glass of port after dinner, she complimented herself on a day well-spent. The visit with the mayor had put the Florentine in the best possible light and had given her casino free advertising in prime time. The Board of Directors was delighted with what they called her "stewardship" of the Strip's flagship club. Most importantly, she had called the hospital in

Salem, and after identifying herself as Jay's mother, had gotten a thorough progress report from the charge nurse on the ICU. Jay had awakened from his coma and no longer required a ventilator. They had moved him out of intensive care onto another floor. If she had believed in God, she would have said a prayer of thanks.

Nonetheless, something continued to gnaw at her. She again gave herself permission to express the unthinkable. *Can I trust Bobby?* Bobby had been her protector since early adolescence. It was Bobby who had stopped her father's abuse, Bobby who had defended their mother until it was too late. Bobby who had conceived their ultimate plan…

But now? Allowing Temperance to live made no sense. That's not the way they did things. What was he thinking? Then the thought she dreaded most—*Is Bobby himself becoming a threat to our enterprise?* That idea tainted her consciousness, spoiled it the way of drop of blood will diffuse in a glass of water and turn it all pink. She shook her head back and forth. The consequences were far too grim to imagine.

Sleep tonight would be a challenge. She needed a massage to smooth away her worries, to put to rest her disturbing thoughts. Perhaps a massage with benefits. She tapped the screen on her phone.

A deep voice responded. "Hello, Sofia. I was beginning to think you had forgotten about me."

"The most talented hands in Las Vegas? Perish the thought! Are you available…for a full treatment tonight?"

"Absolutely, darling. I'll be right over. And I have some new toys you might like to play with."

She smiled in spite of herself. "I look forward to it. See you soon."

23. Behind Enemy Lines

"Easy. The doctor said small sips."

"Yes, Nurse Kate." Jay was lying in bed with his head elevated to facilitate drinking. Every now and then he winced, explaining that the pain came in quick spasms.

"The police were a little surprised at how many conceal carry permits you have. You're legal in almost every State in the Union. How come?"

"After my…acid bath…I don't go anywhere without a weapon. That's my rule." He put the straw to his lips and took another swallow of ice water.

"Seems like the police here shoot first and ask questions later."

"Don't be too hard on them, Kate. I turn around with a gun in my hand, and they have to make a split-second decision. The way police get attacked in this country, they're all a little on edge."

Kate pursed her lips. "All I can say is, that's generous of you."

Jay winced again. "You say this guy targeted you?"

"Yep. Had to be Gemelli's doing, though I can't figure out how she found us."

Jay lowered his eyes. After a moment, he said, "So what's the plan?"

"I canceled our original visit to the winery, but I rescheduled it for the day after tomorrow."

"Without me?"

"Jay, the doctor says you'll be laid up for another few days. I've got a deadline to meet."

"How will you stay safe? That guy must still be out there."

"I'll watch my back. Won't answer the door. Only leave the house in daylight. I won't take any chances, believe me."

He coughed and grimaced. "I don't like it one bit." His expression softened. "Kate, I care about you. I don't want anything bad to happen."

"It already has, if you haven't noticed. Anyway, the really good news is that I've identified one of the bodies in Lake Mead. Two maybe."

"What?" Jay tried to sit bolt upright, but fell back to the mattress in obvious pain.

"Yep. Remember the recent story about the two skeletons found together? One chained to a cinder block? Well, that was Harry Costello, owner of the Cactus Club. Some kids found his Super Bowl ring nearby. He had big plans to expand his place to be the biggest on the Strip. Now the Florentine is. And my hunch is that the other skeleton is the guy who killed him, Tom Romano, Johnny Gemelli's muscle."

"Holy shit!" He groaned in pain. "Hey, give me some warning when you make big revelations like that. They hurt!"

"Okay. Get ready for another one."

Jay grabbed a handful of sheets with each fist. "Go for it."

"And Harry Costello was my father."

His eyes went wide. "Oh, my God! Really? How the hell did you figure that out?"

Kate grinned. "Remember that old picture of the Strip I showed you? Harry spelled it all out on the back. I never saw the note until the frame got wrecked."

Jay relaxed his hands. "You are an absolute wonder, Kate Temperance."

She beamed at him. "I try my best."

A nurse walked in. "Time for some more medicine, Jay, and I'll take your vitals again." She looked at Kate. "Shouldn't be too long before we get those tubes out of him. Then you could help getting him up and walking him around the halls."

"Be happy to." She turned to Jay. "I'm heading home. Got to do some more prep for my interview with Hartford. I'll come back after dinner."

"Sure thing."

She turned and left the room, heading for the parking garage. At the entrance, she pulled a small can of pepper spray from her purse. Looking down the aisles of cars, she saw only an elderly couple walking her way. She dashed to her car, locked the doors, and started the engine. In moments, she was back out in the daylight and headed to the house.

When she arrived, she hurried inside and locked the front door. The house still smelled of cleaning products from the service that she had hired to come in the day before. *Good decision*, she told herself again. Her new computer and new coffee pot were up and running, and she was glad she had copied all her files to the flash drive before she got up close and personal with her assailant. Her first order of business after purchasing the new laptop had been to make a second copy of her files and mail the first one off to Bonnie. The new copy she had hidden in a loaf of bread in the refrigerator.

Ten minutes later, the dominant smell in the house was the fresh coffee brewing in the kitchen. As she sipped one cup after another, she pored over online articles in all the major wine magazines, focusing on the ways they reviewed and rated wines. She learned she was in the heart of Pinot Noir country, and that Oregon was producing wines good enough to compete with the heavy hitters from France. *Yay for our side*, she thought.

Hours passed by. Standing to stretch her back, she saw her coffee pot was empty. Although studying "aroma wheels," circular charts that highlighted the smells and tastes of wine, was useful, she knew nothing could substitute for actually tasting the wines themselves. As the clock in the kitchen chimed five times, she decided what she had to do. The tasting room at Enchanted Hill closed at six. That gave her enough time to sample its wares.

My first foray behind enemy lines, she thought, as she got into her car and drove to the winery. *I'll give Jay a full report tonight.*

The vineyard was a short five minutes from her house. As she turned and drove under the entry arch, her first thought was, *You're not in Nevada anymore, sister.* The driveway curved to the right, then went left up a steep slope covered with lush green vines heavy with grapes. At the crest of the hill was the tower and tasting room complex she had seen on the website, illuminated in the orange glow of the waning autumn sun. Behind it, another hill held what she presumed was the owner's home. All in all, it was breath-taking.

After parking her car, she walked through the enormous front doors into the tasting room, with its high ceilings and mezzanine level above her. Every table was full of visitors, with bottles and glasses of wine and plates of food spread before them. Aromas of food and wine and the buzz of conversations were balm for her spirit after all she had been through in the past week. A voice from behind the bar on the right called to her.

"Welcome! Come here to the tasting bar, and let me get something started for you."

Kate smiled sheepishly and walked toward the woman. "I must look lost. It's my first time here."

"You're not lost, I guarantee," the young server said. She wore a stylish black T-shirt with the vineyard's logo on the upper left side. "You've found the right place. Since it's your first time here, may I recommend our reserve flight? Five of our very best."

"That's exactly what I want, and I'd also like you to tell me about the wines I'm drinking so I can appreciate them more."

"That's what I'm here for." She extended her hand. "I'm Annalise."

"I'm Kate. It's a pleasure to meet you."

Annalise put five large, long-stemmed glasses on the counter. Her lips curled in a playful smile. "Want a little trivia quiz you can use to win yourself a free drink from someone not in-the-know?"

"Sure. I'll use it on my partner when I bring him up here."

"Well, each of these glasses holds a full bottle of wine."

Kate shook her head in disbelief. "No way!"

The server chuckled. "That's everyone's first response. I'll prove it to you." She took an empty wine bottle from behind the counter and filled it with water at the sink. Then with the flourish of a stage magician, she poured the entire contents into a single glass.

Kate was dumbfounded. "I still don't believe it, and I'm looking right at it." She began to laugh. "I'm going to bet more than just a round of drinks with Jay. I'll take him to the cleaners!"

Annalise laughed with her. "Now let's get serious with some wine. We'll start with two white tastings, a Pinot Gris and an Estate Chardonnay, then we'll move on to three Pinot Noirs. I'll share tasting notes with you along the way. Are you ready?"

"Absolutely! Let's get this show on the road."

Forty-five minutes flew by. The whites teased Kate's palate with flavors of lemon and grapefruit, melon and pear. The reds told secrets of dark cherry, cinnamon, and cloves. Kate nodded her head and smiled at Annalise. "I could make a habit of this." She paid for her tasting and left a generous tip for her tutor. "I'll be back," she promised.

"I look forward to seeing you again," Annalise said. "Next time you'll have to order some food. We have a new chef, and he's killing it."

Just then an older gentleman walked up to the bar and spoke quietly to Annalise. "Absolutely, Mr. Amato. I'll get right on it."

Kate paused when she heard the name, and then recognized his face from the website. When he turned from the counter, she approached him and offered her hand.

"Mr. Amato? My name is Kate Temperance. I'm a journalist doing a story for *Wine Spectator*. I have an interview with Mr. Hartford the day after tomorrow."

He shook her hand. "It's a pleasure, Ms. Temperance. Gavin told me you'd be coming." He pursed his lips. "I saw the news on television. Most unfortunate. How is Mr. Scott doing?"

"Much better. We expect he'll be discharged within the next week. Thanks for asking."

"I must run now, but perhaps we can talk a bit after you've met with Gavin?"

"I'd like that very much."

"Till then." He took his leave and disappeared into the kitchen.

Bobby, you sly devil, she thought. *I'm coming for you.* She continued out the door to her car. *And you're going to tell me everything you know about my father and all the other bodies at the bottom of that lake.*

#

Kate parked the car in front of the house and hurried inside. She decided to eat a light dinner and then head back to the hospital to see Jay. In the deepening twilight, she turned on the lamp by the door and was startled by a voice from the living room.

"Don't let me alarm you, Ms. Temperance. I mean you no harm. I'm just here to give you some advice."

"Get out of my house!" she yelled. She fumbled in her purse for her pepper spray and her phone. "I'm calling the police right now!"

"Of course. Feel free. When you're done, please come in here so I may speak with you. I'll only take a few minutes of your time, and then I'll leave."

"What the hell are you doing here? How did you get in?"

"The lock on your front door is quite unsatisfactory. That's one of the things you have to fix."

Befuddled by his unusual answer, she stopped just as she opened the keypad screen on her phone. "Who are you?"

"I'm a security consultant, sent to help you protect yourself from whoever wants to kill you."

"Did Billie send you? The network?"

"I'm not at liberty to say. But please come in and sit down."

She slowly entered the room. The man sat on the couch, smiling and offering his hand. He was dressed in a suit and tie and fashionable wingtip shoes. His dark, neatly combed hair accented his handsome face.

Kate did not take his hand. "Anybody ever tell you you're a ringer for Henry Cavill?"

"My wife sometimes shouts 'Oh, Henry!' while we're making love, and I find it disconcerting." He motioned toward the seat next to him.

"I'll sit over here, thanks. Again, what the hell are you doing here?"

"You must take better care of yourself. For all we know, the man who tried to kill you is still out there, and once things calm down, he'll probably try again." He picked up a piece of paper from the coffee table. "I've taken the liberty of jotting down some notes. Please take a look." He reached toward her. "I won't stand up so as not to alarm you further."

Kate stepped toward him and grasped the note. "Go ahead."

The man took a deep breath. "The lock on your front door is a piece of shit. I've written down the kind of locks you need and the name and number of a locksmith I can vouch for. Also tell him to install better locks on all of the windows. A child could jimmy the ones you've got. And while you're at it, it's best to keep the curtains drawn on all the windows."

Kate studied the list and looked up at him. "What's this about the glass slider off the kitchen?"

"That presents some problems. The one you have is out of date. The newer models have a locking steel bolt in the upper frame. I recommend you have this door replaced. Get a special one with bullet resistant glass." He pursed his lips and pointed to the paper in her hands. "I've included the name of a company that can do that for you. Until then, keep a broom handle in the lower track at all times so the door can't be easily forced open."

"But I don't own this house."

"Of course. I assume you're renting or leasing it. Have the property manager contact the owner. Since these fixes are all upgrades, my guess is you won't have any problem. But act quickly. And please don't sip your coffee where you can be seen from outside."

"Is it Gemelli? Is she the one who sicced her dog on me?"

"Ms. Temperance, you have a knack for getting in trouble. God only knows who wants to kill you. They may have to take a number." He paused. "I'm standing up now to take my leave. Don't be frightened. I'll show myself out." As he reached the door he said, "I'll be watching out for you. A phone number where you can reach me is on that paper. Please add it to your contacts. If you feel threatened at all, call me."

Kate had risen from the chair. "But what's your name?"
The man smiled. "Call me Henry."

24. Rehab

Kate spent most of the next day at the hospital. A nurse showed her how to help Jay out of and back into bed, and how best to assist him in his walks around the halls.

"I'm your rehab assistant," she told him, as she put her arm around his shoulders and helped him stand up. "They said to start with one slow trek around the halls. If you're not too tired, we can do another. If you need a break, we can stop. The goal is to be able to do five or six revolutions without quitting."

Jay grimaced. "Whatever you say." He looked into her eyes. "I don't know how to thank you for all of this."

"You don't have to thank me. You'd do the same for me if the shoe was on the other foot."

He took a deep breath and let it out slowly. "I can't figure out for the life of me why your husband left you."

Kate sighed. "Like I said before, those photos were just a catalyst for something that had been brewing for a long time. He's a pretty needy guy, and I wasn't there enough for him. But enough of that. Let's get you moving."

Fifteen minutes later, one circuit of the hallways brought them back to Jay's room. "Okay. Let's stop for now. I'm tired, and the pain has kicked up a notch." As she eased him back into bed, he turned to her. "I meant to ask you, did you call Billie? Is she the one who sent that guy you call Henry?"

"Nope. She said it wasn't her. I have no idea who sent him."

"Well, at least he seems to be on our side. What about his list of repairs?"

"I got hold of Alla, the property manager, before I left the house this morning. I'm waiting to hear back from her."

He stretched his shoulders and rolled his head. "Would you puff up this pillow, please?"

"You bet." She leaned over to help him.

"You smell good," he said.

"Don't be fresh."

"Just making an observation." His half-grin lit up his face. "So, what's next on your agenda?"

"I'll stay here a while longer, then head back to finish getting ready for tomorrow's interview. I'm seeing Gavin Hartford at ten o'clock."

"Wish I could be there."

"Me, too. I'm getting used to working with you." She looked at him, scarred face and all, with an affection that surprised her. She hadn't felt a stirring in her heart for a man in many years.

#

The pain medication he got after lunch was making him drowsy. Just before he dozed off, he waved goodbye to Kate. Two hours later, he awakened when the nurse came in to take his vital signs again.

"How are you feeling?" she asked.

"Pretty good, actually."

"Glad to hear it. It's almost time to take another walk."

"Sure. Would you hand me my phone first? I think it's on that table over there."

Once she had left, Jay tapped Gemelli's number. "Hello, Sofia."

"Jay! It's so good to hear from you. I've been worried sick."

"Well, I'm out of the woods, getting better by the hour." He paused a moment. "Kate knows Harry Costello was her father and that he was murdered by Tom Romano."

"Shit! Does she know about her mother?"

"I can't say for sure, but I don't think so. She hasn't said anything about it."

"Thank God. What are we going to do? My stubborn brother…" Her voice trailed off before she finished the sentence.

Jay struggled to find how to say what he wanted to without accusing her. Finally, he gave up and blurted out, "Did you send somebody to kill Kate without telling me?"

After a brief pause, she said, "Jay, don't be ridiculous. If I wanted to kill her, I could have done it right here in Las Vegas. You know Bobby wants her to find where we're vulnerable so we can shore up our defenses."

"Sofia, this guy knew who Kate was and where she lived. You're the only one I gave our address to."

"You know we have enemies. I can't be running the biggest hotel on the Strip without stepping on toes. Perhaps someone thought her investigation might dig up something they want to keep buried."

Jay harrumphed. "None of this makes any sense. And I'm lying here feeling like I got used for target practice."

"Would you like me to send you some help? Someone to provide you an extra layer of protection?"

"There's already someone here doing that."

There was a long pause on the other end. "What?"

"Somebody broke into our house. Called himself a security consultant and gave Kate a whole list of home improvements to make our house safer. And he said he was going to hang around to keep an eye on us."

Another long hesitation. "Did he have a name?"

"Not a real one. Kate called him Henry Cavill, after the movie actor." He heard what sounded like a low growl coming from her. Then he went all in. "Sofia, can I trust you?"

"How dare you!" she said and terminated the call.

He stared at the phone in his hand for a moment, then laid it on the bedside table. "That went well," he muttered. *What's going on?* he thought. *Did Sofia really hire someone to kill Kate? And who hired Henry? If Billie denies sending Henry, and Sofia says she didn't, did Bobby do it? But that would mean brother and sister disagree on what to do with Kate. And I'm just collateral damage?*

He lay there torturing himself with scenarios he couldn't explain. Through it all, the one anchor was Kate. Kate, genuinely concerned for his wellbeing. Kate, by his side, helping with his rehab, confiding in him. When the time came and his benefactors tired of her, could he really make her have an "unfortunate accident?" Another question raised its ugly head. *What secrets are Sofia and Bobby hiding from me?*

#

When Kate got home, Alla called her.

"Mrs. Lincoln, the owner, says you can go ahead with those improvements, but you'll have to pay for them yourself since they're above and beyond what would normally be required in that neighborhood. Are you okay with that?"

"Yeah, I thought that might happen. Bulletproof glass is not your everyday slider in Salem, Oregon. But thanks, Alla. I'll go ahead with the project."

She thought she might get some extra cash from the network "to protect their investment." For now, she called the resources Henry had written on his list and set up the next available appointments with them. Then she was back at her computer, studying wine, delighted to discover that she was beginning to understand what had been only esoteric terms to her before. "I can tell *malolactic fermentation* from *carbonic maceration*, Mr. Hartford," she said aloud. "That has to be worth something, right? Can I convince you I'm writing for *Wine Spectator*?"

She let the question hang in the air while she poured herself a glass of bourbon.

25. The Interview

She relished the ride back up the grape-studded slopes to the winery at the top of the hill. The sun shone through a fine bridal veil of clouds, its muted light creating a scene a movie director would envy. Pulling her car to the side, she snapped several quick pictures with her phone before proceeding. *Bonnie will love these*, she thought.

After parking the car, she entered the tasting room, now bustling with activity. Some servers were setting bouquets of fresh flowers on the tables. Others were taking clean wine glasses from the twin dishwashers behind the counter and setting them in the illuminated rack behind and above the bar. Still others were placing food and wine menus on each table and along the bar.

Annalise recognized her right away. "Good morning, Kate! It's a little early for wine tasting, but I'll pour if you like."

"Thank you, but actually I'm here to see Mr. Hartford. I have a ten o'clock appointment."

"Ah, good ol' GW, our Gentleman Winemaker. You just missed his greeting to the staff."

"Oh?"

"It's his ritual with us. Every day, he walks in and says, 'Good morning, my dear friends and fellow servants of the Queen!' It's a hoot. And we all respond, 'And to you, GW.' It's kind of our anchor. It means all's right with the world."

"That's wonderful. I'll have to include that in my article."

Annalise looked puzzled. "Article?"

"I'm writing a piece for *Wine Spectator*."

"Wow! How cool!" Then she pursed her lips. "So, your tasting the other day? Was that like being a 'secret reviewer' or something, trying to get the inside scoop without letting on who you were?"

"Something like that. But more like developing an appreciation for your particular wines. I don't want to write about Pinot Noir in general. I want to write about Enchanted Hill Pinot Noir and all about how your winery operates. Hopefully, Mr.

Hartford will show me all the equipment and machinery it takes to make a great wine.

"I'm sure he will. And you'll love him. I'll call and let him know you're here."

While she waited, Kate walked the perimeter of the tasting room, taking several pictures from different angles. Then she walked out the glass door at the back onto the deck. Here sat the tables with umbrellas she had seen on the website. At the railing, she caught her breath at the vistas before her. Row upon row of vines, laden with dark grapes, made their way to the valley floor. In the distance, she could see the low purple peaks of the Coast Range.

"Quite an impressive view, isn't it?" said a voice behind her.

"Oh, you startled me. I was so captured by..." She extended her arm behind her. "...all this."

The white-haired man in the shirt and tie offered his hand. "Yes, it has that effect on people. I'm Gavin Hartford. You must be Kate Temperance."

"I am. Thank you for seeing me." She was struck by his brilliant blue eyes and shook his hand warmly.

"Ms. Temperance, I must admit, I'm surprised. When I looked you up, your pieces seemed to be more of the investigative kind—looking into crimes and scandals, corrupt politicians. Now wine?"

"I'm a freelance journalist, and I needed a break from the heavy lifting. I approached *Wine Spectator*, and they made me an offer I couldn't refuse."

He smiled at the movie reference. "Indeed. Where would you like to start?"

"Can you tell me a bit about yourself first?" She took a small voice recorder from her purse. "And, if you don't mind, I'll record some things and take some more pictures."

"Of course. Not much to say about me. My partner, Bobby Amato, and I met in Paris many years ago and studied wine-making in Burgundy. We brought clones back to the States, convinced the climate of Oregon would be perfect for Pinot. Now Bobby is the business manager and supervisor of the winery, in charge of all the hiring and firing and making sure Enchanted Hill runs smoothly. I'm the winemaker."

"Family?"

Like a cloud crossing the sun, a shadow passed over his face. "My wife Guinevere and son Jonas are deceased—twenty-five years ago now." He sighed, then brightened again. "So where shall we begin?"

"How about behind the scenes?"

"Excellent!" was his enthusiastic reply. "Come with me to our crush pad—that's our outside production space—where we weigh the grapes, crush them in the de-stemmer. We have a lot of fermentation tanks for Pinot out there as well." He led her through the front door, then continued across to a driveway that curved down behind the large adjacent building. "That's our store on the upper level—books, clothing, souvenirs. I guess what they call 'merch' nowadays. The lower level has some fermentation tanks for Chardonnay, but is mostly our wine cellar. It's like a cool, dark cavern that runs all the way under our tasting room as well. Our lab is down there, too." He smiled at her. "As you know, we measure a lot more than just degrees Brix."

Halfway down the hill, she pointed to six tall white tanks off to the right. "What are those, Mr. Hartford?"

"Please call me Gavin. Those are thirty-six-thousand-gallon stainless steel tanks for finishing our Whole Cluster Pinot Noir. It sits in those for about five months. Do you know about our Whole Cluster?"

She beamed at him. "Your server Annalise was telling me about it. You don't crush those grapes or even take them off the stems. Right?"

"Right. They go from the vines straight into those smaller tanks down there first." He pointed to a row of tanks at the bottom of the hill. "Those are twelve-thousand-gallon tanks. We expel the oxygen from them with carbon dioxide from those cannisters over there." He gestured toward several compressed gas containers. "Since the grapes aren't crushed and there's no oxygen in the tanks, fermentation can't start with the yeast naturally present on the skins.

It has to begin at the intracellular level, inside each individual grape."

"Carbonic maceration?"

He nodded his head. "You've been doing your homework. Finally, the skins burst, releasing the juice. Once it's ready, we call it 'must.' We remove the stems and skins and pump the must into those larger tanks we just walked by. Fermentation is complete in about five months or so. From those tanks to tanks on the bottling line inside the building."

"No oak?"

"No oak for the Whole Cluster. A young, fruity, approachable wine."

"I call it yummy. Annelise gave me a taste of it the other day."

"It's a favorite all right."

Kate walked closer to one of the tanks to read a sign posted there.

DANGER
CONFINED SPACE
ENTER BY
PERMIT ONLY

"What's that about?" she asked.

"The State requires specific training to enter into any of the tanks. You can run out of air very quickly in there." He made a clicking noise with his tongue. "There was an unfortunate accident at a winery here in the valley a few years ago. Someone was found asphyxiated in a fermentation tank. They never did find out how it happened."

Kate shuddered. "I didn't think winemaking could be so dangerous."

To her chagrin, Hartford continued. "Oh, there are any number of ways to die at a winery. A falling barrel might crush someone. A limb might get pulled into a crusher-destemmer."

She was shaking her head back and forth. "Okay, Gavin, now you're giving me chills."

He laughed. "Sorry, Kate. I guess I can have a macabre sense of humor. Come with me to the tanks over here." He stopped before a row of stainless steel tanks. "These are for our Estate Pinot and our Signature Cuvée. We crush and destem the grapes and send the juice here to begin its fermentation journey. Then it's twelve to sixteen months in French oak barrels. Each barrel holds about sixty gallons or three hundred bottles."

Kate let him cast a spell over her. "Show me."

They walked inside past the bottling machine and the Chardonnay tanks and into the wine cellar proper. Kate felt the air temperature drop, as though they were entering a dimly lit cave. Smells of wine and wood filled her nostrils. She saw row upon row of barrels, some rows stacked three high, all lying on their sides.

"The inner sanctum," Gavin whispered with a smile. "A parking lot for Pinot."

"It's amazing," Kate breathed. "What else can I say?"

"Say you'll have lunch with me. We can eat in the private banquet room downstairs from the tasting room. Our chef has some very fine Columbia River salmon."

"Sounds exquisite."

"But first, you must sample some wine in situ, so to speak." He lifted his glass pipette from the barrel on which it was lying. "We call this a 'thief,' and I use it to remove an ounce or two of wine from a barrel for tasting. I've got my glass here, but give me a moment to find a clean one for you."

He walked past several barrels to a small shelf on which sat a box of wine glasses. He returned and handed a glass to her. "We remove the silicone stopper from the bunghole in the barrel, insert the thief, and steal a bit of wine! Here. Taste this."

She swirled the wine, smelled its aromas, and took a sip. "Hmm. It's good, but—"

"But not ready yet. The Queen has another few months to go. Now please come with me to the banquet room."

#

Lunch was a blur. Whether it was the brilliant blue of his eyes or the effects of the superb Pinot they were drinking, her head was spinning.

"This table is koa, Kate. Imported from Hawaii."

She ran her hand over the smooth, opalescent grain. "I've never seen anything like it. It practically glows."

"And these racks of wine around us are our library collection—only the best."

She looked out the windows at the vineyard and the mountains in the distance. They talked of refractometers and hydrometers, pH and Brix, residual sugars and alcohol content by volume. Gavin introduced her to the "Queen" as if Pinot Noir were a living, breathing monarch.

Staring at her across the table, he said, "Pinots are the most romantic of wines, with so voluptuous a perfume, so sweet an edge, and so powerful a punch that, like falling in love, they make the blood run hot and the soul wax embarrassingly poetic."

Kate chuckled. "That's pretty flowery stuff. Did you just make that up?"

"No, my dear. Joel L. Fleishman of *Vanity Fair* said that. And Master Sommelier Madeline Triffon called Pinot 'Sex in a glass.'"

"Well, you're making a believer out of me, I can tell you that." She took another bite of salmon. "And this is marvelous. Please thank the chef for me."

"I will."

When lunch concluded and she had taken her last sip of wine, Kate asked, "Is there any chance I might interview Mr. Amato as well?"

"Of course. I believe he's busy right now with hiring interviews for tasting room servers, but I'll have our receptionist call you with an appointment." He stood and placed his napkin on the table. "I'm afraid I'll have to take my leave now. Duty calls. Feel free to wander the facilities and the grounds."

"Thank you so much, Gavin."

She climbed up the stairs and went out to the parking lot. Once inside her car, she shook her head, as if awakening from a dream or a spell that had been cast over her. As she started the car, one comment of Gavin's came snaking back into her consciousness.

"Oh, there are any number of ways to die at a winery."

26. In the Vineyard with Thor

On a whim, Kate pulled into the overflow parking lot just inside the entry gate to the winery. In her "up close and personal" approach to journalism, she decided to walk through the vineyard itself before heading back to the house. She wanted to smell the grapes before they were harvested, to caress the broad green leaves, to touch the gnarled bark of the older vines. She had to get the "feel" of Enchanted Hill.

Part way up the slope, she walked north between two rows. Noticing that the hill curved around out of sight of the tasting room, she hiked in that direction.

I need more physical exercise, she thought, as her breathing became more rapid. *This is steep!*

Rounding the curve and surrounded only by vines, she trudged on, imagining herself off in a distant estate in Burgundy. The air was clean and fresh and heavy with the scent of ripening grapes. She took pictures of the cone-shaped clusters and sweeping panoramas of the rows. She had never felt so at home in a place before.

Fifty yards farther on, she spotted something like a large white arch straddling the row she was walking along. She had read online about the machine that killed powdery mildew with ultraviolet light. What was it called? *A Thorvald!* She knew the winery only used it at night, so the device was sitting motionless until after sunset. *This I've gotta see!*

Focused on her goal, she hurried down the row, oblivious of the sound of quiet footfalls behind her. *The robot in the vineyard! Bonnie will love this!* The earth was soft beneath her feet as she ran ahead. Vines and grapes flew by. Once she reached the machine, she leaned over with her hands on her knees to catch her breath. Her phone was still in her right hand.

When her breathing had returned to normal, she stood upright and aimed her phone's camera at the futuristic-looking machine. In her haste, she fumbled the phone, and it fell to the ground. "Crap!" she said aloud. As she bent down to pick it up, she heard a *Pop!* behind her and a *Thump!* on the leg of the Thorvald. A tiny hole marred the white finish of the device at the level where her head had been a split-second before.

Kate threw herself to the ground. She rolled around the leg of the Thorvald and tried to get her bearings. Where was the shooter? She saw a man running along the row toward her. Without another thought, she crawled under the guy wire supporting the vines and rolled into the next row. She heard the man curse as she kept diving between the trunks, under one row of vines after another, rolling down the slope, never giving her assailant a clear shot.

Her heart pounded in terror. She spit dirt and debris from her mouth as she struggled to get enough air. What would she do at the bottom of the hill? She would be too exposed if she ran toward her car. Roll back up the hill? But how long could she keep that up before she became too exhausted to move? A desperate moan escaped her lips.

When she rolled out from under the last row of vines, the man with the gun was waiting for her.

"I found it was a lot faster to go back to the entry road and run down the hill instead of doing it your way." He looked over his shoulder toward the gate. "We're in the open here. Let's get back up into the vines." He motioned with his gun. "Walk away from the road toward the end of this row and then up the hill. Let's get ourselves a little privacy."

Tears came unbidden to Kate's eyes. "Please don't do this."

"Oh, but I have to. It's my job. Nothing personal, you understand." Again, he gestured with his pistol. "Move along now."

Kate stumbled on the uneven ground. As they moved back up the hill, away from the road, all hope left her. She would die alone in the vineyard. Her story would go unwritten and unproduced. *How long before a vineyard worker finds my body? Will the Thorvald bump into me on its nightly rounds, shining its mildew-killing light into my lifeless eyes?*

If she had any energy left, she could leap on her attacker and try to scratch his eyeballs out before he made the lethal shot. But she was bone-tired and ached all over. *Maybe sleeping forever among the vines isn't such a bad thing*, her despair whispered to her. *Give up. Lay your body down and close your eyes…*

His gruff voice interrupted her thoughts. "Okay. That's far enough. Lie down there. It'll all be over in a second."

She laid back on the soft, moist earth and closed her eyes. *So this is what it's like, knowing you're about to die? I thought I was supposed to see my life flash before me or something. No such luck, I guess.* She was aware only of a vague disappointment. *Well, fuck me*, was her last thought before she heard *Pop!*

Then another voice. "Kate! You've got to get out of here!"

She opened her eyes and sat up. She saw the crumpled body of her would-be killer lying next to her and another man reaching his arm to help her up. "Henry! What are you doing here?"

"Saving your sorry ass, just like I promised. Now beat feet back to your car and get home while I clean up this mess."

"We have to call the police!" she wailed.

"No way. As soon as whoever sent this guy finds out he's dead, they'll send another one. I want to buy us some time. If the cops come, it'll be all over the news, and we sure as hell don't want that."

"But you just killed somebody!" As the adrenaline of her fright dissipated, her body began to tremble violently.

"I took out the trash, okay? This isn't a person, it's a scumbag hired to kill you. Now if you want to stay alive, get your ass back to your car and get back to the house right away."

"I don't have my phone," she said petulantly. "I dropped it up by the Thorvald."

"I'll get it and bring it to your house. Now get the hell out of here before I carry you back to your car myself. Go!"

Kate got to her feet and staggered down the hill without looking back.

27. Binge-Watching *The Sopranos*

Kate ran from her car to the front door of her house. Once inside, she locked herself in, wishing she had the better locks Henry had recommended. In the bathroom, she stripped off her soiled clothes and stepped into the shower. The hot water massaged her aching muscles as she scrubbed the grime and sweat from her bruised skin. Then she leaned forward against the wall and sobbed. Twenty minutes later, empty of tears, she got out and toweled herself dry. A clean blue blouse and a new pair of jeans made her feel almost normal. The operative word was "almost." She doubted that "normal" would ever apply to her life again.

She had witnessed a murder and hadn't informed the police. Did that make her an accomplice? But Henry's point was a good one. She didn't want another assassin breathing down her neck, and telling the police would be like painting a target on her back. She grimaced as a stab of fear pierced her heart. *What am I doing and where is all this going?*

She poured bourbon into a stout glass and sat on the gray sofa in the living room, sipping and thinking. If Sofia knew she and Jay were here in Oregon, then she must have told her brother. Bobby must have hired one of his "employees" to take her out. But then who was her guardian angel, Henry Cavill, and who had hired him? It didn't make sense.

She reviewed in her mind the things she was sure of, even without proof. Tom Romano had killed her father, Harry Costello, on orders given by Giancarlo Gemelli, Sofia's and Bobby's father. Kate guessed that old man Gemelli had thought her father was positioning his Cactus Club to surpass the Florentine. Even though the coroner hadn't identified the bodies yet, she was convinced that Frankie Gianfrido, Mickey Marchese, and Sal Carminucci had also run afoul of Gemelli's purge. If you crossed Johnny, you were a dead man. End of story. Lake Mead was simply Gemelli's dumping ground.

A sudden knock startled her. A voice came through the door. "Kate, it's me. I've got your phone."

She ran to the door and let him in.

"It doesn't look broken," he said as he handed it to her.

She noticed that his hands were dirty, and there were stains on his pants and shirt. "Thanks. And thanks for saving my life." She took the phone and checked the screen. "I'm going to charge it and then give Jay a call." She hesitated, then asked, "What did you do with the body?"

"Don't worry. It's all taken care of. Just get on with your work."

She shook her head. "Don't worry? Are you kidding? What happened in the vineyard is not something that usually happens to me. It wasn't on my radar."

"Having an assassin come after you is not on anybody's radar." He pursed his lips. "Unless you're a spook for the government, I guess. Anyway, we've bought you some time. Get on with your work so you can get out of Oregon."

"But I like it here. I mean, aside from getting attacked and shot at."

That drew a laugh from her benefactor. "Well, I'm outta here." He stopped at the door and turned back to her. "Did you take my suggestions about your house seriously?"

"Yep. I've got appointments with the locksmith and the glass company."

"Good. Stay safe."

She locked the door as soon as he had left. Then she plugged her phone into its charger. Her expression soured as she recalled yet again the events of the day. *Gavin was right. There are a lot of ways to die at a winery.*

#

The sun was a ball of orange fire sinking behind the hills. Soon the desert night would banish any memory of the day's heat, except for what radiated up from the streets and sidewalks. The galaxy of lights along the Strip grew brighter as the twilight deepened. Sofia answered the phone on its first ring.

"Sofia!" the voice shouted. She pulled the phone away from her ear.

"Calm down, Bobby." It was the voice a mother uses with a stubborn child having a temper tantrum.

"I will not calm down, goddamn it! Now I've got a dead body in my vineyard!"

"What did you say?"

"I said the goddamn collections guy you hired to kill Temperance now has a bullet in his head. On my doorstep, no less! What were you thinking? Do you listen to me at all?"

She drew her hand to her mouth. "I liked James. I'll miss him."

"I swear to God, Sofia, if you send another of your guns to Oregon, I'll come to Las Vegas myself and take you out. Do you understand?"

"I don't like being threatened, dear brother." Her voice sounded firm at first, then hurt and misunderstood. "Don't you see? You're not thinking clearly. Temperance has to go, and the sooner the better. As I told you before, she already knows our father had Costello killed. And that Costello was her father." She paused, as if for dramatic effect. "How long do you think it will be before she finds out about her mother? That would destroy everything we've built."

"Please stop with your doomsday predictions. I'll get rid of Temperance in my own time and in my own way. You stay out of Oregon! I won't tell you again." He ended the call.

Sofia sat there in her office, staring at the phone for a moment before laying it on the desk. "Oh, brother, brother, brother, what am I going to do with you?" she said aloud. "This is not how we used to do things. We were decisive then. We analyzed a situation and fixed it immediately."

She looked at the marble sculpture she had purchased yesterday at her favorite gallery. The statue was two feet tall and sat on a three-foot ebony pedestal. It was a nude male holding a bow at full draw, ready to release its arrow. She loved its proud manhood, stared at the firm muscles of its back and chest, arms and legs. It exuded confidence and determination from every pore.

The opposite of my brother, she thought. *He's grown weak and indecisive. He has no vision, no understanding of our plight.* She sighed and nodded, as if accepting a task not chosen lightly. *It's up to me to save the future of our enterprise.*

#

Kate looked out the slider into the growing darkness. *How long before Bobby sends another goon after me? And what will it be like interviewing Bobby at the winery? Will I be able to keep my cool, or will he make my skin crawl?* "Fuck!" she said aloud. "And there I go again—driving myself crazy." To get her mind off it, she called Jay. "How are you feeling, Mr. Pin Cushion?"

"Not half-bad, considering. They've taken all the needles and tubes out. They're even talking about discharging me in the next day or two."

"That's terrific. Are you up for a visit?"

"Actually, I've just finished five laps around the halls and I'm pretty wiped. I want to hear all about your interview with Hartford, but maybe tomorrow morning?"

"Sounds good. I'll give you an earful." She decided not to worry him with news about the attack. That could wait until morning. His healing was the most important thing now. "Okay, Jay. Good night. Sleep well."

As soon as she ended the call, her phone rang. "Hello, Simon. I didn't expect to hear from you."

"Well, I haven't heard from your lawyer yet, so I was just checking in. You're not going to stonewall this thing, are you?"

"Of course not. I haven't meant to put you off, but I've been so busy, I have to admit that our divorce has been the last thing on my mind."

"It's not the last thing on my mind, Kate. I'd like to get moving on it."

She could hear the impatience in his voice. "Simon, please rest assured I won't be fighting you. I'll hire a lawyer who understands I don't want a shark."

"So, you haven't even found a lawyer yet?"

Something in his tone irked her. "Don't criticize me, all right? I got shot at today, and I'm not in the mood."

"Shot at? What the hell are you talking about?"

She was immediately sorry for what she had said. Her brain scrambled to find a way to undo the mess she had made and end this conversation before it got any worse. "Not shot at, exactly. I got threatened, but it was all a mistake. I've got it all sorted out."

"Sorted out?"

"Look, Simon, I promise to get a lawyer as soon as I get back to Nevada, which should be within the next two weeks. I really can't talk right now. Try me tomorrow." And she touched the red button on her screen to end the call.

"Goddamn it!" she shouted to the empty house. Her whiskey glass was empty, but she knew another drink would only interfere with her sleep. Setting the glass in the sink, she decided to make one more call.

"Hi, girlfriend. Do you have a minute to talk?"

"You know I always have time for you," said Bonnie.

"How are Dan and the kids? Have you sold your house yet?" She hesitated for a moment. "Nobody's been bothering you, have they?"

"You mean like gangsters in a black car? No, we're all fine. Haven't seen the bad guys since that one time they bothered Jeremy. And Toby's swell."

Kate breathed a sigh of relief. "Did my package arrive?"

"It's here. I've decided to lock it in my safety deposit box at the bank. Just so you know, I wasn't happy with the note you sent with it—IF ANYTHING HAPPENS TO ME, GIVE THIS TO THE POLICE." The voice paused. "Is something going to happen to you, Kate? Please tell me."

"I'm not gonna lie, Bonnie. Things have gotten pretty dicey out here. I don't mean to worry you, but I don't know who else I can talk to about it."

"I'm here for you. Talk already."

"Okay. No sugar-coating. Here's the uncensored version." Kate unburdened herself of all that had happened over the last two weeks, sparing no details. The elation of discovering who her father was and what had happened to him was overshadowed by the attacks against her and the injuries to Jay. She heard her friend gasp at the revelations. At last, her body purged of the fear and rage that had been gnawing at her, Kate concluded with a joke they used to share in high school. "And that's how I spent my summer vacation."

"Good God, Kate!" The voice paused. Kate could hear Bonnie take a deep breath. "You make me feel like I'm binge-watching the whole last season of *The Sopranos*!"

"Sorry, sis. I feel like I just vomited all over you."

"No need to feel sorry. I don't ever want you to be afraid to talk to me. It's just—"

Kate heard a hitch in Bonnie's voice and what sounded like a sob. "Don't cry, honey."

Bonnie tried again. "It's just that I feel terrible for abandoning you like that. That's not what friends do."

"You did what you had to do to protect your family. I understand."

Kate heard her take another deep breath and sigh. "Well, Dan and I have had second thoughts."

"Oh? What do you mean?"

"We just took our house off the market. This is our home and this is where we're going to stay. Cruella de Vil can go take a flying leap. Now solve this case and put that bitch behind bars!"

Now Kate was crying. "Oh, Bonnie! I love you. I don't know what else to say."

"Just say you'll be home soon and hang up."

"I'll be home soon."

28. The Noose Tightens

Kate was at the hospital the next day at ten o'clock. Jay wasn't in his room. "Do you know where Jay Scott is?" she asked at the nursing station.

"Oh, he's out on his rounds already. I think he's made three loops so far. If you go in this direction," she pointed down the hall, "you'll probably bump into him."

Three minutes later, Kate spotted him approaching her. He lifted the cane in his right hand and waved.

"Good morning, Kate. How's this for progress?"

"You're looking good, partner. When are they going to cut you loose?"

"If all goes well with my tests today, they'll discharge me tomorrow. I'll still have to take it easy for a while, but at least I'll be home. How'd your interview with Hartford go?"

She pursed her lips. "Probably best not to talk about it out here in the hallway. Let's go back to your room."

"Okay, but I have to make three more orbits first. You can come with me and talk about something else."

They walked in silence for a few minutes, then Kate turned to him. "All this white—the fluorescent lights overhead, the counters at the nursing station, the walls, the stacks of sheets on those carts—makes me feel like we're on an arctic ice floe. I expect to see a polar bear around the next corner."

Jay chuckled. "It's pretty barren in here all right. I actually talked to a nurse about it the other day, and she said the hospital has hired an interior decorator who will be purchasing some paintings by local artists to add a dash of color to the walls. The staff are pretty excited about it."

After they had gone a little farther, Kate said, "I've got some good news. My best friend Bonnie decided not to move away, so she'll be waiting for me when we get back to Nevada."

"I thought you told me she was afraid Sofia Gemelli might do something to hurt her family. That's why she was leaving."

"Yeah, well, she's had a change of heart. She thinks I'll be able to take that bitch down before anything worse happens." She exhaled a deep breath and nodded. "There's nothing I'd like better than to do that. I just hope Bonnie's confidence in me isn't misplaced." Kate didn't see the frown that briefly darkened Jay's face and then was gone.

Fifteen minutes later, they were back in his room. She closed the door. "Good news or bad news first?"

Jay settled into the large stuffed chair in the corner. "Start with more good news. Brighten my day."

Kate sat in the small metal chair opposite him. "I had a great interview with Hartford. He's quite charming. Gave me a tour of the production facilities. Sampled wine straight from the barrel. Treated me to a terrific lunch—Columbia River salmon, no less. Exquisite wine. I definitely have to take you there. And I've got a little game I'll play with you in the tasting room."

"Game?"

"That's all I'm going to say about it right now. Oh, and I almost forgot. I'm expecting a call from the winery today to schedule an interview with Bobby Amato, Hartford's partner, the guy I'm sure is Bobby Gemelli." She smiled. "As they say, the noose tightens."

Jay smiled back at her. "All that sounds like you really scored. What's the bad news?"

Kate grimaced. "I was almost killed."

Jay dropped the cane he had been holding onto, and it clattered to the floor. "What the hell happened?"

"That guy came after me again—the one who got you shot up by the police."

"Oh, my God! Where was he?"

"In the vineyard. After my visit with Hartford, I took a walk through the vines, and Bobby's hired gun followed me."

Jay's eyes went wide as she told him all the details about how Henry saved her. When she was done, he sat there speechless, shaking his head back and forth. "For fuck's sake," he muttered.

Just then, her phone rang. She swiped the screen and put the phone to her ear. After a moment, she said, "That will be perfect. I'll see him then."

Kate could see the questioning look on Jay's face. "Bobby will see me at four o'clock this afternoon."

He stiffened his arms as though he were going to leap from the chair. "Whoa, lady! You just finished telling me that Bobby tried to have you murdered, and now you're going to sit down all nicey-nicey with him? Does that make any gram of sense on God's green earth?"

"I don't think I'll be in any immediate danger inside the winery. Too many witnesses. And like I said, the killer's dead."

"So, you don't think Bobby has any more henchmen up his sleeve? That this isn't some kind of trap to lure you into a dark corner of a wine cellar and put an end to your story?"

"I'm hoping he's in damage-control mode, trying to figure out who the hell screwed up his plans yesterday."

Jay rolled his eyes. "I need to get out of this hospital so I can do some serious drinking. You are driving me crazy!"

She walked over to him and stroked his scarred cheek. "I'll be okay. After all, I have to drive you home tomorrow."

He grasped her hand in his own, then kissed it. "Yes, you do, and don't you forget it." He released her, and she sat back down. "I'm growing kind of fond of you, if you haven't noticed."

"I have, and we're both married—you happily, me not so much, and soon not to be."

Jay averted his gaze.

"Knock, knock," said a nurse as she opened the door. "Gotta do your vitals again, Jay. And have you ordered your lunch?"

"Yep, took care of it after breakfast."

Kate stood to take her leave. She looked deeply into Jay's eyes. "I'm heading home for now. I'll call you as soon as my interview is over."

He blew her a kiss. "I'll be waiting."

#

She got to the winery early and sat in her car behind the tasting room, looking up at the house perched atop the hill. Was that Bobby's house or Gavin's, or did they both live there? She should ask somebody.

She had tracked Johnny Gemelli's son from the glitz of Las Vegas to the green of Salem. Now she was about to sit down face-to-face with the man who had been incognito for fifty years, the man who tried to have her killed, the man she would make reveal the secrets of Lake Mead's dead.

And how exactly am I going to do that? Should I tip-toe around it today, continue the pretense of the wine article I'm supposed to be writing? But my cover is blown already if he's tried to kill me twice. She shook her head and sighed. *Confess, Kate. You don't know what the hell you're doing.* With that, she got out of the car and walked in.

"Hi, Annalise. Today I'm here to see Mr. Amato."

"I'll let him know you're here."

Ten minutes later, a gray-haired gentleman in a dark jacket and blue tie strode toward her with his right arm extended. "Ms. Temperance, it's so good to see you." He shook her hand and smiled. "Gavin said your interview with him went well, and I understand you had a fine lunch prepared by our new chef."

"The salmon was perfect, thank you, Mr. Amato. I plan to bring my partner Jay here as soon as he's well enough to enjoy it."

Amato's face showed concern. "Please call me Bobby. And please tell me, how is Jay doing? Will there be any lasting impairments?"

"He's doing very well. They're discharging him tomorrow. Looks like he'll be good as new within the next couple of months."

"Wonderful! Well, please come to my office. May I get you a glass of wine?"

"That would be lovely. I'm rather partial to your Signature Cuvée."

He nodded. "Excellent choice." Raising his hand toward the bar, he said, "Annalise, would you please bring two glasses of the Sig Cuvée to my office?"

"Right away, sir."

Kate followed him upstairs to a large office off the mezzanine. Bobby opened the door and motioned with his arm. "Please come in and have a seat."

She was not prepared for what she saw. One wall was all glass, providing a panoramic view of the vine-covered slopes. The other three were massive oak bookcases filled with hundreds of volumes. An enormous mahogany desk sat before the glass, with a burgundy leather chair behind it. Two matching armchairs were positioned in front of it. Smells of leather, wood, and paper perfumed the air.

"You have a library!" Kate exclaimed.

Bobby grinned. "Take a look at the bookcase to your right."

Kate read the titles aloud. "*Les Miserables, Notre Dame de Paris, Candide, Les Liaisons Dangereuses, Le Rouge et le Noir, Vingt mille lieues sous les mers, A la recherche du temps perdu, L'étranger, La Nausée, L'Etre et le néant.*" Her eyes grew round with surprise. "These are all in French!"

"Excellent pronunciation, by the way. How many years did you take?"

"Two years in high school and four years in college. I love French, but I haven't spoken it since the two 'immersion' summers I spent there decades ago."

He motioned her to a chair. "I lived in Paris and in Dijon for a number of years. I fell in love with the language and promised myself to stay fluent in it. I read something in French every day. The classics are best—Victor Hugo, Voltaire, Proust, Sartre.

"It looks like an amazing collection. Was living in France what got you into the wine business?"

"Absolutely. I met Gavin in a dive bar in Paris when we were both around twenty years old. We really hit it off together. After we had done enough carousing around the city, we decided that we needed to learn how to make an honest living." Kate could sense the pride in his voice. "We moved out to Bourgogne—Burgundy—and began to study oenology—the science and art of wine-making. And here we are today."

Kate pulled her recorder from her purse. "I almost forgot. I want to record our conversation, if that's all right with you."

"Of course. Feel free."

She started the device. "Do you yourself do any of the winemaking now, or do you leave it mostly to Gavin?"

"We decided it made more business sense to have a division of labor. I run the day-to-day operations of the winery and the tasting room—the hiring and the firing—while he is our resident winemaker and chemist. It suits us."

Just then, Annalise came in with their glasses of Pinot Noir. "Here you go, Mr. Amato." She set them on the desk and left the office, closing the door behind her.

Bobby raised his glass and touched it to Kate's. "May this year's vintage be even better than 2018."

Kate sipped the elixir and sighed. "As I told Gavin, your winery has made a believer out of me. *A votre santé!*"

Bobby bowed his head at Kate's wish to his health. Before she had realized it, forty minutes had rushed past. They spoke of France and Burgundy, the Pacific Northwest and Pinot Noir. The conversation was so pleasant, Kate forgot that she was speaking with a man who had hired someone to kill her. All the culture and gentility were only a façade, a disguise for the savagery lurking beneath his grandfatherly exterior. This was a man who very likely had been involved in some way with her father's murder or with other crimes. Why else try to silence her with a bullet?

Whether it was the disinhibiting effect of the alcohol, or the spark of indignant rage igniting within her, she blurted out, "Bobby, why are you trying to kill me?"

The man choked on his wine. "Kill you? What are you talking about?"

Kate felt like she was hurtling headlong down a mountainside. The words gushed from her mouth. "I'm talking about the man who broke into my house. The same man who attacked me in the vineyard yesterday and now lies dead somewhere. That's what I'm talking about!"

In his haste to stand up, he spilled the remainder of his wine on the desk. The glass shattered. "I know nothing about any attempt on your life! You're out of your mind! You need to leave immediately! Get out!"

She stood up, glaring at him. "You've got something to do with murdering my father. Now you're trying to have me killed. You've been on the run for fifty years, and I'm blowing the whistle. I'm taking you down, Bobby Gemelli!"

The man's face contorted in a mask of shock. "What did you call me?"

"You're Bobby Gemelli, Johnny Gemelli's son. You and your twin sister Sofia know the truth about the bodies in Lake Mead."

"I am not Bobby Gemelli!" he shouted. He picked up the phone. "Security—to my office immediately!"

Kate ran from the room as fast as her legs could carry her.

29. The Existentialist

While the server cleaned up the mess on his desktop, Bobby stood staring out the window into the vineyard, imagining his life to be that shattered wine glass. His thoughts were a jumble of memories and wishes, lies, half-truths, and regrets. The day he had dreaded for fifty years had come to pass, and the tsunami of events it would trigger was rushing toward the shore.

Gavin had warned him, and Temperance's reputation preceded her. She was sharp and unrelenting in her investigations. He had read enough of her previous work to know that her prose was a scalpel, slicing through evasions and distractions, focused only on revealing the truth, whatever the cost. If she was on the hunt, no malefactor was safe, and prosecuting attorneys salivated.

The server addressed him. "Your desk is clean, Mr. Amato. Would you like another glass of wine?"

"No, thank you, Jon."

The man left the office, and Bobby sat back down. *What do I do now?* he thought. *My life is over.* He looked at his bookcase of French literature. Books had always been his lifeline. They were his anchor through the grief that had haunted him since his lover's death. He would immerse himself in stories and essays, seeking the courage to keep living, the strength to put one foot in front of the other.

Bobby was a student of the French philosophers. He believed with Camus and Sartre that life was absurd, bereft of any meaning but what you gave it. Grief had taught him that. He resonated with the morality that Camus proclaimed in *Le Mythe de Sisyphe* and *L'Homme révolté*. It was bedrock for him. A rueful smile touched his lips briefly and was gone. *At least I'm in good company,* he thought. *After his brother's death, Bobby Kennedy had steeped himself in Camus.*

He walked to the bookcase and took down his two copies of *L'Etranger,* the one in French and the one in English. The Stuart Gilbert translation had been his introduction to Camus in high school, and had launched his intellectual journey. Once Bobby had begun reading Camus in French, the English copy became the one he loaned to friends. Now the novella was worn and dog-eared, its spine long-broken. As he lifted it from the shelf, the last page fell to the floor. The final sentence, the one that had riveted him on his first reading of it, leaped off the page.

"For all to be accomplished, for me to feel less lonely, all that remained to hope was that on the day of my execution there should be a huge crowd of spectators and that they should greet me with howls of execration."

He sighed. *My day is coming*. What he had to do would dissolve his partnership with Gavin and very likely get his friend arrested. It threatened the whole business if investors and supporters abandoned the winery. But there was no escape. *This has to stop*, he thought.

He could do nothing more until the winery closed for the evening, so he sat back and waited. He remembered Paris and what he had always referred to as "the undoing." Even from decades away, the pain still made him gasp.

As the twilight deepened, he heard the bustle of the help, preparing to close the winery for the night. They knew he and Gavin often stayed after hours, and wouldn't disturb them.

Thirty minutes later, the building was silent. Looking out his window, he could no longer make out the rows of vines and their precious cargo. *How amazing*, he thought. What had started with a handful of clones from France had burgeoned into acres of dark gold, a living treasure that Gavin and he had coaxed into award-wining wines. They had given the lie to that old joke, "How do you make a small fortune in the wine industry? Start with a big fortune." Despite the odds, they had made Enchanted Hill a financial and critical success.

A deep sigh issued from his lips. *And it's all a house of cards, on the brink of collapsing. Like worrying a thread on an old sweater, that journalist keeps picking away, enlarging the hole, heedless that she is destroying the garment. Her pursuit of the truth is unwavering, no matter how many lives she hurts.* He exhaled noisily. *Did I ever have such integrity?*

That thought gave him pause. What had the psychologist Erikson called the final stage of life? He scratched his chin. It had been many years since he had studied any psychology, but something was tickling the periphery of his consciousness. *Integrity versus despair—that was it.* The heart of the matter for an old man like him. And guilt was the despoiler, ruining everything it touched, condemning him to hopelessness.

Guilt and grief, my bedfellows. He shook his head violently to dislodge the uncomfortable image. *I can end this now.*

Sitting back down at the desk, he removed the bottle of Scotch from the lower right-hand drawer. He reserved it for moments like this. Two fingers of the honey-hued potion would fortify him for what he had to do. Raising the glass to his lips, the burn on his palate steeled his resolve.

Bobby walked out of his office and down the stairs, through the tasting room, bringing the bottle of Scotch with him. It was quiet now, except for the sound of the dishwashers under the bar, cleaning glasses from the day's revelry. Faint aromas of food still lingered in the air. The lights were dim.

He walked slowly but deliberately to the administrative wing and Gavin's office. Gavin's door was open, and he was at his desk, typing on his laptop.

"Why, hello, Bobby," he said as he looked up. "Come in. I'm almost done here. How long have you been standing there?"

Bobby didn't answer the question. Instead, he fixed his eyes on Gavin and said, "We have to talk."

"Of course, of course. Just let me save this file." He made a few clicks with the mouse and closed the laptop. "Fire away."

Bobby cleared his throat. In a voice barely above a whisper, he said, "I have to tell you what happened in Paris fifty years ago. I have to tell you about the undoing."

30. Ms. Pit Bull Meets Phantom of the Opera

It was all Kate could do to keep her eyes on the road. Her brain flew a mile a minute, imagining the worst—cars speeding after her, strangers shooting at her from behind trees, her house being set ablaze while she slept, a bomb exploding in her face as she opened the front door. "What have I done?" she wailed aloud. "What was I thinking?" Her reckless challenge of Bobby might finally be her ticket to an early grave. "I am so fucked!"

Once home, she leaped from the car and ran into the house. Calling Jay was a priority, but first she had to calm herself down. She filled a glass with bourbon and collapsed on the sofa. "Breathe, girl, just breathe."

The whiskey helped. Soon her pounding heart had returned to a normal rhythm. She called Jay.

His voice was light, almost cheerful. "Well, you called, which means you're still alive, which is a good thing. How did it go?"

She could think of no way to break it to him gently. "I screwed up royally." As she told her tale, the silence on the other end deepened. "Jay? Say something for God's sake."

"What do you want me to say? I agree with your assessment. You fucked up!"

Kate could hear him snort his disapproval. Her voice caught in her throat. "What do you think we should do now?"

"I think we should leave Oregon as soon as I get out of the hospital."

"Home?"

"It's probably not safe to go back to Nevada. Hell, his sister is only a phone call away. Let's go East somewhere. Some little hick town in Maine or New Hampshire."

"You're talking about running away? They'll track us down. Anyway, I have a story to write."

"I'm trying to buy us some time—dodge a bullet, for God's sake. You can write your story in a log cabin somewhere. I don't know about you, but I like staying alive. It's kind of on the top of my to-do list."

She was getting frustrated. "I'm sorry, okay? I wasn't thinking straight. I let my emotions get the better of me."

"Apology accepted. I'll see you tomorrow so you can bust me out of this joint." He ended the call.

Kate sat there, stunned. Her eyes filled with tears. Would Bobby send someone after her tonight? She tossed off the rest of her bourbon and walked into the kitchen without turning on any lights. No sense inviting trouble by illuminating herself in front of the glass slider. She felt her way along the counter to the silverware drawer and withdrew a long, sharp fillet knife. That would be her companion in bed tonight, along with her can of mace. Of course, she couldn't imagine falling asleep.

Once in her room, she locked the door and lay on the bed without undressing. She would be ready, whatever happened.

In the darkness, ordinary sounds were magnified by her imagination. The usual sounds of the house settling, the normal creaks of wood and pipes were transformed into footsteps across the kitchen tile, scratching at the door. She strained to hear everything, her muscles tight as a spring. After a half-hour of unrelieved tension, she gave up.

"This sucks," she said aloud. Knife in hand, she went out to the kitchen table and retrieved her laptop. Back in her bedroom, she locked the door again, braced a chair against it, and sat cross-legged on the bed to write more of her report, which now bore the tentative title, "The Lake Mead Murders."

Her fingers raced over the keys as she channeled her anxiety and fear into her writing. This would be her best story ever, even if, ultimately, she was unable to answer all of her questions. She sighed deeply. Even if she wasn't able to bring Bobby and Sofia to justice. That idea triggered her anger again. No! She had to get to the bottom of it. She would buy a ticket for Jay to flee, but she was staying here in Oregon. Her teeth clenched and her jaw tightened. *To the bitter end*, she promised herself.

The hours flew by as she poured her heart into the pages. Finally, her eyes grew heavy. She saved the file and laid her head back on the pillow.

She sat up abruptly to find the bedroom full of daylight. Exhaustion had gotten the better of her. Her watch showed nine o'clock. "Not dead yet," she said aloud. "Any day spent above ground is a good day."

The chair was still propped against the door. She stripped off her clothes, picked up the knife from the bed, and took it with her into the shower. She wouldn't get caught like Marion Crane in *Psycho*. The hot water was just what her body needed. That and clean clothes.

She stepped out of the shower and wiped the fog from the mirror. "You got this, girl," she told her reflection. Soon she was dressed in new jeans and a flattering teal blouse, ready to start the day. Leaving the knife on the bed, she slung her purse over her shoulder and pulled the chair from the door. Holding the mace at arms-length, as she had held the gun at the shooting range with Jay, she cautiously left the bedroom. The house was empty. Her stomach growled. Rather than fix something in the kitchen, she decided on a breakfast sandwich from the nearest drive-through.

She opened the front door and looked up and down the street. Everything was quiet. She locked the door and bolted to her car.

#

Jay sat in the wheelchair, looking grumpy. "Do I have to?"

"You know the rules. We have to roll you out the front door, then you can get up," explained the nurse. "Is your girlfriend bringing the car around?"

He began to say, "She's not—" but then stopped himself. *Girlfriend?* The word bounced around in his mind. "Yeah, she should be out front by now."

It was a short trip to the automatic doors that slid open at their approach. There under the front canopy was Kate with the car, running around to open the passenger door. Jay stood up and steadied himself with his cane.

"Thank you for everything," he said to the nurse, who nodded her head and wheeled the chair back inside. He turned to the driver. "Hi, Kate."

"Hi. Let me throw your bag of clothes in the trunk."

Jay eased into the seat as Kate joined him on the other side. "Nobody's taken any shots at you today, I hope?"

"Nope. Not yet anyway. But the day is still young." She drove away from the entrance and back to the highway.

"Did you check out airline tickets?"

She pursed her lips, then let out a loud sigh. "You can leave, if you like. I'm staying here. I've decided to see this thing through. I'm going to finish what I've started."

His voice rose. "Finish what you've started? You'll finish on a goddamn slab in the morgue!"

She kept her eyes on the road and stiffened her jaw. "My mind is made up. You can stay or go."

Neither spoke for several minutes. Jay finally broke the silence. "You are the stubbornest, most frustrating woman I've ever met. Lucky for you you're so damn cute."

Kate smiled in spite of herself. "The locksmith will be out later today to install better locks on the front door and all the windows. The glass company had to do a special order on the bullet-proof slider. That should be here next week."

Jay laughed. "New locks. Bullet-proof glass. Some job we do!" He shook his head. "We make quite the pair, you and me. Ms. Pit Bull meets Phantom of the Opera. Shit!"

There was little traffic, and they were home in fifteen minutes. Jay got out and looked up and down the street. Kate did the same.

"I'll get your bag from the trunk."

She hurried to meet him at the front door. Once inside, she locked the door again and took Jay's bag to his room. When she returned, she found him sitting on the couch. She sat down next to him.

"Are you hungry? Can I get you anything?"

"I'm fine, thanks. Just glad to be home, such as it is." He leaned into her and put his head on her shoulder. "I was kind of abrupt with you yesterday. I'm sorry."

"No apology necessary. I was an ass. I've made our situation worse." She turned to face him. "I would have no hard feelings if you wanted to take off."

"And miss all the fun? I feel like Chevy Chase in that silly holiday movie where everything has gone wrong, and his family wants to bail out. Remember it? He tells them nobody can leave, that they're going to have 'the hap-hap-happiest Christmas since Bing Crosby tap danced with Danny-fucking-Kaye.' We're in this together, come hell or high water."

She put her arms around him. "Thank you," she whispered.

Her phone buzzed. "It's the winery. What now?" She swiped the screen. "Hello?"

"Hello, Kate. This is Annalise at Enchanted Hill. Mr. Hartford asked me to call you."

"Hi, Annalise. What does he want?"

"He'd like you to come to the winery as soon as you can. Something terrible has happened."

31. Tanked

A police car with its lights flashing greeted the couple as they drove through the gate to the winery. The officer standing there motioned the car to stop, and Kate rolled down her window. He peered inside.

"I'm sorry, ma'am, sir, but the tasting room is closed to visitors today."

Kate could see her face reflected in the man's sunglasses. "We're not coming to the tasting room. The owner, Mr. Hartford, told us to come and meet with him."

"And you are…"

"Kate Temperance and Jay Scott."

"Oh, yes, Mr. Hartford told me he was expecting you." He pointed up the hill. "Go directly to his office in the administrative wing. Stay away from the production facilities out back. We've still got that area taped off until we've finished our investigation."

"What's happened?"

The police officer shook his head. "I'm sure Mr. Hartford will tell you all about it." He stepped back from the car to let them pass.

Kate glanced at her partner. "What do you suppose is going on?"

"I don't know, but it can't be good."

As they neared the top of the hill, they saw several other vehicles parked in front of the building across from the tasting room. Most were police cars, but one was a white van with a blue inscription on the back panel that read MARION COUNTY MEDICAL EXAMINER AND CORONER.

"Oh, shit," muttered Jay.

They hurried inside the front door of the tasting room, where Annalise met them. Her eyes were red and puffy.

"Hi, Kate," she managed, her voice choking back a sob.

"Hi, Annalise. This is my partner, Jay Scott. What's happening?"

"Nice to meet you, Mr. Scott. Sorry, but I'm in no shape to talk right now. Let me show you to Mr. Hartford's office. He'll explain everything." She took them down the hall and knocked on his door. Once the voice inside acknowledged their presence, she walked away.

"Come in."

Gavin was standing behind his desk, looking out the window into the vineyards. The laptop on his desk was closed. The walls were hung with the gold and blue ribbons Enchanted Hill had won for its wines, along with framed articles and covers from *Wine Spectator* and *Wine Enthusiast*.

"Gavin, I've brought my partner, Jay Scott, with me."

Gavin turned around and extended his right arm. "Nice to meet you," he said as they shook hands. "May I call you Jay?"

"Please do."

"I understand you've been through quite an ordeal. I'm glad to see you're on the mend." He sighed and averted his gaze. "I'm afraid I have some very bad news." His voice sounded rough with emotion. "My partner and lifelong friend, Bobby Amato, is dead."

Kate's eyes went wide with surprise. "Oh, my God! What happened?"

"The Medical Examiner is still investigating." Gavin motioned to the chairs on the other side of the desk. "Please sit. I'll tell you what I know." He all but collapsed into his chair. Kate and Jay took the seats facing him.

"Bobby came to my office last night after the tasting room had closed and everyone had gone home. He and I would often stay late to finish wrapping up our chores, answering emails, that sort of thing." He took a deep breath and continued. "But last night was different. Bobby was very upset. Agitated." Gavin looked directly at Kate. "He said you accused him of trying to have you killed. Is that true?"

Kate buried her face in her hands. "Yes." Her mind was reeling. Had her allegations pushed Bobby to the brink? Was she wrong about him—was he not Gemelli after all? Or was this proof that she had touched a nerve, found him after all these years?

Whatever the case, it felt like she had blood on her hands. Then other emotions filled her body—hope and relief. If he was Gemelli, she wouldn't have to keep looking over her shoulder, fearing what lurked in the shadows. The man who had tried to kill her would be dead.

Gavin furrowed his brow. "He said you called him Bobby Gemelli. When I asked him who the hell that was, he said Gemelli was the son of the owner of the Florentine Casino in Las Vegas. That the son disappeared fifty years ago, right after his father was murdered."

Kate nodded her head. "That's all true."

"So, tell me, Kate Temperance, you aren't really writing an article for *Wine Spectator*, are you?"

After a moment's hesitation, she lowered her eyes and took a deep breath. "No, I'm not. Gemelli is one of several disappearances I'm looking into, some of which I'm sure were murders."

Gavin turned to her partner. "And you, Jay? What is it you do?"

"I work for KLKE-TV in Las Vegas. I'm an investigative reporter also. We'll be doing a true-crime feature from Kate's story."

Gavin ran his hands through his white hair and looked up at the ceiling. "Undercover reporters who have no qualms about lying. Huh! And I've lost my best friend."

Kate's heart went out to him. "If it's not too difficult for you to say, may I ask how he died?"

Gavin leveled his gaze at the two people before him. "He brought a bottle of Scotch with him when he came to my office. Said he had to tell me about what happened after we met in Paris fifty years ago, back when we were young bucks on the prowl. We started drinking and swapping stories. One thing led to another. Before long, we were both three sheets to the wind." He pursed his lips and shook his head.

"You both got drunk?" Jay asked.

"Pie-eyed. I passed out right here at my desk. But Bobby could always hold his liquor better than I could. When I came to later, he was gone. I assumed he had gone home and prayed to God he didn't get in a wreck on the way. I staggered up the hill to my house and went to bed."

Kate pursued the question. "Where did he go?"

Gavin shook his head back and forth. "He went out to the crush pad and crawled into one of the Whole Cluster tanks I showed you last time. Must have fallen asleep in there. A worker found him this morning. Yanked him out, gave him CPR. But he was gone. Suffocated."

She winced. "Oh, crap! I'm so sorry, Gavin. I don't know what to say."

"You don't have to say anything, Kate. Please give me your email address and your house address. I'm sure the police will want to talk to you, especially after they take my statement. In fact, I expect them in here any minute. I can't imagine what's taking them so long." He opened his computer and logged on. When he entered Kate's address, he noticed a message sent from Bobby's computer late last night. He opened it and gasped.

"Dear God in heaven!" he exclaimed as he read it. He looked up a few moments later. His eyes were moist with tears. "You were right, Kate." She heard disappointment and disbelief in his voice. He turned the laptop so she and Jay could read it. "And here's the conclusion to your story."

32. The Ferryman of Hades

Kate and Jay crowded in together so they could both read it. "Fuck!" she whispered.

Dear Gavin,

I hope you can forgive me for a half-century of lying to you. After all this time, I really thought I had escaped my past, but I was wrong. Temperance is right. My real name is Bobby Gemelli. It's a long, sordid story, so I'll try to give you only the Cliff's Notes version here.

My father, Johnny Gemelli, wanted to make his casino, the Florentine, the biggest in Las Vegas, and heaven help anybody who got in his way. All his enemies wound up dead.

Tom Romano was his enforcer, the guy who did all his dirty work. I helped. I rowed the boat out onto Lake Mead every time to dispose of the bodies. Remember your Greek mythology? I was Charon, ferrying the souls of the dead across the river Styx to Hades. But I shouldn't joke about it, my dear friend. It made me an accomplice to murder.

And it gets worse. When my twin sister Sofia and I were teenagers, I found out my father was sexually abusing her. I confronted him about it. I told him I would kill him if he ever touched her again. He stopped. Then just after Sofia graduated from Harvard Law School, I walked into his office and found him arguing with her about something. He slapped her so hard she fell to the floor, bleeding from her nose. I completely lost it. I jumped on him and got him in a choke hold. I held on way too long. All I felt was rage, and all I wanted to do was punish him for everything he had ever done to my sister. Finally, he quit breathing.

My sister and I freaked out. We didn't know what to do. I didn't want to go to jail. With her law background, she thought I could get off on self-defense, but if the police opened an investigation, I worried they might find out about my job as the oarsman on Lake Mead. Sofia told me to turn myself in and hire the best legal team money could buy. But I was too afraid. I decided to make my father's death look like a mob hit. Sofia did her best to stop me. She became frantic trying to make me give up my plan and go to the police. I'm ashamed to say that I finally had to threaten her to make her leave me alone. It was not my finest hour.

Anyway, life since then had been good. I loved our time in France together. I loved our vineyard. Then Kate Temperance came around, digging up all the bodies. I tried to have her killed, but she didn't have the decency to die.

I'm too old to keep running. I hope our investors and customers don't back out of the winery now and you can maintain its success. I know it'll be a challenge. You're a hell of a winemaker, and this year is going to be a great vintage.

Gavin, you've been the best friend a man could ever have. I can't thank you enough. You were always there for me in the good times and the bad. I'm sorry I let you down.

Love,

Bobby

Kate didn't speak. She looked at Jay, then turned the laptop back around to Gavin.

"You were right all along," Jay said to her. "Your instincts led you here to Oregon and to this guy. You tracked him down when no one else could." He turned to their host. "I'm sorry for your loss, Gavin. It's hard for me to imagine what you're going through right now, how all this makes you feel. What a shock."

"It's an earthquake. A man I loved. A man I thought I knew turns out to be someone else entirely. I don't know how to process that."

Jay sighed. "I hope you can find some measure of peace after the dust settles. It sounds like he loved you till the end. And I do hope your winery survives this mess. It certainly deserves to."

"Thank you. But I know it will be a completely different place without him running it."

Jay clicked his tongue and drew in a breath. "I feel awkward asking this, but I do have one request, if I may." He looked at Kate, then back at Gavin. "Would you send that email to Kate's address? It would be the perfect coda for the piece we're doing."

Gavin nodded. "Of course. You're reporters, and you have a job to do." As he looked at his computer screen again, he said, "I'm guessing the police haven't gotten into Bobby's computer yet, but once they see this email, I'm sure they're going to want to talk to both of you. I hope that doesn't delay your return to Nevada. You probably want to get back there as soon as you can."

Jay nudged his partner. "I sure do. Nothing like sleeping in my own bed. How about you?"

"Fine by me," she said, but her tone was noncommittal.

Gavin stood. "I guess we're done here. I'm going to walk over and see what the Medical Examiner has come up with. Do you want to hang around for a little bit and see if the police want to talk to you today? Kate, why don't you take Jay downstairs and show him the banquet room? If the police want to interview you, that would be a good place to do it."

All three left the office, and Kate took Jay to the banquet room. The two stood before the window, looking over the rows and rows of grapevines.

Jay put his hand on Kate's shoulder. "From the looks of it, I'll bet they'll be harvesting soon." He turned to the wine racks on the wall. "What's with all these bottles?"

"They call it their library collection—the oldest and the best." She pointed at the koa table. "This is where I had that salmon lunch with Gavin that I told you about."

"Hey, I have to ask you. Do you feel any closure around this thing? Any vindication? You didn't exactly do a victory lap upstairs when you read that email."

A shadow crossed her face. "It almost seems too easy, too neat. All tied up with a bow."

"For God's sake, Kate! Easy? How many weeks—months!—have you been tracking this guy? How many miles have you logged? He's been your obsession, remember? He cost you your marriage and almost your best friend. That doesn't sound anything like easy to me."

"Does Gavin seem a little too eager to get us out of Oregon?"

"Shit, Kate! Your investigation was the catalyst that just torpedoed his whole life. His best friend is dead, his winery is in crisis. If I was him, I'd want you out of here, too."

"But we don't have all the pieces of the puzzle yet. Have you forgotten there's a dead body out there somewhere? I didn't tell the police when it happened, and I sure as hell don't want them to find out about it now. Gemelli made a reference to sending a killer after me in his email, and I don't want the police to trip me up about it. They're like sharks once they smell blood in the water."

Jay frowned. "Like I told Gavin, I was looking forward to sleeping in my own bed again. So that's not happening any time soon?"

She shook her head. "I have no idea. And speaking of dead bodies, who the hell is Henry, anyway? Where did he come from? Why did he save my life? And where the hell is he now?"

Jay almost spat the words at her. "Damned if I know."

#

When Sofia saw who was calling, she let a few rings go by before she answered it. "Hello, Bobby. I didn't expect to be hearing from you so soon after our last conversation. And if you're wondering—no, I haven't sent anyone else after Temperance."

"I wasn't calling about that. I wanted to let you know what's happened before you hear anything about it on the news."

"Is Temperance dead at last, fingers crossed?"

"No, my partner is."

"Bobby Amato? He was your best friend. What happened?"

"He had an unfortunate accident in a Whole Cluster tank."

She smiled. "Are you up to your old tricks again, you rascal?"

"It's not funny!" he snapped back. "I loved that man like the brother I never had."

Sofia began tapping her fingernails on the desk. "So why did he die?"

"He was the vulnerability—the chink in our armor—I was looking for. He knew everything. About me, you. About our father and Tom. About Temperance's mother and father. Everybody."

"Oh, my God." Her impatient tapping stopped, and she spread her palm on the desk. "Did he spill any of it to Temperance?"

"Jay assures me he didn't, at least not that Temperance has said anything to him about it."

She sighed with relief. "So, find a convenient way for her to have an accident, too, and be done with this whole messy business.

Jay is well enough to handle it, isn't he?" She heard a grumble on the other end.

"I don't think we can trust him anymore. After you sent your gun out here without telling him, and after Temperance has been nursing him back to health, he's changed."

"Goddamn it, Bobby!" Her fist came down hard on the desk. "I'm betting you never told Jay you assigned somebody to protect her, did you? Now you're telling me we can't rely on Jay anymore—the boy that's been a son to us? You have fucked this thing up so badly!"

"Me?"

"You! I told you we should have killed Temperance long ago, and none of this would have happened. You've lost your best friend, I've lost a man I trusted, and we're both losing a son."

"It's not my fault, goddamn it! You're so high and mighty, sitting in your casino. Now get your ass out here to Oregon so you can identify the body and prevent them from doing any forensics. I want Amato as Gemelli in a crematorium yesterday."

"Good. I'll be there. And you can spread his ashes around your fucking vineyard." She ended the call and returned the phone to her purse. Then she lifted the handset of the phone on her desk. "Sylvie, would you tell them to get my jet ready at the airport? I need to leave for Portland, Oregon, as soon as possible."

"Yes, ma'am. Will you be gone long? You have that meeting with the Chamber of Commerce on Friday."

"I'll be back in plenty of time for that, thank you."

I will save my empire, dear brother, with you or without you.

33. The Undoing

DECEMBER 26, 1973. PARIS, FRANCE. *Le Chat Noir* was the only bar open, such as it was. Calling it a dive would be high praise for the dark, smoke-filled room beneath the seedy *Hotel Parcours*. Its only decorations were grainy, black and white photographs of cats, adorning the paneled walls. The oak counter was scuffed and scratched with a hieroglyphic of pain—jobs lost, loves estranged, dreams abandoned. It was the kind of bar people visited not to celebrate their triumphs but to drown their defeats.

The young man hunched over the counter lit another cigarette and took a big swallow of his Kronenbourg 1664. His clothes looked as though he might have slept in them. His black hair was unkempt, and the charcoal shadow of five days without shaving made him look older than his twenty-one years.

Only one other customer sat at the bar, five stools away, nursing a longneck. His sandy hair framed a handsome face. A winter jacket lay on the stool beside him. His muscular chest looked as though it might pop the buttons from his long-sleeve blue shirt. "Got another cigarette?" he called to the other patron. "I'm fresh out."

"Sure. Help yourself," the man said as he took a drink from his Kronenbourg. He pulled the pack from his shirt pocket and set it on the bar.

The man in the blue shirt walked over and took the stool next to him. "My name's Bobby. What's yours?"

The dark-haired man never took his eyes from his bottle of beer. Exhaling a long stream of smoke, he said, "Bobby."

"No shit! What are the odds? And you sound American, too."

"Yeah, but I'm not really up for talking tonight. Okay? I just want to drink till I fall asleep."

"Sure, buddy. No problem. I won't bother you." He took a Zippo from his pocket and lit his cigarette. "You come here often?"

"Every night."

"Then I'll see you tomorrow."

Two beers later, a disheveled Bobby Amato left the bar and shuffled down the street to the studio apartment he was renting above *Les Provisions*, a small, neighborhood grocery store. Snow on the sidewalk from a freak storm would have made the journey treacherous, even if he wasn't drunk. The first fall seemed to awaken him a bit. The second jarred him into slowing his progress to mere inches per step. From the cone of one streetlight to the next, he slid and stumbled his way home, his breath making white puffs in the unusual cold.

He couldn't talk to a stranger tonight, even one from America. The wound was too fresh, the cut too deep. Louise had been gone only two weeks.

Her funeral had been held at *Sacré-Coeur*—a small local church that shared the name of the basilica on Montmartre Hill. Recalling it now drew tears from his eyes and a sob from his chest. Just as her burial awaited a thaw in the frozen ground, getting on with his life awaited a thaw in his heart.

Once back in his apartment, he flopped onto his bed without removing his clothes and was asleep in seconds.

#

The next morning, when he was halfway between sleep and waking, he had a vision, at least that's what he chose to call it. There at the foot of his bed, he saw Louise in her yellow flowered dress, her blonde curls sweeping over her shoulders. She held a finger to her lips in a gesture to keep him silent while she said, in clear and perfect English, "I'm not sick anymore, Bobby. You be well, too, my love," and then she was gone.

Bobby arose and stripped off his dirty clothes. He showered and shaved and dressed in a clean outfit. His grief was excruciating, but he made a promise to Louise that he would learn to live with it. At some level, he knew that grief would be his companion for the rest of his life.

That evening, he entered *Le Chat Noir* to find the other Bobby sitting on the stool he had occupied the previous night. This time, he greeted him with a handshake. "Hello, Bobby."

"Hi, Bobby," the man responded. "Thanks for the cigarette last night." He reached into his jacket pocket. "Here's a pack for your troubles."

Amato objected. "It was only one cigarette, for Pete's sake. I don't need a whole pack."

"Trust me. Where I come from, you stay generous to your benefactors and current with your debts."

"And where do you come from?"

"The land of the casinos and the low lives that haunt them. Let me buy you a drink, and I'll tell you all about it. What are you having?"

"Kronenbourg 1664."

Bobby motioned with two fingers to the bartender. "*Deux Kronenbourg, s'il vout plait.*"

"*Oui*," the man behind the bar replied.

Drink in hand, Bobby prefaced his tale to Amato by saying, "Please start calling me Gavin so you get used to it. I'm changing my name from Bobby Gemelli to Gavin Hartford."

"Why on earth would you do that?"

"As they say, therein hangs the tale. The short version is that I left Las Vegas suddenly, and I need to disappear. The long version will take several more beers."

"I've got nothing but time."

Each man lit a cigarette, and Gavin launched into his story. "You've heard words like 'mob' or 'mafia,' right?"

"You mean 'gangsters'? I've lived here in France for the last ten years, but I've watched a fair amount of American cinema."

Gavin nodded. "Good. So, my father was a gangster. He owned a casino called the Florentine in Las Vegas. His goal was to make it the biggest of them all, and anybody that got in his way wound up dead." Gavin's cigarette flared red on the end as he took a long drag. "But the mob is big—lots of families. It's like an octopus. Somebody took out a contract on my father and they got him. My sister found him in his office one day with a bullet in his head."

"Shit! So, it's not just in the movies."

"Hell, no! It's real."

Bobby frowned. "You don't sound sad about losing your father."

Gavin nodded again. "Damn straight. He was not a nice guy. The world is a better place without him in it. Anyway, my sister took over the operation of the casino, and I beat feet out of Dodge. I was afraid the mob might come after me next. You know, the king is dead. Now let's get the heir apparent, too."

Bobby lit another cigarette. "I'm guessing that changing your name will make it harder for them to find you?"

"That's the plan." He took a swallow of beer. "But enough about me. Tell me about yourself, Bobby."

He hesitated a moment, until he recalled the vision of Louise. He imagined that talking about it might be part of her encouragement of him to stay well. "My last name is Amato. I've lived in Paris since I was eleven-years-old. Mom and Dad came here to work in the Embassy. When they moved back to the States a year ago, I stayed behind. I had fallen in love with—" Suddenly, his stomach felt like he was falling too fast in an elevator. His breathing hitched for a moment, then returned to normal. "I had fallen in love with Louise. She was a Paris-born university student, studying literature at the Sorbonne. At night, when she had finished her homework, we would take turns reading French classics aloud to each other." He averted his eyes for a moment and dabbed them with a napkin. "I started taking courses at the Sorbonne myself, just so I could be near her. We were inseparable."

Gavin finished his beer and signaled the bartender for another round. "What happened?"

Bobby shook his head back and forth. "She developed a very aggressive cancer. By the time she was diagnosed, it had spread throughout her body. She died two months later, just two weeks ago."

"Oh, my God! I am so, so sorry, man. How are you holding up?"

"This is the first time I've been able to talk about it with anybody." He lit another cigarette and inhaled deeply. "Mom and Dad came out for the funeral, but they had to go back home to the States. They gave me a bit of money to live on till I can find a better job. I've been waiting tables at a *brasserie* not far from here. You'll have to come by. Still taking classes, too. I think reading French literature keeps me connected to Louise."

After that, they drank in silence for a while. Bobby drained his bottle and ordered another. He turned to Gavin. "How long you planning on staying in Paris?"

"I'm not sure. At least a year or two, maybe more. I have to figure out this whole 'work-permit-visa' thing. I know nothing about it."

"I can help you with that. No sweat."

"Thanks." Gavin held up his bottle. "Looks about empty. I'll finish it off, then I gotta crash. Nice talking to you, Bobby. Tomorrow?"

"Yep. I'll be here."

#

Winter became spring. Gavin took a job at the same *brasserie* where Bobby worked, even though his sister Sofia wired him money regularly. He spoke with her on the phone once a month.

As the friendship between Gavin and Bobby deepened, they rented a two-bedroom apartment together, not far from the Eiffel Tower. They also began to explore higher caliber bars than *Le Chat Noir*.

With the advent of summer, they found *Le Tigre*, a new restaurant and bar that proudly proclaimed in French and English, "We serve every libation known to man. If you cannot find it here, it is not made on planet earth." *Le Tigre* was considerably more expensive than their old hangout, but neither objected. It was their Friday treat—dressing up after a long week of hard work, rubbing shoulders with *le beau monde*. A night of exquisite dining and heavy drinking.

Late one warm Saturday morning, after an especially adventurous evening at *Le Tigre*, Bobby sat in the kitchen with his third cup of coffee, waiting for Gavin to wake up. Finally, he could wait no longer. "Okay, up and at 'em, sleepyhead. We're wasting a perfectly good day off."

"Oh, my aching head!" groused Gavin as he stumbled from his room. "Why did you wake me up?"

"Drink some coffee. Here." He poured a mug for his friend and handed it to him. "Do you have a bathing suit?"

Gavin sat down and took a sip. "This is what I needed." As the caffeine began to kick in, he said, "Actually, I do have a bathing suit. I always travel with one. I told you I grew up in Las Vegas. The only way to survive summer there as a kid is to spend it in a swimming pool. I even worked as a lifeguard for a while during high school. Why? What's up?"

Bobby topped off his own cup. "I'm going to take you to the most beautiful swimming pool you've ever seen—*La Piscine Pontoise*. It's in the Latin Quarter, not far from *le boulevard Saint-Germain*. All the students from the Sorbonne swim there."

"What's so beautiful about it?"

"It's art deco. Wait till you see it." He took another sip of coffee. "All blue and white inside, with these yellow-blue Aztec murals. Two mezzanines surrounding the pool with changing rooms—*les vestiaires*—you can lock your stuff in. There's a sunroof. They even have night swimming, all lit up. Very cool."

Gavin winced. "I'm pretty hungover. Can we do it another time?"

"This will be a great hangover cure. Believe me."

And it was. Less than an hour later, they entered the dazzling complex, changed into their trunks, and dove into splendor. The two men swam until they were exhausted, then just sat in the water, their arms on the edge of the pool, watching what Gavin called the bikini-clad "mermaids" all around them. He nudged his friend. "An old high school chum of mine would say, 'This is better than living.'"

Bobby smiled. "I'm inclined to agree. Let's do another lap."

How the accident happened neither knew for sure. Gavin thought that when the rowdy group of adolescent boys leaped into the pool, one of them might have struck Bobby on the head. Gavin turned and noticed that Bobby was no longer swimming with him. Instantly, his lifeguard training kicked in like muscle memory. He was underwater in a flash, pulling Bobby's motionless body back to the surface. Before the regular lifeguard on duty could rush to help, Gavin had Bobby out of the pool. He felt no pulse. He immediately began CPR, alternating two rescue breaths for every thirty chest compressions. Frantic moments later, the prostrate man coughed up a lungful of water.

"Just breathe, Bobby, just breathe," urged his rescuer.

"*Il va bien?*" asked the lifeguard, who knelt beside Gavin.

"*Oui, il va bien.*"

Bobby sat up, still coughing. When his breathing returned to a normal rhythm, he looked Gavin in the eyes. "You saved my life. How can I ever thank you?"

"Your breathing is thanks enough. Let's go change and head home."

"I'm with you."

#

As one day bled into the next, both men were getting restless. Late one night, while Bobby was reading *L'Etranger*, Gavin poked his book. "I don't want to be waiting tables for the rest of my life. What about you?"

Bobby put the book down on the end table and lit a cigarette. "You're psychic. I was thinking the same thing. Any ideas?"

Gavin nodded his head. "I learned two new words today—oenology and viticulture—the studies of wine-making and grape-growing. I'm not sure how many university classes we'll have to take but—"

Bobby interrupted him. "What an idea! I love it! And maybe we can skip the classes and do it the old-fashioned way—sign on to a vineyard out in Burgundy and learn like an apprenticeship. Real-world stuff instead of textbooks."

"Sounds good, but how would we go about it? Where would we start?"

"I'll bet my parents still have connections from back in their Embassy days. It seemed like they knew everybody in France. I'll call them."

A week later, Bobby's mother called him back. He hastily scribbled information on a scrap of paper by the phone. When their conversation was complete, Bobby whooped for joy.

"We've got it, partner. Jacques Rochefort owns Domaine Cece, just outside of Dijon. He's willing to take us on." He vigorously shook Gavin's hand. "Welcome to the wine industry!"

Gavin embraced his friend. "We need to celebrate. Friday night we're off to *Le Tigre* to tie one on!"

On Thursday, Gavin received a call from Sofia. Bobby looked up from his book to see his friend's face darken, but he could not hear the other side of the conversation.

"Oh, no!" said Gavin. "That's horrible! Was it necessary?" He sat down hard in a kitchen chair and exhaled a deep sigh. "Hopefully that's the last."

As he hung up the phone, Bobby asked him, "Bad news?"

"Yeah." He put his hand on his forehead.

"Anything I can do to help?"

"No, thanks. It's family matters."

#

When Friday arrived, they dressed in their finest and were greeted at the door of *Le Tigre* by a young woman in a stunning black strapless gown. "*Deux ce soir*? Two for tonight?"

"Yes!" bubbled Gavin. "We're celebrating our new jobs at Domaine Cece in Bourgogne."

"Congratulations to both of you. Please follow me."

The walls were a collage of French Impressionism, lending brilliant colors to the dark paneling. Candles like twinkling stars sparkled on every white-clad table. In the back, on a small stage, a dark-haired woman in a low-cut red dress crooned jazz favorites into a microphone, accompanied by another woman at the piano.

As Gavin and Bobby took their seats, the lady in black said, "I'll have your server bring you a glass of *Veuve Cliquot* to begin your celebration. On the house."

The two men grinned at each other.

When their Champagne arrived, Bobby raised his glass, and Gavin tapped it with his own. "Now that's what I call a welcome."

They decided it was a night for caviar and oysters to complement their Champagne.

Time was a blur. They lost track of how many bottles of Champagne they had drunk, how many oysters they had consumed.

Gavin looked as though he were trying to focus on Bobby's face, but was not having complete success. "You don't look anywhere near as drunk as I feel. What's your secret?"

Bobby took his wallet from his pocket. "I drink less, and I drink more slowly. Let's ante up. We'll have them call us a cab, unless you would rather walk."

"I need the fresh air," Gavin slurred. "If I can lean on you for balance, let's walk."

The night was clear and warm, but the stars could not penetrate the glow of the city lights. In the distance, the dark finger of the Eiffel Tower pointed to the heavens.

As they stumbled along, Bobby laughed. "Did you know you can't take pictures of the Eiffel Tower and publish them?"

"What?"

Bobby was still chuckling. "It's protected by French copyright law. Buildings are classified just like works of art, and the copyright doesn't expire until seventy years after its creator dies. You'll be able to take pictures of the tower starting in 1993, when Eiffel's copyright runs out."

Gavin stumbled again. "That's just crazy," he slurred. After another lurching step, he said, "Can we take a break? I need a cigarette and a rest."

Bobby guided him to a stoop in front of an apartment building. Across the street, the yellow cone of a streetlight provided some dim illumination. "Here you go. Sit down. I'll light a cigarette for you."

Gavin puffed on the cigarette Bobby handed him and coughed. He turned to his friend and said, "Bless me, Father, for I have sinned. It's been five years since my last confession—"

"Whoa! Whoa! Gavin, I'm not your priest. You can't confess to me."

"But if I'm gonna die, I need forgiveness!"

Bobby put a calming hand on his shoulder. "You're not going to die. You're just very drunk. I'll help you get home."

Gavin shouted. "Just listen to me! Forgive me! I'm a murderer and an accomplice to murder!"

"You're not a murderer, Gavin. Like I said, you're drunk. I have to get you home so you can sleep it off."

"I killed my own father!"

Bobby's heart skipped a beat. He took his hand off Gavin's shoulder. "What did you say?"

Tears were streaming down Gavin's face. "He slapped my sister. I jumped on him and choked him out. Then I shot him to make it look like a mob hit. My sister killed one of his bodyguards."

Bobby stood up and looked at Gavin as though he were a complete stranger. His mind recoiled at the revelations, and a deep sense of revulsion sickened his stomach. "Why are you telling me this now?"

"Because my sister just killed someone else. To protect us."

Bobby was tempted to put his hands over his ears to stop hearing the disclosures, but could not, drawn to them like an observer to an awful accident.

Through his sobs, Gavin continued. "You have to understand. I was the ferryman. I rowed the boat while Tom did my father's dirty work." He turned his head and vomited on the stoop. Then he wiped his mouth on his shirt sleeve. "We dumped the bodies in Lake Mead. I can't remember how many. One of them was Harry. We didn't know his girlfriend Samantha was pregnant."

Bobby's mind was reeling. His dearest friend was a man he didn't know. His dearest friend had a heart blacker than he could have ever imagined.

"Samantha somehow figured out my father had Harry killed. She went to my sister Sofia, who runs the Florentine. Told her she needed money to take care of her new baby Kate, or she'd go to the police. Sofia was afraid that if the police started digging, they might find out everything."

Bobby finished Gavin's exposé. "So, your sister had her killed. To protect herself and to protect you."

"Yes. She loves me." Gavin leaned back on the stoop as though he were a sprinter out of breath, the last of his energy depleted. His head lolled to the side and saliva dripped from the corner of his mouth.

Bobby's eyes filled with tears of heartbreak and outrage. A brother and sister—twin scorpions—willing to do anything to protect themselves. The man who had saved him from drowning—the man to whom he owed his life—had taken untold lives from others. The man he could talk to about Louise, the man on whose shoulder he could cry when his grief overwhelmed him, that same man cast a shadow of indescribable evil. *Dear God, how do I answer him?* he thought. *And will he remember anything about this when he sobers up tomorrow?*

Bobby sat back down next to Gavin and took his hand. "I can't give you absolution for your sins. You'll have to get that from a real priest. But I can promise you never to reveal this to anyone. Never to speak of it again." Now he grasped Gavin's hand in both of his. "You have undone our friendship, but I still owe you my life. I will honor that till my dying breath."

He wrapped his arms around Gavin's shoulders and helped him to his feet. "Now let's get you home."

The next afternoon, when Gavin finally staggered out of his bedroom, rubbing his eyes, he said, "How did we get home? Did you get us a cab?"

"No, we walked. It took us a while, but we made it. Here. Have a cup of coffee." He filled a mug and handed it to him.

"Whew! My brain is wiped. I don't remember anything after that last bottle of Champagne."

Bobby's lips curled in a rueful smile. "Some things are best left forgotten."

Gavin raised his mug in a toast. "Amen to that, my friend."

34. All in the Family

The next day, Kate called Billie to bring her up-to-date on the latest developments. The producer asked for details, and Kate shared what she knew. Billie congratulated her.

"Sounds like your story has good bones—no pun intended—but like you said, there are still a lot of holes in it. Are you going to be able to fill in those holes?"

Kate took another sip of her morning coffee. "I'm not sure yet. I'll go back out to the vineyard today and take a bunch of pictures now that the police are gone. I'll send you some to see what you think."

Billie's voice sounded genuinely concerned. "Were the police hard on you yesterday?"

"No, they were completely professional and respectful. They let me off easy."

"So what answers are you looking for now?"

Kate squinted her eyes as she drew on her mental notes. "First, I'd like to know who the hell Henry is and who sent him. I'm only alive today because of him. I'm also more than a little curious about who the other dead body is. Bobby says in his email that he hired somebody to kill me. At first, I thought that Sofia had found us, but I guess she hasn't. And I don't want her to."

"Right. She's a black widow spider if there ever was one."

"My sentiments exactly. I just got out from under her brother's crosshairs. I don't want her drawing a bead on me now."

"Hmmm. Sounds like gun-talk to me."

Kate chuckled. "I have Jay to thank for that."

"Speaking of him, where is he and how is he doing?"

"He's doing well. He can walk pretty much without the cane until he gets tired by the end of the day. He took off to fill the car up with gas before we drive back out to the winery."

"Well, give him my best. Hope you get home soon."

#

"You handled yourself very well when you were out here with Temperance."

Jay held the phone to his ear while the attendant pumped gas into the car's tank. "Thanks. I had to keep reminding myself to call you 'Gavin.' I almost tripped up once or twice." He took a breath. "But before we go any further, I have to be honest with you. I'm not sure how I should understand you and Sofia keeping me out of the loop. I presume she's the one who sent somebody to kill Kate. And I'm guessing you're the one who sent the guy Kate calls 'Henry' to protect her. Why did you both leave me out?"

"Are you ready to make Temperance have an accident?" Gavin countered.

Jay hesitated a moment before responding.

Gavin jumped in. "See? Your pause tells the tale. She's no longer just a target to you, is she? She isn't just a job anymore. You have feelings for her."

"I-I," Jay stammered, unsure what to say.

"It's nothing to be ashamed of, son. It happens. Just don't get in the way when we make our move. That would change the whole complexion of this thing. Understand?"

Jay nodded his head, as though not recognizing Gavin couldn't see him. "Yes," he said in a voice without emotion.

"Good. I expect to be seeing Sofia shortly. She's identifying Bobby Gemelli's body as we speak. Then she'll be coming to the winery to pay me a visit. A little family time. I understand you and Kate will be coming out here as well?"

"Yeah. I'll keep an eye out and steer Kate clear of Sofia."

"Of course. It wouldn't do for Temperance to see my sister here. Keep me posted and I'll...keep you in the loop."

The gas station attendant called in the window. "That'll be forty-five dollars and fifteen cents."

Jay handed him two twenties and a ten. "Keep the change, buddy."

"Thanks, mister."

As he drove away from the station, Jay pondered his telephone conversation. Gavin was right. He did have feelings for

Kate, however undefined they might be. At this point, he couldn't imagine arranging her death—her murder. Could he "stay out of the way" when Gavin or Sofia tried to kill her?

#

Kate drove around the winery's tasting room to the back parking lot. They passed a black Suburban and parked several spaces down from it. She turned to Jay in the passenger seat. "I wonder where they're visiting from? It's a rental car. I saw the little barcode sticker on the side window."

Jay got out and looked back toward the SUV. "An expensive rental, I'll bet." He glanced toward the side door to the tasting room, the entrance to the administrative hallway where Gavin's office was. "What do you say we walk down to the crush pad first and spend some time there? Take some pictures. Get closeups of the tank where Gemelli bought it. You can show me around since I never got the grand tour that you did. Then we can go into the tasting room later and maybe have a bite to eat."

"Sounds like a plan."

They took their time walking around the building that housed the merchandise store. Halfway down the hill they passed the giant white tanks on the right. "Pretty soon those will be filled with the juice from the smaller fermentation tanks down there." She pointed. "I'll show you," Kate sounded like a docent in an art museum. Then her tone became more somber. "That's where Bobby Gemelli died."

When they reached the crush pad, one of the tanks seemed to be getting special attention from a cleaning crew. "That must be the one Bobby crawled into." She started taking pictures.

One of the workers spotted them and raised his hand. "You shouldn't be here without a tour guide from the winery. If you'll stay there, I'll call one for you."

Jay nodded his head. "Sure. This is Kate Temperance, and I'm her partner Jay Scott. Maybe Mr. Hartford spoke about us? We're doing a story for our TV station in Las Vegas."

"I thought it was for *Wine Spectator*. Anyway, he said we're supposed to give you the red-carpet treatment. I'll get somebody right away."

A few minutes later, Annalise came down the hill. "Hi, Kate. Jay. You saved me from having to stand behind that bar all day. I thought about taking today off, but then I thought it would be better to stay busy."

"You really miss him, don't you?" said Kate, recalling the young woman's tears from yesterday.

"He was like a grandfather to us." Her breath caught for a moment. "And I'm so confused. I've heard rumors from other tasting room staff. They're saying he wasn't Bobby Amato at all but Bobby Gemelli, somebody in the Mafia—that he killed people. You don't believe that, do you?"

Kate wasn't sure how to respond. It was like Gemelli was two different people. Annalise knew the kindly old man who managed the business of Enchanted Hill. Kate knew the shadowy figure from Las Vegas who tried to have her killed. How could she reconcile the two? She reached out and took the woman's hand. "I'm so sorry for your loss, Annalise."

"Thank you, Kate." She took a tissue from her pocket and dabbed at her eyes. "He never told us he had any family, but now they're saying his sister from Las Vegas is here to see where he died."

"What?" Kate's eyes went wide with surprise. She turned to Jay. "What would she be doing here?"

Jay shrugged his shoulders. "Maybe the police asked her to come and identify the body?"

"But why come here to the winery? Doesn't it seem a little grisly to want to see the fermentation tank where your brother suffocated?"

Annalise interrupted them. "Wait a minute, Kate. Do you know his sister?"

Just then, Gavin and Sofia Gemelli emerged from the wine cellar and walked out onto the crush pad. Sofia scowled.

"Kate Temperance." She made the name sound like a curse. "Why am I not surprised to see you? I suppose you're here to besmirch my brother's memory, as you'd like to do with my father's?"

Kate frowned. "I'm glad to see you, too, Sofia. Have you killed anybody today?"

"The day is young, my dear," the silver-haired woman snapped back. "Just give me a reason."

Annalise stood there, aghast, looking from one to the other. "You do know each other!" she yelled.

Sofia addressed her. "My darling, had not this trollop stuck her nose into other people's business, Bobby might still be alive today. You would not be in the throes of grief."

Annelise's face contorted into a mask of anger and betrayal as she riveted Kate with her gaze. "You've been lying to me from the day we met. How could you?"

Sofia looked at her as a mother might at her injured child. "Oh, my dear, it's what Kate Temperance does for a living. I'm so sorry you had to find out the hard way."

Annalise turned on her heels and ran up the hill.

"See the effect you have on people, Ms. Temperance?" It sounded as though Sofia had just proved a geometry theorem. "It should give you pause."

Jay tried to come between the women as a peacemaker. Gavin looked on with a smile as Kate erupted at her nemesis.

"Your brother couldn't kill me and neither will you! His toady is lying out there somewhere with a bullet in his head! I won't quit till you're in prison!"

"But Ms. Temperance," she replied, in a voice dripping with condescension. "Mr. Hartford just read my brother's suicide note to me, and it clearly exonerates me of any wrong-doing. For what shall I go to prison? For lying to the police about what really happened when my father was killed fifty years ago? I was under duress and feared for my own safety—that my crazy brother would hire someone to shut me up permanently if I tried to talk. Or perhaps I should go to prison for trying to protect my family from reckless fools like you?" Her smile was that of a monarch bestowing her largesse on plebians unworthy of her generosity. "Ms. Temperance, I hope you can see at last that you are not a Pulitzer-Prize-winning journalist, but a mere hack, a gnat on the body politic. Now, if you'll excuse me, I would like to see where my brother died. Please give me some privacy."

Kate's shoulders sagged as though some skeletal piece inside her had suddenly broken. She could think of no response. She turned and began to walk back up the hill and around toward the tasting room. Jay followed.

Once the two reporters were gone and out of earshot and no crush pad workers were in the immediate vicinity, Sofia turned to Gavin. "I don't think she's a threat to us any longer, Gavin." She pursed her lips. "I was afraid your judgment might be compromised because of her uncanny resemblance to your late wife Guinevere. It's remarkable, isn't it?"

"It is. Her hair. The way she holds herself. Her sharp intellect." He sighed. "We never escape grief, do we? It just takes different shapes as time passes. I think about our mother, as I'm sure you do. I think about Guinevere and my son Jonas. And I'll always remember Bobby. I'll miss him for the rest of my life."

"I can imagine. The business decisions we must make to maintain an empire." She shook her head back and forth. "As difficult as it must have been to execute, your plan was masterful. That note you created on Bobby's computer and then sent to yourself? Brilliant! You should think about writing a novel."

"Why, thank you, Sofia. What a lovely compliment. Is all forgiven between us?"

"Yes, all is forgiven, dear brother. But there is one more thing."

"Yes?"

"I still want Temperance dead."

Gavin embraced her, then kissed her on the cheek. "I agree, Sofia. We are family after all."

35. Where the Heart Is

FRIDAY, DECEMBER 7, 1973. Bobby and his sister Sofia sat in a dim corner of the restaurant, sipping cocktails under a haze of cigarette smoke. A small rock band was tuning their guitars on the stage off to the right of them, muting the sounds of the two men arguing at the bar. Sofia withdrew a letter from her purse and handed it to her brother.

"This arrived in the mail today. It's postmarked four days after Mom...disappeared."

Bobby withdrew the letter from the envelope and held it by the candle's light to read it.

> Dear Sofia,
>
> Please forgive me for running away and leaving you and your brother with that monster. He wants to divorce me and marry his latest whore. When I told him he would have to make it worth my while, especially since I know all his secrets, he went crazy. I'm writing this from the hospital. They're discharging me today. I didn't want to call you because I was afraid you'd want to come and visit me. I need to disappear.
>
> Now that you've graduated, get as far away from him as you can. Maybe practice law on the East Coast near where you went to school.
>
> I worry about your brother. He should forget about wanting to run a casino and run away from Las Vegas as fast as he can. Tell him.
>
> I'll send you another letter when I settle down somewhere. I won't be able to tell you where I am, but at least you'll know I'm alive.
>
> Love you with all my heart,
>
> Mom

Sofia took a sip of her martini and looked at Bobby. "What secrets is she talking about?"

Bobby looked down at the table, then back up at his sister. "I'm not sure you want to know."

She reached over and touched his hand. "I do want to know. Tell me."

He took a deep breath and exhaled slowly. "While you've been away at school, Dad's been settling some old scores. He's trying to grab control of some of the other casinos." He raised his Manhattan to his lips. "He's been eliminating anybody that gets in his way."

Her eyebrows rose and her eyes became large circles in the candlelight. "Eliminated as in…killed?" she whispered.

Bobby nodded and took another sip.

"You haven't been involved in that, have you?" Sofia asked.

He could hear the worry in her voice, and he grimaced, his face a mask of shame.

She leaned across the table. "What have you done? Have you killed somebody?"

"No, no, I haven't killed anybody myself. But…" He struggled to find the words of his confession. "It's Tom Romano who does the killing. I just row the boat while he dumps the bodies in Lake Mead."

"Sweet mother of God," she said. "So, you're an accomplice to murder."

His shame morphed into anger. "Don't sound so high and mighty about it. You were miles away at school, away from this whole mess. What was I supposed to do? I thought if I did what he asked me to, he'd stay calm and wouldn't keep slapping Mom around." The shame returned. "And maybe he'd let me run a casino."

Sofia leaned back in the booth and drained her glass. The light from the candle glistened off the tears in her eyes.

"Welcome home, sis," Bobby said. The words were a self-reproach and an accusation.

Sofia clenched her teeth. "Now he's going to kill our mother if he can track her down. He's a wild animal."

Bobby finished his drink. "And there's nothing we can do about it."

Sofia put both her hands on the table and stared at her brother. Her lips curled in a wry smile. "Yes, there is. We'll kill him before he finds her." She said it as though she were simply ordering another cocktail.

Bobby's jaw dropped. "Are you serious?" His voice was a low growl. "You just criticized me for being an accomplice, and now you want to do the deed? Are you crazy?" What he saw in her eyes—an unquenchable fury—sent a chill through his body.

"I'm not crazy. I'm mad," she said in measured tones. "His dirty hands all over me for years. If you hadn't stopped him, I know he would have raped me. He was grooming me for that. And now he's chased our mother away in fear for her life? He has to be stopped. He's a rabid dog, and he has to be put down."

"Do you hear what you're saying?" He quickly looked around the restaurant to make sure they could not be overheard, pleased the band had begun playing a tune. "Killing our own father?"

"Do you have the stomach for it, brother? Or has Daddy cut your balls off?"

Bobby stood up from his seat, uncertain what to say or do next. He was angry at his sister's taunt, but compelled by her logic. How could anyone be safe in a home presided over by a dragon—by a monster who apparently knew no bounds? Bobby was convinced his father would kill his mother if he had the chance, but would he kill Sofia if he felt the "need?" Or him? *You can't reason with a rabid dog*, he thought. *Maybe my sister is right.*

Sofia looked up at him. "Please order us some more drinks and come sit back down. We have a lot to talk about."

#

The following Sunday, brother and sister were ready. They had rehearsed their plan many times. What they were about to do had to be done quickly. They knew that the two bodyguards at the door to their father's office always took turns going to ten o'clock Mass at the Catholic Church. The one left behind in the casino today had won a very unfortunate lottery.

The black-suited man stood at the door with his arms folded across his broad chest. On his left cheek was the shadow of a scar from an old knife wound. His moustache was neatly trimmed and his dark hair slicked back.

As Bobby and Sofia approached the guard, Sofia distracted him. "Did you know that on December 12th in 1901, Guglielmo Marconi sent the first radio transmission across the Atlantic Ocean?"

The man furrowed his brow in confusion. "What did you say?"

It was all the opening Bobby needed. He leaped behind the man and wrapped his arm around the guard's neck. The man thrashed and squirmed in the pincer-like grip of the sleeper hold. He bounced his legs off the floor as he thrust backward against his attacker, flailing his arms helplessly. Bobby held on. As the frantic movements diminished, Bobby tightened his grasp. He was the python squeezing its hapless prey. Ten seconds later, the man went limp. Bobby did not release him for another sixty seconds. He laid the body on the floor and checked for a pulse. Once he was assured the man was dead, he took the guard's pistol from the holster under his suit jacket.

Sofia knocked on the massive oak door and turned the gold knob. "Daddy?" she called. Without waiting for a response, she opened the door and walked in.

Giancarlo stood up from his desk. "Sofia, what are you—"

Bobby stepped out from behind his sister. In one quick motion, he raised the gun and fired. The man collapsed into his chair. His head crashed forward onto the desk. A red pool began to form around it.

Sofia checked her watch. "The other guard will be back in about twenty minutes. C'mon."

Bobby wiped his fingerprints from the pistol and dropped it to the floor. "We're coming to the real hard part, Sofia. I don't want to hurt you."

Sofia was adamant. "We have to make it look convincing. Tie my hands behind my back. Hurry." When her wrists were bound, she nodded in affirmation. "Good. Now do what you have to do."

"Okay," he said, sighing in reluctance. "Sit down in that chair so I don't knock you over. Now close your eyes." He punched his sister in the nose, rocking her head back.

"Fuck, that hurt! But we've got a gusher," she said, as she watched the blood from her nose and lip splash down the front of her dress. "Quick. Help me lie down on the floor over there in the corner. Then run!"

Bobby was out the door and racing to the airport long before the second guard returned. Their entire plan had taken less than five minutes to execute. It would be hours before the guests of the Florentine learned the horrifying news of a mob assassination right above them as they were heedlessly playing poker and slot machines, ordering drinks from the wandering waitresses, wondering if they had enough money left to pay for their hotel rooms.

36. Oh, Henry!

Kate was silent until they reached the car. "I don't want to go into the tasting room. I just want to go home." She got in the driver's side, while Jay slid into the passenger's seat.

"Hey, don't take it so hard. What that bitch said about you isn't true." He leaned over and touched her shoulder. "You're a terrific investigative journalist, and this story will be another big notch in your career. It may win you the Emmy or the Pulitzer, even if it's not as complete as you'd like it to be. I think Billie will really be able to run with it."

She started the car and turned toward him. "Thanks, Jay. I appreciate your vote of confidence. I really do. I'm just not feeling it right now."

"I understand. It may be time for a little bourbon."

Kate smiled in spite of herself. "It must be five o'clock somewhere."

His half-grin was slim comfort. "What was that old expression? The sun is over the yard arm?"

A few minutes later, they arrived at the house. Once inside, Jay went to the cabinet in the kitchen where they kept the whiskey, while Kate took a seat in the living room. "Make mine a double," she called.

"I'm bringing the bottle with me. We'll plunk it down on the coffee table."

With glasses in hand, Kate made a toast. "Here's to Oregon, a lovely State if there ever was one. In fact, I may have to rethink my residence in the desert."

"Hear! Hear!"

Her face grew somber. "All kidding aside, I'm ready to go back to Nevada. I don't think the Willamette Valley is going to give up any more secrets." She took another sip. "Let's work with what we've got and start putting it together."

"I'm with you, partner. Let's see if we can get tickets out of here for tomorrow."

Kate opened her laptop and let her fingers fly over the keys. "Ouch! Looks pretty busy. Lots of people are leaving Portland to deposit their hard-earned cash in 'Lost Wages'. Oh, wait a minute. Here we go. Looks like there's still two seats tomorrow afternoon. Shall I book them?"

"By all means. Can't wait to get back to that 'but it's a dry heat' desert. Enough of this lush greenery, moderate temperatures, wonderful wine."

Kate chuckled. "Pass me that bottle, sir."

#

The next morning, Kate was up early to make them both breakfast. When Jay walked into the kitchen, he was greeted by the aromas of freshly-brewed coffee and bacon sizzling in the pan.

"What's this?" he said. "I didn't know you were so…domestic."

"I'm not. I just thought we might as well use up some of the food in the refrigerator. We can't take it with us. I'll call the property manager later and let her know our plans."

"Good idea. I almost forgot. After breakfast, I'll take my shower, then I've got to pick up some shirts I left at the laundromat." He poured himself a mug of coffee and took a tentative sip. "Wow! Now that's what I call a good cup of Joe."

"How do you like your eggs?"

"Why don't you just scramble a bunch of them?"

"Works for me. You take care of the toast."

When they sat down to eat, Kate looked at Jay with affection. "You're a good partner, and I like working with you. We'll have to do more of it."

"Thanks, Kate. The feeling's mutual."

She sighed. "You know, I never want to take this for granted."

"What?"

"The ordinary," she explained. "The simplest, every-day things. Being able to get out of bed and walk upright. Being able to eat without a feeding tube. Hell, being able to shit and piss without medical help. Know what I mean?"

"Yeah, like recognizing you're well before you get sick, instead of not being tuned into your health until it's gone south."

"Exactly. I almost died in that vineyard, but my past didn't flash before my eyes. It's all about the present. This moment, right now, eating breakfast with you and enjoying it."

"Zen 101?" he joked.

"C'mon. You know what I'm talking about." She raised her mug and took another sip of coffee. "If one of those bullets that hit you was one inch higher or lower, you wouldn't be sitting here with me. I'd be scattering your ashes somewhere."

Jay nodded his head. "Amen, partner. You're one-hundred-percent right." He beamed at her. "And I like philosophy with my breakfast."

After the meal, Jay brought their dishes to the sink. "I'll wash these. It's the least I can do."

"Thanks. I'll jump in the shower. Don't worry. I'll be quick, so I'll save plenty of hot water for you."

#

With the dishes washed and morning ablutions completed, Jay prepared to leave for the laundromat. "You can stay and pack, Kate, but first, I want to give you something." He went to his bedroom and came back with his pistol. "Here, take this."

"What do I need that for? Bobby's dead, remember?"

"Hey, humor me, okay? I'll feel better if I know you've got this with you." When she took the gun, he said, "I want to review our lessons. Pop the magazine out."

Kate did as she was told.

"Now work the slide and eject the cartridge in the chamber. Good. Pick that round up, load it back into the magazine, and ram the clip home. Perfect."

"It's all coming back to me. I can do this, Mr. Teacher."

"Of course. You're a good student. Last but not least, work the slide and seat a round in the chamber."

In one swift motion, she loaded the gun. The slide clicked home with authority. "Done."

"One other thing. Remember what I told you. If you have to use this, don't do anything fancy like aiming for the head. Just point at the center of body mass and keep pulling the trigger as fast as you can."

She made a mock salute with her free hand. "Aye, aye, cap'n."

"All right. I'm out of here. I'll be back as soon as I get my shirts."

Kate locked the door behind him. She walked into the living room and aimed the pistol at imaginary targets. *This calls for another trip to the range when we get back*, she thought. Just as she was about to go to her bedroom to begin packing, she heard a knock. She hastily put the gun behind a pillow on the couch and went to the door. She looked through the peephole. "Oh, Henry!" she exclaimed, as she opened the door. "I wondered if I'd ever see you again. You just missed my partner. He's off to the laundromat."

"I know. I saw him leave."

"What?" Something in his tone wasn't right.

"Let's step into the living room, shall we?" He shut the door as Kate backed away. "I see you had the locks changed like I suggested. Good for you. What about that glass slider?"

Kate's alarm sent a flood of adrenaline into her bloodstream, elevating her heart rate and respirations. *Fight or flight*, she thought, in a crazy association to an old science lesson in high school. "Um, the slider is on order, but we'll cancel it. Jay and I are going back to Las Vegas today."

He frowned. "I'm sorry to have to change your plans, Kate. Please go sit on the couch."

"Henry, you're scaring me. What's going on?" She sat on the couch and slid her hand under the pillow that hid the pistol.

"Want to know my real name?" he said, sitting down in the chair opposite her. As he did so, he drew a gun from behind his back. "It's Patrick. Patrick Reilly. A good Irish name."

"I still don't understand…Patrick. What are you doing here?"

"Kate, think of me like a contractor. You know, like the guy you hired to change the locks on your front door. I get hired to do jobs, too. And I do what I'm told." He was aiming his pistol at her.

A spark of anger ignited in her breast, pushing aside the fear. "So, what have you been told?"

"It's like an about-face. First, Bobby Gemelli hires me to protect you because he thinks his sister has sent somebody to kill you. Now my orders have changed. He wants me to take you out."

"Bobby Gemelli is dead. He suffocated in a fermentation tank at the winery."

Patrick smiled. "Please understand. I like you, Kate. In an ordinary world, we could be friends. But I'm a businessman, and this is my job. I promise I'll do it in a quick way so you won't suffer, and I won't spoil your face, so you can have an open coffin."

Kate's brain was racing, searching for a way out. *What can I do? What can I do?* Her fingers flexed around the grip of the gun under the cushion. She inserted her index finger into the trigger guard. She hollered at him, "How considerate of you, you dumb fuck! At least it'll be recorded for posterity on that camera I had installed over the door."

"Wha—?" He turned his head for a split-second.

It was all the distraction Kate needed. In a flash, the pistol was out. She pointed it at him and pulled the trigger. The first round caught Patrick in the sternum. A look of total surprise washed over his face as his own gun dropped from his hand. The next round hit him in the stomach. He pitched forward and fell onto the coffee table. Kate kept pulling the trigger again and again. Finally, the slide rammed back and stayed open. The magazine was empty. Kate's nostrils filled with the acrid smell of burnt gunpowder. Her ears were ringing. Patrick's dead body lay there twitching.

Kate dropped the gun. She tried to stand up, but her knees buckled, and she collapsed to the carpet. Grasping the arm of the sofa, she pulled herself to her feet. Then she bent over and vomited her breakfast all over Patrick's corpse. She staggered into the kitchen.

#

Ten minutes later, Jay smelled the gunpowder as soon as he opened the front door. He raced in and saw the bloody body in the living room. "Kate!" he cried. "Kate!"

"In here. In the kitchen." She was supporting herself against the counter by the sink. A bit of vomit still clung to her lower lip. Her body was trembling convulsively.

Jay rushed to her. She collapsed into his arms. "Oh, Jay. Jay. I've killed somebody. I can't stop puking." As if to emphasize that, she pushed away from him and leaned over the sink, retching violently. Nothing came out.

"Dry heaves, darling. Your stomach's empty." He embraced her and tried to comfort her shaking body. "Easy. Easy. You did great. You're safe."

"But I killed Patrick!" she wailed.

"Who's Patrick?"

"Henry's real name. He said Bobby sent him to kill me." She was sobbing uncontrollably.

Jay's body stiffened. "What did he say?"

"He said Bobby Gemelli first hired him to protect me, then changed his mind and wanted him to take me out."

"Fuck," muttered Jay under his breath. He pulled her closer and felt her tears wet through his shirt.

Kate struggled to speak, her breath hitching in gasps. "So, Bobby Amato wasn't Gemelli after all."

"Whoa, Kate. Whoa. Slow down." He tried to divert the inevitable track of her logic.

"I won't slow down! That can only mean Gavin Hartford is Bobby Gemelli. That he faked Amato's suicide. That he murdered Amato so he could keep hiding in plain sight."

Jay opened his arms so he could grasp Kate by the shoulders and look into her eyes. "First things first. We have to call the police and report that body in our living room. And we have to get our story straight. You didn't shoot Patrick."

"What?"

"You don't have a permit for that pistol. I do. If you tell the police you shot him, they'll probably arrest you and have you charged with illegal possession of a firearm."

"For fuck's sake!" She had stopped weeping, and her body had stopped shuddering.

Jay continued. "So, you went to fill the car with gas. When you were gone, this guy came to the door—the same guy that broke in here the first time. Only this time, I took care of him just as he drew his gun on me."

"But then we have to tell them that Bobby Gemelli isn't dead, that his sister lied to them when she identified Amato's body."

"Kate, stop. We have no proof. Amato's body has already been cremated, and they took his ashes."

Kate slapped his arms away from her. Her mouth was wide open, her eyebrows arched. She shook her head back and forth. "How could you possibly know that?" she shouted. "Unless, unless—"

Jay could see her face contort as she tried to make sense of his blunder, finally jumping to the only conclusion possible.

"You're one of them!" she shrieked. "I was right about you from the beginning. You're their spy! You told them where we were living so they could target me. You fucking Judas!"

"Kate, I can explain. Wait."

But she had already grabbed her purse and run out the front door.

"Kate, come back!" He rushed to the door, in time to see her leap into the car and speed away.

37. The Apple Falls

"Where to, Mr. Scott?" the Lyft driver asked. He looked to be in his mid-twenties, and he sported a full beard that reached down to the first button on his Hawaiian shirt.

Jay climbed into the back seat. "Enchanted Hill Winery, please."

"Beautiful. And you're being smart. You can drink up there all afternoon, then give me a call, and I'll come back to get you."

"Thanks, Nazareth. I'll do that." He fastened his seatbelt and looked at the driver. "How'd you come by a name like that, if you don't mind my asking? Don't think I ever met a 'Nazareth' before."

"I don't mind at all. You're not the first to ask." He pulled the car away from the curb and drove toward the highway. "My father bailed on my mother about two months into her pregnancy. She was so desperate—no job, no money—abortion seemed to be her only option." Jay watched Nazareth get more animated as he told his story. "Anyway, this holy roller group was picketing the clinic when she got there. Long story short, she got mixed up with them. They promised her room and board, free medical care, adoption services when she delivered. And all the babies got Bible-type names. Thank God, she found out just in time they were selling babies on the black market. She grabbed me and ran."

"Holy crap! What a crazy story! So, what happened to your mother?"

Nazareth was laughing. "She married this pot-smoking dude in a band you never heard of. Pete was actually a good dad. Took care of us pretty good until about fifteen years later when the cancer got him. And the sonofagun had a great life insurance policy. So here I am today. I only drive part-time when I need to get away from my desk at T-Mobile. And I send my mom a check every month."

"Good for you, man." Jay turned when he felt his face darken. "There's nothing like having good parents. They make all the difference in the world."

"Amen, brother."

They were at the winery in a few minutes. Jay got out at the front entry. He took his phone from his pocket. "I'll leave you a nice tip and a good review, Nazareth. Thanks."

The man gave a friendly salute and drove away.

Jay walked in and approached the bar. About half the tables had guests, eating and drinking. The murmur of conversations filled the open space. "Is Mr. Hartford in his office?" he asked the auburn-haired server behind the counter.

"Let me call and find out." A moment later, she hung up the phone and said, "He's not answering his phone. Would you like me to leave him a message?"

"No thanks. I'll just walk around." He went down the stairs and checked the banquet room. A young man in a Lord Huron T-shirt was just leaving.

"Can I help you, sir?"

"Yeah, I was looking for Mr. Hartford."

"You just missed him. I think he said he was heading to the cellar. Want me to call his cell phone?"

"That won't be necessary. Thanks." Although Jay had Gavin's cell phone number, he now had second thoughts about announcing his presence before he confronted the man.

Jay left the room, walked down the hall, and entered the wine cellar. The smells of wine and wood were especially strong today. He walked past the barrels of Chardonnay. He saw Gavin at the Pinot Noir with a pipette in his hand, lowering it through the bunghole in a barrel to retrieve a sample of wine. Gavin raised his head as Jay approached.

"Why, hello, Jay. I didn't expect to see you here. Would you like a taste?"

"You sonofabitch! What the fuck do you think you're doing?"

The white-haired man frowned. "I'm sampling a barrel of Pinot, of course."

Jay shouted at him. "The Medical Examiner just removed a dead body from my living room!"

"My, my. That does sound serious. It was Kate Temperance, I hope."

"It was your stooge Reilly, for God's sake."

Gavin put the pipette down and returned the stopper to the bunghole. He stared at Jay. "You killed him?"

"I didn't kill him. Kate did." He repeated himself as though addressing an inattentive student. "Kate Temperance killed him!"

Gavin screwed up his face as though he had just eaten something distasteful. "That little strumpet lives a charmed life, I swear to God." Lifting his eyes back to Jay, he said, "I don't much like your tone of voice."

Jay's jaw tightened. "You'll like my fist in your teeth even less."

Gavin raised a hand. "Calm down, son. You're taking a business matter way too personally."

"I'm not your son. Not anymore," he said through gritted teeth.

The old man frowned. "That's really hurtful, especially after all my sister and I have done for you."

"Has Sofia gone back to Vegas?"

"No, she's staying with me at the house for a couple of days. Perhaps you'd like to tell her yourself about your change of heart? What's the term they use nowadays? That you're 'unfriending' us?"

"Go take a flying leap."

"How crass. Certainly, you can be more creative than that, Jay. And where is Ms. Temperance, by the way?"

"I haven't a clue. She took off when she discovered I'd been helping you. She called me your 'spy.'" He scratched his chin. "Let's see. The last label she flung at me on her way out the door was 'fucking Judas.' That about says it all."

"So that explains why you're here dumping all your shit on me. Your girlfriend broke up with you in a way that would do a high school drama queen proud."

Jay moved toward him, then restrained himself. His fists clenched reflexively. "She's not my girlfriend. She's my partner. We work together."

Gavin laughed. "You're smitten by her, by a woman twenty years your senior. Perhaps with your ugly, acid-burned face you can't get a girlfriend your own age?"

Jay lost control. He yelled something unintelligible and leaped on the man. The two fell in a snarling heap onto the floor. Jay straddled him and punched him twice in the face. Then he rolled off him and lay on the floor, trying to catch his breath. Gavin curled into a fetal position, moaning softly, bleeding from his nose and lips.

Jay regained his feet and brushed himself off. "You just couldn't leave it alone, could you? Maybe you'd stop laughing if I went to the police and told them all I know about you and…Lady Macbeth." He extended his hand to help Gavin up, but Gavin pushed it away and said something too quiet to hear.

Jay got down on one knee and leaned his ear toward the man. "What did you say?"

Gavin spit a mouthful of blood onto the floor and whispered, "I said you've signed your own death warrant, asshole."

Jay stood up. "That's your answer to everything, isn't it? Something bothers you, offends you, gets in the way of something you want to do—just kill it. From the descriptions I've heard, from what Kate and I have learned, you're just like your father. Like they say, the apple doesn't fall far from the tree." He bent over and grasped Gavin by the shoulders. "Now get up. Tell me where we can get ice for your face."

With Jay's help, Gavin struggled to his feet. "There's a small refrigerator under the wet bar in the banquet room."

"Okay. Lean on me, and I'll take you there."

The two stumbled down the hall, making slow progress toward the banquet room. Jay was glad they encountered no one else on the way. Once in the room, Jay sat the older man in a chair while he retrieved some ice.

Gavin pointed to the cabinets. "There are hand towels in the far-left cupboard. Wrap a few cubes in one. Wet another so I can wash the blood off my face."

Jay brought the wet one to Gavin. "Hold still. I'll take care of it. There's no mirror here, so you can't see to do it yourself." He gently dabbed at Gavin's face. "Looks like the bleeding's stopped. Nose doesn't look broken. Lip's a little swollen. You may get a black eye out of it." Two more wipes with the towel and he said, "There you go. All clean. Now I'll get you the ice."

Once Gavin had the icepack in place, Jay sat down opposite him. "Look, I'm sorry. I don't usually hit...men more than twenty years my senior. But I have a request. Would you and Sofia please stop trying to kill Kate Temperance? Give it a rest, for God's sake."

Gavin slowly shook his head back and forth. "She's trying to ruin us. You understand that, don't you?"

"I understand we were booked to fly back to Las Vegas today, with a story that would have satisfied the network and leave you unscathed. In fact, the publicity—the tale of dead bodies in Lake Mead, a suicide at a winery in Oregon—the audience would have eaten it up. The notoriety would have been worth its weight in gold to the Florentine. Bookings out the wazoo." Jay snorted in disapproval. "But no. You had to go after Kate again. Now she knows Bobby Gemelli isn't dead. She just can't prove it."

Gavin leaned forward. "How does she know that?"

"Your hired gun Reilly got careless."

"Damn it! She knows about me. She knows about you. If you didn't love her, you'd want Temperance dead, too."

Jay winced. "Have you been listening to anything I've said? Be patient. Call off your dogs. I can convince her to go with the story she's got, then finally turn her attention elsewhere and start something new." He took a deep breath and sighed. "You told me Bobby's been cremated already and you've taken care of the ashes. There's no way Kate can prove you aren't who you say you are, so long as you leave her alone. Can you do that?"

Gavin strummed the table with the fingers of his left hand, while he continued to hold the ice pack against his face with the right. "I'll tell Sofia. Now go get me a glass of the Sig Cuvée."

As soon as he had left, Gavin took the phone from his pocket and tapped his sister's number. "Hello, my dear." He paused as he listened. "Well, I've been better. Our erstwhile son Jay just punched my lights out." Another pause. "No, I don't need the emergency room. I'll be all right. I may wind up with a black eye." Silence. "Unfortunately, we'll have to add him to our take-out order. Mm hm. He and Temperance have to go."

room. I'll be all right. I may wind up with a black eye." Silence. "Unfortunately, we'll have to add him to our take-out order. Mm hm. He and Temperance have to go."

gently dabbed at Gavin's face. "Looks like the bleeding's stopped. Nose doesn't look broken. Lip's a little swollen. You may get a black eye out of it." Two more wipes with the towel and he said, "There you go. All clean. Now I'll get you the ice."

Once Gavin had the icepack in place, Jay sat down opposite him. "Look, I'm sorry. I don't usually hit…men more than twenty years my senior. But I have a request. Would you and Sofia please stop trying to kill Kate Temperance? Give it a rest, for God's sake."

Gavin slowly shook his head back and forth. "She's trying to ruin us. You understand that, don't you?"

"I understand we were booked to fly back to Las Vegas today, with a story that would have satisfied the network and leave you unscathed. In fact, the publicity—the tale of dead bodies in Lake Mead, a suicide at a winery in Oregon—the audience would have eaten it up. The notoriety would have been worth its weight in gold to the Florentine. Bookings out the wazoo." Jay snorted in disapproval. "But no. You had to go after Kate again. Now she knows Bobby Gemelli isn't dead. She just can't prove it."

Gavin leaned forward. "How does she know that?"

"Your hired gun Reilly got careless."

"Damn it! She knows about me. She knows about you. If you didn't love her, you'd want Temperance dead, too."

Jay winced. "Have you been listening to anything I've said? Be patient. Call off your dogs. I can convince her to go with the story she's got, then finally turn her attention elsewhere and start something new." He took a deep breath and sighed. "You told me Bobby's been cremated already and you've taken care of the ashes. There's no way Kate can prove you aren't who you say you are, so long as you leave her alone. Can you do that?"

Gavin strummed the table with the fingers of his left hand, while he continued to hold the ice pack against his face with the right. "I'll tell Sofia. Now go get me a glass of the Sig Cuvée."

As soon as he had left, Gavin took the phone from his pocket and tapped his sister's number. "Hello, my dear." He paused as he listened. "Well, I've been better. Our erstwhile son Jay just punched my lights out." Another pause. "No, I don't need the emergency

Spying a foot path on the right, she began to descend into the bowl. After a straight leg, the trail veered sharply to the left, as a skier might slalom down a steep slope. Through the trees, she saw the path continue behind the falls to wrap around the entire bowl. She felt a rush of pleasure.

Minutes later, cool mist brushed her face. She was in a stony alcove, with the waterfall right in front of her and the rock behind. The tumbling water was a lacey veil shimmering in the sunlight, creating a rainbow that hung angelic in the air before her. Her mind had stopped whirling. Embraced by ineffable beauty, she was at peace.

How long had she been standing there? Minutes? Hours? A family of hikers interrupted her reverie. Refreshed, she smiled a greeting at the three young children and their parents, then continued on her way around the bowl and back up the trail to the parking lot.

The drive back home gave her more time to think without the storm of emotion that had initially impelled her to drive off. How could she stay safe? Certainly, she could flee back to Nevada or anywhere else, for that matter. But she had no doubt the Gemellis wouldn't stop trying to kill her until they succeeded. *Once a target, always a target*, she thought. She would have to stop them. But how? It struck her like a thunderbolt. *I have to prove to the police that Bobby is still alive and Sofia lied to the Medical Examiner. There's no other way.*

She couldn't imagine that Jay would try to kill her. He may have been a pipeline of information to the Gemellis, but everything within her said he could never physically harm her. She would speak with him, assess his loyalties. If need be, she would move out on her own without letting him know where.

That was all the plan she could formulate for now.

#

Jay was in the kitchen preparing dinner when she arrived home. "Looks like we missed our plane," he said.

38. In the Valley of the Shadow

Kate didn't know where she was going, she was just driving. She had emptied her reservoir of tears and fanned embers of inner rage into white-hot incandescence. Why hadn't she trusted her initial instincts? Why had she let a man with a ruined face win her over? And what on earth could she do now? The thought of driving to the airport and leaving Jay behind occurred to her, but she realized she was already too late to make the flight. Should she go there and take the next available plane anywhere?

For no particular reason, she began following signs for Silver Falls State Park. Soon she was outside Salem among rolling hills, driving past acres of grass seed farms, now blackened by post-harvest burning to eliminate pests and disease. Before long, she saw meadows and slopes covered with row upon row of small Douglas firs, which she recognized as future Christmas trees for homes across the country. With every mile, she felt her fury subsiding, calmed by vistas of forest and glen, away from the violence that haunted her.

Twenty miles from town, she drove through the park entrance, paid her fee, and left her car in the lot closest to the South Falls. She remembered reading about the falls when she was doing her research on the Willamette Valley. It was almost two hundred feet high, one of ten waterfalls along a trail that circumnavigated the park. She needed this experience—the cool, mountain air; the sound of water rushing headlong over basalt cliffs; the rich, loamy smells of wet earth. Her soul thirsted for it, ached to have it cleanse her of murder. It was absolution without a priest, in a cathedral of towering trees.

She walked the path toward the waterfall, drawn by its roar. High overhead, a vast canopy of massive Douglas firs filtered the sunlight and lowered the ambient temperature by ten degrees. The thunder of falling water grew until she was on a cliff bounded by a guard rail, looking over the edge into the pool below. She had to get closer.

A sour expression curled her lips. She tossed her purse on the table. "Blame it on your mentors."

Jay turned from the stove and stared at her. "Any chance we can talk?"

"I'm listening."

"Look. I apologize from the bottom of my heart. Bobby and Sofia have been lifelines for me. I lied about my wife. She bailed out with the kids years ago. My health insurance ran out. The Gemellis took me in and treated me like a son."

Kate's frown deepened. "I think the term is 'groomed.' They had a useful mole at the network, so they could always stay a step ahead of whatever was going on. I'll bet you even had something to do with Nolan and his daughter."

Jay lowered his gaze. "Nothing I'm proud of," he muttered.

She pursed her lips and shook her head back and forth. Time for the question. "Did they ask you to kill me?"

Now Jay's back was to her. His voice was a quiet recital of shame. "They wanted me to make sure you had an 'accident' when the time came." He turned around and faced her. "But they know I can't do that—wouldn't do that. I care too much about you. That's why they hired those other guys."

"You *care* about me?"

"Is that so strange? You're smart, beautiful, and the most dedicated woman I've ever met. And I'm not trying to flatter you or flirt with you. It's not about sex—it's about your integrity. You have it in Spades, and I admire that."

Her expression softened. "Apology accepted. Now what? Where do we go from here?"

"First, we eat dinner. I took a Lyft to the grocery store and got us some Ahi tuna. Once I steam some asparagus and toss a salad, I'll sear the fish. It'll only be a few minutes."

"Sounds good to me. I like a man who can cook. My husband was pretty good at it." She took a deep breath and lowered her gaze. "I haven't thought about Simon in a while. It makes me sad. I didn't pick up on the cues until it was too late." She exhaled and focused back on Jay. "Can I fix you an Old Fashioned while you're busy?"

"I'd love one."

Dinner was a gourmet treat. As they finished the last of the food and alcohol, Kate asked the thousand-dollar question. "How do we stop the Bobbsey Twins? They're like the fucking Eveready bunny."

"More like Arnie the Terminator. They won't stop until you're dead." He wiped his lips with a napkin. "I tried to persuade Gavin otherwise today, but I don't think he bought it. My guess is I painted a target on my back, too."

"What did you do?"

"I took a Lyft out to the winery and told him to let you go with the story you have. That there's no way you can prove he's not who he says he is. He should leave you alone, let you run with what you've got, and then you'll move on to something else. Of course, that was after I gave him a bloody nose."

Kate looked incredulous. "A bloody nose?"

"Yeah. He pissed me off."

She chuckled. "I wish I could have seen that."

Jay's head swung back and forth. "I don't think I helped our cause. I threatened to go to the police and tell them what I know."

"Holy shit! What were you thinking?"

"Obviously, I wasn't." His half-smile shined on her. "Truth be told, I think we have that in common sometimes."

Kate pursed her lips and furrowed her brow. She raised her hand. "Wait a minute! Maybe that's our best shot. You go to the police and spill everything. It will at least get an investigation going." She stood up in her excitement. "They'd take Gavin's fingerprints! And we'd have him! Fingerprints don't change with age. His fingerprints must be on file somewhere. And that would prove his sister lied to the Medical Examiner about the body. It would blow the case wide open! Two birds with one stone!"

Jay did not look happy. "Slow down, Kate. Slow down. You don't understand. I've done some...very bad things for the Gemellis. They'd turn around and nail me. I'd spend the rest of my life in prison."

"Fuck." She sat back down, her emotion expelled like helium from a burst balloon. "Any other ideas?"

"I need some more whiskey first. Can I get you some?"

"By all means."

While he poured three fingers-worth into each glass, he asked, "Just for the record, do you think Bobby Amato killed himself by falling asleep in a fermentation tank?"

"Hell no!" she snapped.

"Neither do I. That's beyond bullshit."

Minutes later, they sat in the living room, glasses in hand. With her right foot bouncing on the floor, her brain raced through ideas, searching for anything that might help them out of their dilemma. *How can I prove Gavin Hartford is Bobby Gemelli before I'm decorating a slab in the morgue? And how can I do it without sending Jay to prison?* She looked at her partner, sitting in the chair opposite.

"What if I go on broadcast news and just tell the world Gavin is Bobby, and dare him to prove me wrong? I'd say something like, 'I dare Gavin Hartford and Sofia Gemelli to submit to DNA testing!' DNA would prove they're related and that Sofia lied."

Jay took a sip of his drink and grimaced. "And they would slap you with a defamation lawsuit so fast your head would spin. Many hundreds of thousands of dollars later, you still wouldn't see any DNA from them."

Kate stuck her forefinger in her glass and stirred the ice cube around. As she licked her finger, she said, "So how long before we're both dead? Before a speeding car runs us off the road? We get caught in a B&E gone bad? A 'random' shooter picks us off?"

Jay sighed. "The clock is ticking for sure."

"Well, I for one am not content to sit here in their sights, waiting for that trigger to be pulled. DNA is the only way to go. I just have to figure out how to get it from Gavin and Sofia. You on board?"

He raised his glass. "I'm with you, partner." As he sipped the whiskey, he sighed again. "How well do you remember your Sunday school lessons?"

"Not at all. My grandmother never took me to church."

"Then you might have heard it at a funeral. There's a Psalm, I think it's the twenty-third, that goes something like, 'Yea, though I walk through the valley of the shadow of death…'"

Kate nodded. "Yep, sounds like the Willamette Valley to me, all right."

39. Launching the Astronaut

THREE DAYS AGO. Bobby cleared his throat. In a voice barely above a whisper, he said, "I have to tell you what happened in Paris fifty years ago. I have to tell you about the undoing."

Gavin looked puzzled. "The undoing? What are you talking about?"

"That night in Paris when you got really drunk."

Gavin chuckled. "As I recall, there were lots of nights I got really drunk. Which one are you talking about?" His broad smile contradicted the sober expression on Bobby's face.

Bobby looked around the office, saw the trophies of their success hanging there, the accolades and prizes for the best Pinot Noir in the valley. He looked at the man who had saved his life all those decades ago. In his heart of hearts, Bobby knew what he was about to reveal would ruin everything. The years of hard work, overcoming the near-bankruptcy in the early days of the winery, the courage the two shared in the face of all the nay-sayers who proclaimed no good wine could come from Oregon. Their great adventure was all for naught. In a shattering realization, he regretted not abandoning Gavin when he had had the chance, before they had become so entangled as to be inseparable. The two had become one, and Bobby would forever share in Gavin's sins.

"That night we celebrated at *Le Tigre*. Jacques Rochefort just gave us an apprenticeship at Domaine Cece. Our wine career was about to begin. Do you remember?"

"I remember a hell of a lot of empty Champagne bottles sitting on our table. Lots of empty oyster shells. A lot of caviar down the hatch. I don't know how the hell we ever got home."

"So let me tell you."

Gavin pointed to the chair in front of his desk. "Go ahead, Bobby. Take a load off."

Bobby lifted the bottle of Scotch and put it on the desk. "Got any glasses?"

"Sure do." Gavin opened the deep desk drawer on the right and pulled out two whiskey glasses. "For special occasions. Does this conversation qualify?"

"Most certainly," Bobby said, as he poured the amber liquid into the glasses. "Most certainly."

Bobby told all—how Gavin had wanted absolution from him for all the killing that had poisoned his soul, murders that had started with his being an accomplice, the ferryman for Tom Romano disposing bodies in Lake Mead. "I know your father abused your sister until you stopped him. You said you finally lost control when he hit her that time in his office. You choked him out and then made it look like a mob hit, even though your sister didn't want you to." He took a big swallow of Scotch. "But it wasn't over. Sofia had Samantha, Kate Temperance's mother, killed when she tried to blackmail her." Bobby was shaking his head back and forth. "Now you and your sister have your sights set on Kate. I can't let that happen. It has to stop."

The smile on Gavin's face was incongruous with their conversation. "I'm amazed that I can lie even when I'm drunk—a talent I didn't know I had."

"What do you mean?"

"I mean I didn't choke my father out when I lost my temper. There was no temper involved." He took a sip of whiskey and pursed his lips. "Sofia and I carefully planned the whole thing. We had a strategy. We did it on a Sunday morning. One of my father's two bodyguards was always away at church. I choked out the other one and then put a bullet in my father's head." He took another drink. "My sister stayed behind. What better way to cover our tracks than have her tell the police the story we had already concocted for them?" He sounded as though he were describing the winning touchdown in a football game. "She took over the casino, and I flew to Paris. The rest, as they say, is history."

Bobby's eyebrows arched and his mouth opened. He chugged the rest of his Scotch and poured himself more. "Have you no feelings? You describe killing your own father like you're telling me about a lousy summer vacation you had."

"The man was a monster. Killing him instantly was a gift he didn't deserve." He emptied the remainder of the bottle into his glass. "And yes, I have feelings. I love my twin sister—always have. We've been there for each other since we were barely out of diapers." He took a breath. "And I love you. You're the brother I never had, my dearest friend in the world. The rest is just business, something you probably can't understand with all your sentimentality."

"You're right. I can't understand how murder is just a business decision. When I learned that about you, it undid our friendship."

"But you stayed around. You never left me. We tackled the wine industry side by side." He swept his arm in a wide arc. "We built all this together."

Bobby nodded his head in affirmation. "I made a pledge to you on that drunken night in Paris. After all, I could never forget that you saved my life at the swimming pool. I swore I would never betray your confidence. But I have to break that promise tonight, unless you give up your vendetta against Temperance. The killing has to stop now. No more murders. None. Understood? Don't make me go to the police."

Gavin frowned. "I understand." He held up the empty bottle of whiskey. "Fear not, I have a spare."

"I've had plenty already."

"No, you haven't. Not tonight." There was an edge to his voice. He opened the drawer and took out his bottle. "And it's a bit higher grade than the one you brought. Drink up. Let's talk about the good times, when we were the cocks on the block."

They did. As the effects of the alcohol deepened, they laughed about their adventures in Burgundy. French girls loved the two young Americans, who never complained about the most menial jobs at the vineyard, even if the task was just cleaning the toilets. As their experience grew, they were given jobs on the slopes, planting and pruning, and later, in the laboratory, learning the chemistry of winemaking. Hours were spent in the cellar, discovering what to look for in the barreled wines they sampled using the glass pipette.

Degrees Brix and pH, refractometers and hydrometers, racking and riddling—all became second nature to both of them. Rochefort fed on their enthusiasm, and rewarded them with special bottles of wine to share with the girls who always seemed to find them. Both agreed those were the best years of their lives.

By this time, Bobby was slurring his words. "That may be the most I've ever had to drink. I'm not sure I can get up." He tried to stand, but fell back into his chair.

Gavin smiled. "Now I'm the almost-sober one. Let me help you."

The two men staggered to their feet. Gavin put his arms around Bobby's shoulders and said, "You're not in any shape to drive."

It looked as though Bobby were trying to form words but was having difficulty doing so. His mouth opened and closed. Finally, he said, "You're telling me. I can't even walk."

Gavin coached him. "There you go. One foot in front of the other. Let's go outside and get some fresh air."

Slowly, they made their way out the front entrance. The air was cool, and the night sky was punctured with brilliant stars. The Milky Way spread a white smudge across the heavens.

Gavin helped his friend stumble forward. "The air feels really good tonight. Let's head down to the crush pad."

Bobby's head leaned over on Gavin's shoulder. "Over to the grass first. I'm gonna heave." He vomited into the decorative shrubbery and wiped his mouth on his sleeve. "I have to lie down somewhere."

"Not here. I have just the place."

The two made slow progress down the hill to the crush pad and stopped before the Whole Cluster fermentation tanks. The lower hatch on the middle one was open.

"Ever been inside one of these? It's kind of cool—like being in a space capsule heading to the moon."

Bobby hesitated. "Nope. Haven't been. I'm too claustrophobic."

Gavin became insistent. "Well, climb aboard, astronaut. The adventure of a lifetime awaits."

Bobby began to struggle against Gavin's hands. "No! I don't want to. Besides, they're all clean and waiting for the harvest."

"I said get in, goddamn it!"

Gavin grabbed him around the hips. In a quick upward motion, he thrust the hapless man into the narrow opening. Bobby reached out with his arms and flailed with his feet. He grasped the sides of the hatch to stop himself. He kicked back in vain as Gavin pried his fingers away and pushed. Bobby fell into the tank. He rolled around and leaped back toward the hatch. Gavin slammed it shut in his face.

Bobby's shouts were muffled to a whisper by the heavy steel. "Gavin!" he wailed. "Gavin, I can't see my hand in front of my face! Please let me out!"

"I can't do that, Bobby. I love you, but now you've gone and ruined everything." He leaned his forehead against the cold hatch and felt Bobby pounding on the other side. Tears began to stream down his face. "This is all your fault. Why couldn't you keep business and personal life separate? I can't let you destroy everything we've worked for, everything my sister and I have built. I love her, and I have to protect her."

The voice pleaded again. "It's dark, Gavin. Please open the hatch. I'll suffocate."

Gavin was weeping now. "I know you will. It breaks my heart." He attached the hose from the carbon dioxide canister and turned on the valve. Gas hissed into the tank. "Just breathe, Bobby, just breathe." He sat down heavily on the ground and buried his face in his hands. "I've always loved you. I always will."

Twenty minutes later, Gavin stood up. He turned off the valve and detached the hose. Then he opened the hatch, careful to avoid breathing the carbon dioxide that poured invisibly from the tank. He could not bear to look inside.

His final chore of the night would be to erase the digital evidence from the security camera system. But first, he walked slowly back up the hill to the tasting room, then up the stairs to the mezzanine and Bobby's office. From past experience, he knew Bobby kept all his passwords in a little notebook in the middle drawer of his desk. Once he found the password to Bobby's computer, Gavin opened the laptop and composed an email to himself. He read the conclusion again.

    Gavin, you've been the best friend a man could ever have. I can't thank you enough. You were always there for me in the good times and the bad. I'm sorry I let you down.

    Love,

    Bobby

    How had it come to this? How could his world go so horribly wrong? He pulled a handkerchief from his pocket and wiped the tears from his eyes. "Goodbye, Bobby," he whispered aloud in a voice hoarse with emotion. "I love you." With a world-weary sigh, he read the email one more time and hit SEND.

40. The Going-All-In Caper

An hour after dinner, Jay again asked the question they had been pondering all evening. "So how are we going to get their DNA?"

Kate's eyes widened as an idea occurred to her. "During my tour with Gavin, he took me into the cellar under the winery and had me sample wine he took from barrels with this glass pipette he called a 'thief.' I don't think anybody else there uses it. I'll bet it's covered with his DNA." She smiled. "If I can get in there and find it, maybe the thief can steal his identity for us."

Her partner laughed. "It's probably worth a try." He looked at his watch. "The winery closed two hours ago. I wonder if we could get into the cellar from the crush pad. There may be a few staff there getting everything ready for the harvest."

"But what about Sofia's DNA, assuming she's still here?"

Jay stroked his chin. "Gavin said she was staying with him for a couple days before going back to Vegas. If I could get into the house and find the bathroom she's using, there'd be hairbrushes, toothbrushes."

Kate became thoughtful. "There's a lot of 'ifs' in our plan, including a really big one—if they catch us, will they kill us on the spot?"

"Maybe we should bail out while we still can—beat feet back to Las Vegas and set up some kind of defense for ourselves there."

"We've been over all that before," Kate countered. "The Gemellis won't stop. You kill one hornet or one ant, and the nest hatches out a replacement. Gavin and Sofia will keep sending hired guns after us until one of them succeeds. We won't be lucky forever."

Jay nodded in agreement. "You're right. Reminds me of a story I was doing at Caesar's Palace a couple years ago. I remember every detail like it was yesterday. I'm watching this guy play Texas Hold 'Em. He's on a winning streak—stacks and stacks of chips.

And he's arrogant about it, making snide remarks to the other players, keeping up this macho trash talk." Jay chuckled. "Anyway, he's sitting on pocket kings, with an ace of hearts, a seven of spades, and a deuce of clubs on the table. And the turn is a seven, so he's got two pair."

Kate was now on the edge of her seat, caught up in the story, waiting for the denouement.

"The dealer goes for the dramatic, looking stone-faced at each player and finally flipping the last card. Wouldn't you know it, the river is a king. Now our guy has a full house, sure the card gods are still smiling on him, and that he's got the winning hand. He goes all in. Everyone folds but the guy across the table from him. 'I call,' that guy says very quietly as he shoves his chips in. Now we're talking many, many thousands in that pot. Our friend turns over his kings and shouts, 'Beat my kings full of sevens, sharky!' And grinning from ear to ear, the other dude turns over his pocket aces. 'Aces full of sevens, dickwad! Eat shit and die!'"

Kate burst out laughing. "Oh, my God!"

"True story. I swear."

"So, we've survived so far, but we don't want to get cocky about it. Our luck won't last forever."

Jay was bouncing his head up and down. "Amen to that!"

"And given the amount we've been drinking, I don't think we should try to pull off our grand caper tonight."

Jay agreed. "Neither do I. We need to be sharp."

Kate tossed off the last of her whiskey. "Until tomorrow, partner."

#

Over breakfast the next morning, they refined their plan. Sipping her second cup of coffee, Kate said, "What about security? Suppose they've got cameras at the entrances? Alarms of some kind?"

"Shit. I'll bet they do. I hadn't thought of that."

Kate continued. "How about we do this? Let's go out to the winery fifteen minutes before it closes. Shouldn't be any alarms on then. Park in the employee lot. I'll slip into the cellar through the crush pad and hide there till everyone's gone. You stake out the house."

"And do what?"

"I'll text you once I'm safely back to the car with the pipette and the glass Gavin drinks from. Then you call Sofia and Gavin and tell them you've had a change of heart—that you can't forget all they've done for you. And you have to warn them about me. Tell them I'm in the wine cellar and they better get to me quick—I'm stealing DNA evidence. Say you're heading there yourself to stop me. When you see them leave the house, slip in and get what we need. Then meet me at the car."

"Sweet mother! That's a lot of moving pieces. You really think we can pull that off?"

"I don't have a clue, but I'm fresh out of ideas. Like you said, we're going all in. But we're not being cocky about it. We know our fortunes could change in a heartbeat." She thought for a moment. "Let's go out and buy some of those light nitrile gloves they use for food prep and painting—keep from contaminating our samples. Plastic bags, too."

Jay looked hard into Kate's face. "I'm bringing my gun. I hope I don't have to use it, but I need a little cold steel companionship while I'm watching their place." He embraced her and held on for a long, breathing minute. "You have to stay safe. We both have to."

#

They were glad there was no rain in the forecast. Kate pulled their car into the employee lot and turned to her partner. "Take no chances. They're nurturing several rows of young plants that go right up to the back of the house. Lie on the ground among them, where you should be able to get a view of the door they'll use to run down to the winery."

"You take care, too, Kate. Watch yourself. Abort the mission if you're discovered by somebody. Let's keep our phones on silent so we can text each other safely."

They left the car and headed in different directions, Jay toward the right around the tasting room and Kate toward the left to reach the crush pad. The sun was low in the sky, casting long shadows among the rows of vines. The fragrance of the nearly-ripe grapes perfumed the air with sweet fruit. Kate was down on all-fours, crawling between the trunks of the older vines. She reached up, plucked a grape, and plopped it into her mouth. "Damn, that's good," she whispered.

In minutes, she was at the end of the vines, looking toward the array of stainless steel tanks that filled the small paved space. It reminded her of a giant chessboard, each tank a pawn positioned to protect the Queen in the wine cellar behind them. A conveyor belt awaited the arrival of fruit for the Whole Cluster initial fermentation tanks. Another belt was prepared to deliver grapes to the crusher-destemmer machine.

She crouched lower as she saw a worker emerge from the entrance to the wine cellar. He seemed to be talking with someone behind him out of her range of vision. Their conversation was inaudible. The other man joined him, and the two walked down the paved driveway toward the employee lot.

Kate scooted toward the destemmer and hid behind it. Another staff person came out onto the crush pad. As soon as he was gone, she rushed to the door before it was locked and any security system might be turned on. She ducked inside, and hid behind a Chardonnay tank. Three more staff approached, chatting about their plans for the evening. Hunkered down, she was all but invisible. Once they had left, she approached the entrance into the wine cellar proper, listening intently. When she heard no sound, she slipped inside and quickly ran toward the wall to the right, past several rows of wine barrels and away from the main walkway. She sat on the floor behind the last barrel to catch her breath.

The rich smells of wood and wine were almost overpowering. The air temperature was cooler than outside, and the chill made her shiver. As she and Jay had agreed, she sat and waited. A half-hour later, hearing no sound and certain all the staff had left, she stood up to begin her search. She tried to remember where she and Gavin had been standing when he offered her a barrel taste. Down one row and up another, she looked for the evidence that would bring belated justice for her father and mother, and free her from the fear that clutched her heart.

The lights overhead were small and dim, creating an eerie twilight. The cellar felt like a dark cavern deep beneath the earth. She was the cicada again, climbing from the dark to the daylight. When she emerged, pipette and glass in hand, she would burst the husk of her old life, spread her wings, and fly free of the murderous family that pursued her.

Now she saw that the tops of the barrels had labels indicating their contents. She was surrounded by Signature Cuvée. A few rows farther, and she was keeping company with Estate Reserve. Still no pipette or glass.

Where were you sipping last, Gavin? she thought. *Is this plan going to work?*

In the next row she found it, sitting atop a barrel of the Reserve. *There you are, you little thief!* She pulled the gloves from her pocket and slipped them on. Just as she was opening the plastic bag she had brought with her, she felt her phone vibrate in her pocket.

Take cover. Gavin coming.

She spun around, looking for a place to hide. "Fuck!" she whispered.

41. Of Chance and Necessity

Gavin and Sofia were sitting down to dinner in his house on the crest of the hill. He had rubbed four lamb chops with a mixture of herbs and lemon zest, marinated them in a blend of olive oil and juice from the zested lemons, and grilled them to a perfect medium rare. She had sautéed summer squash and sweet onions and prepared a green salad. Gavin opened one of their favorite Cabernets with a flourish.

He lifted his glass in a toast. "Here's to you, my dear. So glad we've mended our fences. I've missed you."

She raised her wine and repeated the greeting. "I've missed you, too. It's been much too long. I had begun to worry about you."

"As you can see, I'm the picture of health." He took a sip. "This is lovely. We make it from grapes that come from the Rogue Valley, south of here." A shadow passed over his face. "I miss Bobby terribly. Suppose I always will. The dearest friend I've ever had." He took another drink and looked into his sister's eyes. "But I couldn't let him hurt you. Or me, for that matter. He threatened to expose us and ruin everything we've devoted our lives to."

Sofia nodded. "Most people don't understand how difficult it is to run a family business like ours. The demands of our chosen profession trump any personal relationship. The decisions we are forced to make are not for the faint of heart."

Gavin picked up his knife and fork and sliced a piece of lamb. "But did we choose our occupation, or did it choose us? Would we be doing this if our father hadn't pushed us in this direction?"

Sofia frowned. "What direction is that? I run a casino, and you run a winery, perfectly legitimate operations."

Gavin pursed his lips. "You know what I mean. Because of our past, we're compelled to use strategies that…well, sometimes put us outside the law." He put the forkful of meat into his mouth. "This is really good," he said. "You should try a bite."

Now Sofia was laughing as she picked up her utensils. "If by 'strategies' you're referring to occasionally killing people, then of course. But all business is cutthroat, striving to eliminate the competition and increase profit. We just do it straightforwardly. And usually, it's quick and painless."

As he cut another piece, he said, "Do you ever have any regrets?"

Sofia tried a forkful of salad. "Regrets? About my life? Well, I've always wished I had had the chance to practice law, even if only for a few years. But as you said, I was 'compelled' to take over the casino. I've also wondered about never having a long-term romantic relationship. Not that I'm suitable marriage or mother material, by any stretch of the imagination."

Gavin grew more thoughtful. "I suppose I regret ever letting Tom Romano persuade me into being his oarsman, dropping those bodies into Lake Mead."

"But if you hadn't done that, it's unlikely you would have wound up in Burgundy, studying winemaking. And you've become a master winemaker. Not only that, you love your work."

"You're right, of course. What a tangled web of chance and necessity. And so totally unpredictable from the starting point." He took another sip of his wine to wash down a mouthful of the tender meat. "There's no way I could have imagined as a fourteen-year-old boy protecting his sister from a beast of a father in Las Vegas, Nevada, that I'd wind up producing world-class Pinot Noir in Salem, Oregon. It boggles the mind."

"And yet here you are. And the odds of your guessing your path through life would have been astronomically larger than your chances of winning the lottery."

"Maybe I have won the lottery, Sofia. I'm here with a sister I adore, eating a delightful meal, drinking a lovely wine that I produced." He furrowed his brow. "I just wish Bobby could be here to enjoy this with us."

She raised her glass, and he followed suit. "Here's to Bobby," she said. "May he rest in peace."

Just then an alert sounded on Gavin's phone. He withdrew it from his pocket and opened the app for his remote camera system. "Dear God, that woman Temperance is like a mosquito in your tent, keeping you awake all night with its buzzing." Looking at Sofia, he added, "And yes, you were right all along. We should have taken care of her long ago. Now she's in the wine cellar, doing God knows what."

Sofia acknowledged the admission and asked, "Is there someone you can call?"

"Not that would get here fast enough. I'll have to take care of her myself."

"More business decisions," she said with a smile. "Need any help?"

"I shouldn't. Please enjoy your meal. If I'm not back in fifteen minutes, walk down and see what's keeping me."

He threw his napkin down on the table with a huff and went to his bedroom to retrieve his pistol. Once he had worked the slide and seated a cartridge in the chamber, he tucked the gun under his belt at the small of his back. "I should be back momentarily, darling," he called to his sister as he walked out the door.

The brisk night air refreshed him. He gazed at the stars overhead and picked up his pace. *Can I dispatch this creature once and for all so Sofia and I can get on with our lives?* he thought. *This is insufferable.*

He unlocked the large glass doors and let himself into the tasting room. As quietly as he could, he reached the stairs and descended to the wine cellar. What could Temperance possibly be after among the barrels of wine? It made no sense.

With the gun in his right hand and his arm extended, he tiptoed down the main walkway, pausing at each row to see if his nemesis might be lurking there. As his eyes got used to the dim light, he could see farther down the rows into the shadows, looking for an irregular shape that was out of place among the barrels. Row after row yielded no results. He realized she might be moving silently, either keeping ahead of him or slipping behind him after he had cleared a row. Pulling the phone from his pocket, he saw her on a camera he had just passed.

"Ms. Temperance," he called, as he stuck the gun back into his belt. "I'm considering calling the police and having you arrested for trespassing. Is that what you really want?"

No answer.

"Ms. Temperance, let's not keep playing this game of cat and mouse. You have a story to write, a deadline to meet. I have a wonderful dinner to finish. I'm afraid you're wasting both your time and mine."

"What I really want is to be safe," she said, still hunkered down behind a wine barrel. "Not to have to look over my shoulder because I'm afraid someone is trying to kill me."

Gavin responded in a calm and reassuring voice. "Then you'll be happy to know I've convinced my friend, Sofia Gemelli, to call off her vendetta against you. She was behind it from the very beginning, afraid you were trying to ruin her casino business. Afraid you would hurt her brother Bobby and his winery."

Still out of sight in the shadows, she replied "That's not what your man Patrick Reilly told me when he came to my house. He said you wanted him to kill me."

"My dear, I'm sure he told you Bobby Gemelli wanted you dead, not me. And we both know Gemelli has preceded us into the great beyond."

He heard her snarl in the darkness, "That sounds like a crock of shit to me."

Gavin pulled out his gun again and silently stalked toward where he had last heard her voice. The shadows deepened as he got farther from the main path through the cellar. *This madness ends now*, he thought.

42. Killing the Queen

Kate held her breath and strained her hearing to detect his approach. She had already removed her shoes so she could move more quietly. Now she turned on her phone's video and sound recorder, hoping she could catch anything Gavin might say, hoping he would make a mistake and reveal he was really Bobby Gemelli.

The wine cellar was darkest against the wall at the end of the rows of barrels. She stayed in that shadowed corridor and slipped as quickly as she could away from where she had last heard her adversary.

The voice was arrogant. "Ms. Temperance, this is getting tiresome. Please come out. I'm sure we can arrive at some mutually satisfactory arrangement. Perhaps I might review your report to ensure its accuracy before the network produces it."

She heard him struggle to find possible enticements to lure her from hiding. He sounded desperate to get her to come out.

"I could persuade Sofia to give you an on-screen interview to add to the drama. I'm sure she would even be willing to pay you a substantial sum since the story would be such an advertising boon for the Florentine."

More bullshit, but this time she could hear his waning patience.

"Please, Ms. Temperance. Bobby is dead. You have his suicide note. And you have a truly exciting tale to tell—dead bodies in Lake Mead, a killer you've tracked all the way from Las Vegas, Nevada, to Burgundy, France, and ultimately to the Willamette Valley in Oregon. Epic material!"

She knew he was a snake, that he would never let her leave the winery alive. In the plastic bag she held was DNA evidence that he was not who he claimed to be. But would that evidence ever see the light of day? Would the cicada ever reach the sunlight?

"Have it your way," came the voice. "I'm calling the police now."

He sounded disgusted with her, but also anxious. She hoped he would call the police, but she didn't believe for a minute that he would. She was a threat to the entire Gemelli empire. He would have to kill her.

She heard the scrape of a shoe. She stood up to run, but it was too late.

The voice was a feral growl. "Stop! Move another muscle, and I'll shoot."

Kate turned to face him, a scant ten feet away. Even in the dim light, she could see the gun pointing at her. The face behind the gun was a mask of hatred.

"What are you doing trespassing in my winery?"

She saw no point in being disingenuous. "I'm here to prove you're Bobby Gemelli and not Gavin Hartford."

"Dear God in heaven, give it a rest! Bobby is dead, his ashes have been scattered, the story is over."

"Fuck you."

"I'll have you prosecuted to the full extent of the law!" he shouted.

"I would welcome that. Call the police. Go ahead." She spat the words at him. "I know you won't, you sonofabitch. Your man, Patrick Reilly, told me Bobby wanted me eliminated *after* Bobby was supposedly dead." She stood up straight and tall and hurled the words at him. "You're Bobby Gemelli, and you killed Bobby Amato to cover your tracks."

He yelled something unintelligible. Aiming the gun at her chest, he snarled, "You couldn't let it go, could you? You couldn't back off and walk away. Now you'll be just another dead body they find out in the woods next month or next year, rotting away, feeding maggots. Are you happy now?"

Resigned to her fate, she said, "No, I'm not, but you could improve my mood before you kill me."

"How might I do that? And why would I?" The gun never wavered from its point of aim.

"Take pleasure in announcing your accomplishments. Hell, you've won the Olympic Gold in Criminal Behavior. You've fooled the whole world for fifty years. Own it!"

He smiled. "I hadn't looked at it like that before, but you're right. It's been quite an achievement."

"Now admit once and for all that you're Bobby Gemelli. What have you got to lose? I'm as good as dead already."

He took a deep breath. "Of course, I'm Bobby Gemelli, but I like the sound of Gavin Hartford better."

"Then please tell me…Gavin. Did you kill Harry Costello, my father?"

He pursed his lips. "No, I just rowed the boat for Tom Romano. He did the killing. Only that night was a disaster." He shook his head back and forth. "Harry wasn't giving up easily. He got in a fight with Tom and knocked him out of the boat. I reached for the gun Tom dropped, but Harry was all over me. I shot a hole in the bottom of the boat. When the boat sank, Tom got tangled up in Harry's chain. Both of them went down together. It was awful. Worthy of the Coen brothers, I suppose."

Kate frowned. She had a final question she had to ask him. She squinted her eyes and furrowed her brow. "Do you know if my mother committed suicide? She was pregnant with me when my father died."

A mirthless smile curled his lips. "No, she didn't, my dear. My sister called me when I was living in Paris. She said Samantha tried to blackmail her. Sofia had no choice. She had to have your mother killed."

Kate expelled a deep breath. At last, she knew what she had begun to suspect. She stared into his eyes. "In the end, was it all really necessary?"

He cleared his throat and frowned, as though forced to explain something patently obvious. "Oh, my dear, you clearly don't understand family and the demands it imposes."

"You never gave me a chance to—you killed them," she snapped.

He uttered a low growl. "You've lost all the important relationships in your life—your husband, your best friend. You sacrifice family for what you call 'truth.' I sacrifice truth for family. Which is nobler? Truth or family?"

Her face contorted in anger. "Is that how you justify the evil you and your sister do? Some 'All is fair in love and war and family' bullshit? Well, I'm not buying that story."

He chuckled. "But we are all stories. You must know that. There is no meaning in life but what we give it—and we give it the stories we tell to ourselves and others."

She gritted her teeth. "What the hell are you talking about?"

The smile on his face was devoid of humor. "I'll tell you another story. Do you remember Scott Peterson, the man who murdered his pregnant wife Laci on Christmas Eve of 2002 and dumped her body in the San Francisco Bay?"

She shuddered. "That was horrible. How could anyone forget that?"

"It was indeed gruesome—just the kind of story reporters love to tell. Her decaying body and her fetus washed ashore the following April. Still gives you the shivers, doesn't it?"

She felt like slapping him across the face, and would have were it not for the gun he was still pointing at her. "Goddamn it! What the hell is your point?"

"Do you know his father's first words to the jurors at his son's murder trial?"

"No."

"He said, 'I love him very much. I have great respect for him.' This for a man who had committed a truly spectacular murder—a killing so grisly it defies comprehension." Gavin shook his head back and forth. "He went on to tell them that Scott was a friendly boy who sang at a senior citizens home on Sundays, tutored young students, and distributed clothes and food in Tijuana, Mexico. I'm sure that's still the story he tells himself about his son the butcher."

Kate clenched her teeth again. "But that doesn't exonerate him."

"Exonerate? Ms. Temperance, we live in an indifferent universe, as blind to our depravity as to our innocence. No absolution required."

Her voice was venom and revulsion. "And how did you come upon that philosophy, Oh Wise One? The School of Hard Knocks?"

For a moment, the barrel of the gun lowered slightly. "I was taught that when my wife took her own life after my son's overdose. But I don't expect you to understand. I'm sure it's easier for you to see me as a soulless monster." He raised the gun again and pointed it at her left breast. "And perhaps I am. After all, I was forced to kill the best friend I ever had. And to kill my own father."

She looked at him with utter contempt. "I knew you must have killed Amato. That was no suicide. And your father? That's why you ran away to Paris. You are a madman, and it embarrasses me to be breathing the same air as you."

"That won't go on for much longer, I can assure you," he replied. "This madman still holds the gun. Let's take a walk outside, shall we?" Waving the pistol, he motioned her to walk toward the exit to the crush pad.

Suddenly, Jay shouted, "Stop right there or I'll blow your fucking head off!"

In an instant, Gavin leaped toward Kate and grabbed her around the neck, using her as a shield. "Good evening, son. I was expecting you to join our party. Welcome."

"Cut the crap, old man. Let her go, or I swear to God I'll shoot you."

Gavin yanked on Kate, briefly lifting her feet off the ground. "I don't believe you, son. You don't want to risk shooting your girlfriend, do you?" He pressed the barrel of his gun against her temple. "In fact, if you don't want me to shoot her, I suggest you drop your gun."

Kate was afraid to move. It was all she could do to breathe with the steel-like hold around her throat. "Please," she managed in a hoarse whisper.

Jay held his pistol at arm's-length. He moved from side to side as though looking for a way to take a safe shot. Kate saw uncertainty in his eyes. Even if given the chance, could he shoot the man he regarded as Father? She knew Gavin saw that doubt, too, and capitalized on it by calling him 'son' instead of 'Jay.' She also knew that the next seconds would be critical. If Jay let down his guard at all, she was sure Gavin would shoot him.

Now Gavin taunted him. "You can't do it, can you, son? We've been through too much together, you and I. You can't shoot your father."

"You're right…Gavin. I can't shoot you." But instead of dropping his gun, he wheeled toward the row of barrels next to him. "But I can shoot the Queen!" The cellar rang with rapid gunfire, each bullet smashing into another barrel. Geysers of Pinot Noir erupted from the bungholes. Fountains of red wine spurted like heart's blood from bullet holes in the stricken barrels.

"No! Not the Queen!" Gavin shrieked. "Don't shoot the Queen!"

It was all the distraction Kate needed. She kicked her heel as hard as she could against Gavin's shin and thrust an elbow deep into his ribs. Gavin howled as he dropped his gun. Kate wrenched free from his grasp and sprinted down the row into the shadows.

Gavin's face contorted in animal frenzy. He leaped at Jay, but his feet slipped in the deepening pool of wine. The two men collided and fell to the floor in an angry, writhing mass. Punching and clawing at each other, they rolled in the puddles between the barrels until their clothing was saturated. Jay finally landed a wine-wet fist to Gavin's nose, and the older man released his grip. Jay pulled away. Dripping Pinot from his shirt sleeves and pants, he staggered to his feet.

"Stay down, old man," he cautioned.

Gavin lay there gasping for breath, his blood mingling with the Queen's. "You've ruined a perfectly good suit," he complained, as his hand splashed in the wine. "Not to mention—" He rolled on his side and counted the broken barrels. "240 gallons of Sig Cuvée. 1200 bottles of the Queen's best. You bastard."

Jay leaned over him. "I'm sick to death of your 'Queen' bullshit. It's fucking wine, for God's sake. Four fucking barrels. Send me a bill."

Gavin struggled to sit up. "You'll be hearing from my lawyer."

Jay clenched his teeth and pointed his finger at Gavin's face. "The only lawyer you'll be talking to is the one trying to defend you from murder charges." He stood up straight. "Now where's my goddamn gun?"

He never heard Sofia enter the wine cellar. His back was to her as he searched the floor for his weapon. She had a small 9 mm. pistol in her hand, the one she usually carried in her purse. Extending her arm, she aimed the gun at Jay's back.

The cellar echoed with gunfire.

43. Blood and Wine

Kate stood there shivering with a post-adrenaline letdown, hands still tightly grasping the gun Gavin had dropped when she ran from him. The pistol was empty now, its slide locked in the open position. The acrid bite of gunpowder briefly masked the pungent smell of the wine.

Gavin had rushed to his sister as she fell and caught her in his arms. He collapsed to the floor, cradling her head in his lap. In a quiet voice, he whispered a lullaby in her ear, oblivious to all else, helpless to prevent her blood from spilling into the wine around them.

A moan from Jay startled Kate. He sat in a puddle of wine, leaning against a barrel, clutching his left arm. She let the gun fall from her hands and ran to his side.

"You're shot! You're shot!" she cried.

"It's a through-and-through. See?" He lifted his hand so she could see where the bullet had pierced his bicep. "Missed the bone, but it hurts like hell."

In quick motions, Kate removed her blouse and tore the sleeve from it. "Here. Let me wrap it with this to try to stop the bleeding. Now hold it in place while I get another piece of cloth to tie it on with." She grabbed the lower hem of the shirt and ripped a length of cloth from it. She tied it as firmly as she dared around the makeshift bandage.

Jay winced. "You're quite the field nurse, Ms. Temperance," he said. "And very sexy, I might add."

Kate blushed. "Don't be fresh, mister." As she put her torn blouse back on, she said, "It looks like you went swimming in a fermentation tank, for goodness' sake. You're dripping wet. And red."

"Yeah, Gavin and I did a few laps around the pool." He looked toward the man he had once regarded as a father, the man he could not kill even to save his own life. Gavin sat there rocking his dead twin in his arms, weeping. The scene was a perverse Pietà, two murderous siblings bound together by love and death.

Then Jay turned his gaze back to Kate. "I owe you my life. If you hadn't come back and picked up his gun, I'd be the one lying there."

"We're partners, remember? And we've got to get you some real medical treatment. Can you get up?"

Jay stood, balancing himself against the barrel. "I'm a little shaky, but I think I can make it to the car."

"You won't have to. While you and Gavin were fighting, I called 911. I expect them to be here any minute." She cocked her head. "There they are now."

Both heard the wail of sirens approaching up the hill.

"I told them to come around to the service entrance so they wouldn't have to fuss with the big gate."

"Great. Now gather up the guns and put them on that barrel over there, far away from us. I don't want a repeat of what happened to me before."

She rushed to do the job before the police arrived. With that task accomplished, they waited. The only sounds were Gavin's sobs and the occasional drip of wine from a pierced barrel. The smell of Pinot suffused the dim cellar and soon became unpleasant.

"Police!" came the shout from the crush pad. "Police!" came another shout down the stairs from the tasting room.

Kate answered. "We're in here, officers. Unarmed."

"Hands where we can see them!" shouted the first officer there. He approached them warily, service weapon drawn and held at arm's-length.

Kate pointed to Jay. "My partner, Jay Scott, has a gunshot wound to his left arm." Then she motioned to Gavin and his bloody burden. "That woman, Sofia Gemelli, is dead. She was the owner of the Florentine in Vegas. I shot her in self-defense just before you arrived. That's her brother holding her. Bobby Gemelli, better known as Gavin Hartford. All the guns are right there on that barrel."

Gavin looked as though he were in a trance. His eyes stared ahead, unfocused. He seemed not to notice the bustle of the arriving police. He rocked back and forth in a gentle rhythm, as if trying to put an infant to sleep. Leaning over, he whispered in Sofia's ear, "I'm singing your favorite song, darling. I hope you like it."

Soon, the wine cellar was swarming with people, everyone talking at once and filling the chamber with an excited buzz. More police backup appeared, along with two detectives, three EMTs, and the Medical Examiner, who was dressed in a long white lab coat. With practiced efficiency, she snapped on rubber gloves and knelt down by Gavin. With as much compassion as the circumstances would allow, she tried to persuade him to release his sister so she could begin her examination.

The two detectives chatted briefly with the first officers on the scene. The younger one went to help the M.E. extricate Sofia from Gavin. The other went to Jay, as the EMTs finished dressing his wound. The man's thinning hair was disheveled, and the unshaven scruff on his face was turning gray. His shirt was stained with sweat.

"Sorry I'm late for the party." A look of recognition lit up his face. "You again! Scott, isn't it? I never forget a face."

"Nobody forgets mine, Detective," Jay quipped. "No matter how much they'd like to."

"And what the hell is it with you and bodies?" He was jotting notes on a small scratch pad. "First, you get yourself shot full of holes—excellent recovery, by the way. Then that body at the place you're leasing." He leaned toward Jay. "And just between you and me, I'm not buying your story of how you unloaded a whole magazine into that stiff. That's not something an experienced guy like you would do. Hell, you had him dead to rights after the first few rounds. You were just wasting good ammunition." He tipped his head toward Kate. "Now her. Ms. Investigative Journalist? Her I could see blowing him all to hell. Like she just did with—" He looked down at his pad.

Jay answered for him. "Gemelli, Sofia Gemelli. Daughter of the late-great Giancarlo Gemelli of Las Vegas fame. She took over the Florentine after her father's untimely death." He nodded toward Gavin, still sitting on the floor, looking abandoned, while the other detective tried to talk with him. "And that's her brother, Bobby Gemelli, better known as Gavin Hartford."

"Wait a minute." The detective was flipping back through his pages. "Wait a minute. We took Bobby Gemelli out of here in a body bag three days ago."

"Nope. That was Bobby Amato, Gemelli's best friend. They met in France years ago. Sofia wanted my partner, Kate Temperance, to think her brother Bobby was dead, so she faked the ID at the morgue." As an afterthought, he added, "And Amato wasn't a suicide."

"Holy shit on a shingle. I'm gonna need more note pads." He drew his lips up into a pout. "I'll get statements from the whole goddamn bunch of you. My workday just got a whole lot more complicated."

Jay gave him his half-smile. "Look at it this way. At least you won't get bored."

The man snorted in response and moved on to talk with Kate.

#

After the questioning was over, two police officers remained behind at the crime scene while their colleagues left. Kate looked at a very sodden Jay. "You're still red," she said, as she put her shoes back on.

"I'm glad you noticed. I've got a classy new bandage, too, and a bag of them that should last a week." He lifted his arm to show her. "But I'm pretty cold. Shall we go home?"

"By all means. The police have our address if they have any more questions for us."

The two walked down to the employee parking lot under a canopy of stars. Somewhere in the trees beyond the vineyard, an owl hooted. A minute later, they heard the howls of a pack of coyotes.

"The natives are restless tonight," Jay said. He reached for Kate's hand, and when she didn't resist, he held it all the way back to their car. "Thank you for saving my life tonight. You could've run away, but you didn't. You came back for me."

"You did the same for me, as I recall, and wound up in the hospital because of it. I'm still in one piece." She leaned into his shoulder. "I was afraid I was going to lose you. I couldn't bear that."

As Kate unlocked the doors, Jay spoke in a voice barely above a whisper. "May I kiss you?"

She smiled back at him. "I'd like that."

He gently touched his lips to hers, and she responded in kind. Then she wrapped her arms around him, while he pulled her close. They stood like that, locked together, for several moments. She kissed him again and said quietly, "Sometimes I feel like it's just you and me, alone in a lifeboat together, adrift on an ocean without a map or a compass."

He nodded. "You've got fancier words than I do, but I get it." He began to shiver in the cold. "I've done a lot of bad things in my life, Kate, things I regret. It's like I've spent my life adding to the world's sum total of darkness. But you—you diminish the dark by shining a light. I'd like to be able to do that."

She grabbed him by the shoulders, careful of his wound, and looked him in the eyes. "You're already doing it, Jay. Trust me." Then she embraced him again. Finally, he pulled away with a sheepish look on his face.

"Would you please take me home before I freeze to death out here?"

Kate chuckled. "I'll crank up the heater on the way."

Neither spoke on the short drive home. Once there, Jay announced, "I'm off to the shower. And just so you know, I may never drink a glass of Pinot Noir again."

Kate laughed. "I was thinking the same thing. I'll shower, too, and maybe we can meet in the living room for a nightcap afterwards."

Kate finished her shower first. After toweling off, she put on a robe and walked out to the cabinet where they stored their liquor. She poured two glasses of whiskey, then walked back to Jay's bedroom. She could hear the water still running, so she entered and set the glasses on his night stand. Once the shower stopped, she could hear him drying himself, humming a tune. Wrapped in a towel, he opened the bathroom door to find her standing there.

"Kate, you surprised me. I didn't expect to see you in my bedroom."

"Well, I thought you might need some help putting a new bandage on that arm after your shower."

"Sure, thanks. I've got the bandages in here with the antibiotic ointment they gave me. They also want me to get checked out at the hospital's Urgent Care Clinic tomorrow afternoon. They booked an appointment for me to make sure everything's okay."

He retrieved the materials and gave them to Kate. She carefully applied the ointment, covered the wound with a large sterile pad, and wrapped an ace bandage around Jay's upper arm. "There you go. All done."

Neither planned what happened next. In the silence, Kate was staring into Jay's eyes as if she might find answers there for the emotional storm that had engulfed her. The hot shower that had finally washed away the blood and the wine of this terrible night had left an emptiness within her. She felt like a marathon runner collapsing after just crossing the finish line.

Their lips and tongues found each other. Kate's hands explored Jay's chest and back as his towel fell away. She felt a deep stirring as he opened her robe and caressed her breasts. Drawing him into a tight embrace, skin on skin, she felt her awful tension melting away.

Without speaking a word, she pulled down the cover on the bed and slid under the sheets. She felt welcoming heat radiating from his body as he climbed in alongside her, and she snuggled closer. At first, he ran his fingers from her lips, down her neck, and over her left breast. Then he started kissing her, from the top of her head down the entire length of her body. With every touch of his lips, her body tingled with excitement, till she ached to have him inside her.

When she finally opened herself to him, he entered her tenderly until their bodies were one, moving rhythmically together, enflaming passions she had not known for a long time. Motions that began slowly became more eager and insistent, as she surrendered to the ecstasy of the moment. She arched her hips and met each of his thrusts with moans of pleasure. When release came at last, it quenched an almost desperate thirst she had been unwilling to acknowledge before.

She lay there for several minutes, cleansed of her mental turmoil, breathing deeply, her hand resting on Jay's chest. As her heart rate returned to normal, she sat up in bed, propped on a pillow. She pulled Jay to her and cradled his head in her lap. With a gentle finger, she traced the bas-relief of scars on his face, his topography of pain. "Does it hurt after all these years?" she asked. "Your face, I mean?"

He turned his head and looked into her eyes. "Only when it frightens a child."

She sighed. "I can't imagine what that must be like for you." Nodding her head, she said, "Your face is beautiful to me, and you're a fantastic lover. That was wonderful. I think I really needed that."

Jay beamed at her. "I adore you."

They sat like that for several comfortable minutes, neither speaking.

Kate ran her fingers through his hair and stroked his cheeks. "I feel at peace," she said. "Warm and alive." Then she chuckled. "Oh, I forgot. I had brought our nightcaps in here and put them on your bedside table."

Jay shook his head. "They'll keep till tomorrow. I'm ready to crash. You?"

Kate agreed. "I'm wiped out, but I don't want to go back to my room and be alone. Not tonight. May I sleep in here with you?"

He grinned as much as his scars would allow. "Absolutely."

They cuddled together and were asleep in minutes. It was the safest Kate had felt in weeks.

#

They both slept in the next morning, exhausted from the night before. Kate was the first to awaken. She looked at Jay as he slept, his chest rising and falling. His body was lean and muscled from his regular work-outs. Before the scarring, his face would have qualified for the cliché "ruggedly handsome."

What must it have been like—the assault, the years of surgeries and treatments, the abandonment by his family? Her situation was different, although her pending divorce bore some similarities. Of course, she had lost her birth family, too, but she was too young to have any memories of her mother, and she had never known her father. *Jay and I are in a lifeboat after all,* she thought. *But we're safe! I have to call Bonnie and tell her the good news. Life can get back to normal at last.* She paused. *Or does "normal" even apply to the lives of investigative journalists?*

Jay began to stir. She saw his eyelids flutter and open. "Good morning, sleepyhead. It's almost noon. What time is your appointment at the clinic?"

He squinted his eyes in the sunlight streaming through the window. "Three o'clock, I think."

She leaned over and kissed his forehead. "Can I interest you in a Denver omelet?"

"Sure can. I'll be out in a minute to help."

"After breakfast, we'll plan our trip back to Vegas. I'll call Billie and let her know we'll be home soon."

"I'll miss the green, I can tell you that."

She became thoughtful. "What do you suppose your life will be like without…" She hesitated.

He finished the sentence for her. "The Gemellis? Hopefully, I'll learn to shine a light, like you do. Fingers crossed."

She nodded. "Fingers crossed. And I'll have a lot of writing to do."

Jay smiled at her. "Do you have a name for your story yet?"

"Mm hm. I'm calling it 'The Lake Mead Murders.'"

44. The Lake Mead Murders

ONE MONTH LATER. "Sign's still out, Hal," Kate said as she entered Vincent's.

"Oh, hi, Kate. Thanks. I'll put it on my list. Bonnie's at your booth over in the corner. Want your regular?"

"Is a bear Catholic? Does the Pope shit in the woods?" she quipped.

"Coming right up, hon."

When Kate reached the table, Bonnie stood up and ran to her. The two embraced as though Kate had been lost at sea for a year and had just found her way home.

Bonnie spoke first. "Do you actually have time for me today? I mean, all I've heard from you since you got back are little snippet phone calls—'Sorry, I can't talk now. I have a deadline to meet. I'll call you later.' And then you don't. You've been burrowed into that office of yours like a tick on my dog Toby. Are you coming up for air? Did you finish your friggin' story?"

"Yep. I did. Sent it off to Billie this morning. Waiting to hear back from her about what she thinks. I'm all yours—free as a bird!"

"Well, thank goodness! After lunch we can go back to my place and relax by the pool." Her grin spread from ear to ear. "Wait till you see my new swimsuit. Dan isn't sure he wants me out in public in it." She chuckled. "He's showing three houses this afternoon and Jeremy will be at football practice, so the place is ours. I mixed us up a pitcher of margaritas, and they're chilling in the refrigerator as we speak."

"I've missed you so much, Bon." Kate hugged her again, just as Hal approached the table.

"Here's your Old Fashioned, Kate. You ladies let me know when you want to order some food."

The women sat down. It looked as though they might burst from the pressure of all they wanted to say, but they remained silent for a moment, staring at each other as if they were the lone survivors of a plane crash.

Bonnie raised her wine, and Kate lifted her cocktail. As they touched glasses, Bonnie said "Welcome home, dear sister. Welcome home." Then she added, "You did it, just like I knew you would."

"I did. And the medicine my shrink is giving me is helping with the nightmares."

"Shrink? Nightmares? What's going on?"

Kate took another sip of her drink. "I haven't told you, but I'm sure you heard part of it on the news. About Sofia being killed?"

"Yeah. They said Cruella was shot at some vineyard in Oregon."

Kate cleared her throat. "Enchanted Hill Winery. And the police were afraid there might be some Gemelli connections alive and well in Nevada who might not take kindly to her being killed, so they never released the whole story."

"The whole story? What's the whole story?"

"I'm the one who killed her. And another guy, too."

Bonnie almost spilled her drink. "Holy shit! Holy shit! What—who?"

Kate frowned. "I killed the guy Bobby Gemelli sent after me…and I killed Sofia Gemelli when she tried to kill my partner, Jay."

Bonnie looked as though she might run out of the restaurant. "Dear God in heaven," she muttered. "Do I know you?"

"It's me, Bon, but I've been through the ringer. Killing people isn't as easy as they make it look in the movies. Trust me." She sighed as she raised the cocktail to her lips. "Sometimes I see their faces as I'm drifting off to sleep or just when I'm waking up. I hear things, too—doors opening, footsteps—or I feel like someone is standing over my bed. But like I said, the pills are helping, and my doctor is good at what she does. Says it's post-trauma stuff."

Bonnie appeared to be at a complete loss. "Oh, sis. I-I never imagined…I don't know what to say."

"Just say you still love me. That's all I need."

"You know I do. I'll always love you. You're my best friend in the whole world."

Kate relaxed, as though a great weight had been lifted from her shoulders. She reached across the table and grasped Bonnie's hand. "I was so afraid you might…"

"Hey, I apologize for running out on you before. I won't ever do that again. We're in it together—for the long haul."

"Thank you, Bon. That's just what I needed to hear."

They were silent for a few minutes after that, as though simply basking in each other's company. Then Kate spoke.

"Before I give you all the gory details on the Gemellis, bring me up to date on you and your family. How are the kids? How's the real estate business going?"

Bonnie shared recent events, glowing with the success of the Ballantine Realtors partnership she shared with her husband Dan. "Business is good, Kate, and the kids have been absolute angels. Susie is loving Brown and getting the grades to prove it. She may change majors—thinking about chemistry, if you can believe that. She's even talking about medical school after she graduates." She took a sip of her wine. "Jeremy has a four-point at Rosemount and is becoming a girl-magnet. I've gotta keep my eye on him," she said with a smile.

They shared small talk for a while until Kate's phone rang. "I have to take this," she said. "It's Billie at the network." As she listened, her eyes grew wide and a broad grin spread across her face. "That's fantastic! And the execs are all behind it? Fast-tracked? Oh, wow! When? I'll be there bright-eyed and bushy-tailed! You've just made my day, Billie. Hell, you've just made my whole week. See you soon."

Bonnie sat staring at her. "Well, tell me! Tell me! Don't keep me in suspense. What's going on?"

"The studio loves my story! They've mobilized a small army to fast-track it and get it into production as soon as possible. And get this—they're making it into a series, dedicating a whole episode to each of the bodies."

Bonnie furrowed her brow. "But I thought they hadn't been able to identify who all the bodies were and how they died. You told me that yourself—how hard it is to work with those water-logged bones."

"Yeah, they're fudging things a little bit, I know. But they also can't prove the bodies *aren't* who the network people say they are." She chuckled and took a sip of her whiskey. "But we can run with honest-to-goodness stories on all the people who went missing from the Strip back then. I've dug up a lot of material on the five I call 'the little league.' The 'big league' of course will be Bobby and Sofia, and the series will conclude with their stories. Strictly big-budget."

"And a big-budget paycheck for you, I presume?"

Kate leaned over the table and whispered in Bonnie's ear. Her friend chirped in surprise.

"You can't be serious! That much! Holy shit—pardon my French!"

Kate was beaming. "Maybe an Emmy this time, Bon. A Pulitzer may be a little too much to hope for, but it can't hurt to dream. Billie says we've got a good shot at it. And they want me to introduce the series. It'll be this sweet face that everybody sees first."

Bonnie put on a mock-sober face. "Okay, now promise me you'll get me into the studio when they film your part. I want to be there, in the green room or whatever they call it."

"You got it, Sweet Pea."

Bonnie grimaced. "I thought I told you—"

Kate was laughing. "I couldn't resist. I won't do it again. I promise." As her laughter subsided, she became more serious. "Just for the record, the divorce is a done deal. Simon and I have parted company, but we're on good terms. It's a friendly split."

"I'm sorry, Kate. Divorces are never easy, even the friendly ones. You know I'm there for you, if you need a shoulder to cry on." Bonnie picked up the menu in front of her. "Getting hungry?" she asked as she took another sip of her Chardonnay.

As though she didn't hear her, Kate said, "And I might have a new boyfriend. We're not quite sure yet where our relationship is going."

Bonnie spit the mouthful of her drink onto the tablecloth. "Would you please give me a little warning before you drop a bombshell like that? That's the way clothes get ruined." She dabbed at her lips with a napkin as she checked the front of her blouse. "Now do tell. Is he cute?"

"Well, that's not exactly the word I'd use to describe him. But I think he's beautiful."

"Uh oh. He's an old, fat, rich dude?"

"Nope. Twenty years younger than me. And he's dynamite in bed."

Bonnie started fanning herself with the menu. "Oooh, girl! Did the temperature just go up in here or is it just me? You are something else. I'm all ears."

Kate told Bonnie all about Jay, from their first meeting in Billie's office to their harrowing adventures in the Willamette Valley. Bonnie hung on her every word.

When Kate finished, Bonnie was still staring at her. "Dear God in heaven. I don't know what to say. You've left me speechless."

"Then let's order some food. Split a salad?"

"And I need another glass of wine."

#

Relaxing by the pool later was just what Kate needed. Her marathon project to deliver her story to the network had succeeded far beyond her wildest expectations. Between that and her ongoing recovery from her trip to Oregon, she felt wired, like a guitar strung too tightly. It felt good to laugh as Bonnie strutted like a runway model in her new eye-popping bikini. Lying in a chaise lounge in beach hat and sunglasses, sipping cool margaritas, was the perfect refreshment for her soul.

"So, when am I going to meet Mr. Scott, this new love interest of yours?" Bonnie asked as she lifted the brim of her hat and looked over at her friend. "And pass me the lotion please."

Kate handed the tube of sunscreen to her. "Like I said, we're not completely sure about things yet. You'll be the first to know once we figure it out."

"Well, when you do, how about if Dan and I invite the two of you over for dinner some night?"

"Sure, that'd be great."

Just then Bonnie's phone rang. She sat up. "The one problem with being a realtor—you're always on call. This is a client I have to talk to. Back in a minute." She walked inside as she swiped the screen. "Hi, Jan."

Kate lay there under the large umbrella, waiting to get warm enough to plunge into the pool. It felt so good to finally be able to spend time with Bonnie. Nonetheless, she was finding it hard being back in Nevada. As Jay had predicted, she missed the green hills of the Willamette Valley. When she let her mind wander, she saw vineyards and forests, grass seed farms and Christmas trees. She felt drawn to the place, as though it had awakened something inside her she hadn't known was there. She even imagined she heard the wind whispering through Douglas firs when she went to bed at night.

Bonnie came back and filled her glass again. "Jan wants to see a place tomorrow. She's got a good budget, and she knows what she's looking for. A great client." She settled back into her chaise lounge. "Now, where were we?"

Kate took a sip of margarita and looked over at her. "Ever get tired of Nevada? The heat, the desert? The pool is nice and all, but…" Her voice trailed off.

"Funny you should ask. Dan and I were just talking about that last night." She took a big draft of her drink. "Damn! I make a good margarita. Anyway, the only thing that's really holding us here is Jeremy finishing high school. Once he's done with Rosemount, anything's possible. Why? What's up? Got a little wanderlust after your travels?"

"I have to admit, I really fell in love with Oregon."

"Where it rains all the time?"

Kate laughed. "It doesn't. Now I never went exploring—I only know a little something about the Willamette Valley, where I was. But I've heard great things about the coast. The whole thing is National Seashore. And I'd like to visit the mountains. Supposed to be great skiing there."

"You're not thinking of moving to Oregon, are you?"

"Would you consider it?"

"Whew! I'd have to get another real estate license. I don't know. We just got our business started here. That would be a big move. I don't know what Dan would have to say about it."

"Whisper 'salmon fishing and elk hunting' in his ear and check his reaction."

Now it was Bonnie's turn to laugh. "Yep. You're something else."

As the alcohol relaxed them both, Bonnie said, "Can you tell me anymore about your story and what happened? I mean, if it doesn't upset you too much?"

"To coin a phrase, Lake Mead was like 'the Elephants' Graveyard for Gangsters.' Nobody knows how many bodies Giancarlo Gemelli dumped there. His son Bobby was the ferryman for Tom Romano, who did the actual killing." She refilled her glass. "Row, row, row your boat."

"I think I prefer being a realtor to being an investigative journalist. I don't know how you do it."

"Well, I answered the two questions that have bugged me since I was a little kid—who my father was and how my mother died."

Bonnie turned toward her. "I'm all ears."

"Harry Costello—the guy with the Super Bowl ring I told you about?—he was my father. And Sofia had my mother killed."

Bonnie reached out and touched Kate's hand. "I don't know what to say. The Gemellis took out your whole family."

"All except for my grandmother, who probably spent the rest of her life watching her back, worried they'd come after her. That's why she never said a word about it to me, if she knew anything at all."

Bonnie was shaking her head. "This just boggles my mind. I really can't wrap my head around it. And I clearly haven't made enough margaritas." She paused. "One last question and I'll go squeeze some more limes. Did you ever find out who killed Giancarlo?"

"Bobby told me he did."

Bonnie's eyes went round. "Well, I'm not very fond of using the f-bomb, but I can't think of another word that's more appropriate. Fuck!"

"Amen to that, sister. Now I'll come and help you with our next pitcher."

#

When the time finally arrived for filming Kate's introduction to the series, the studio was decorated for Hanukkah and Christmas. Two fir trees with hundreds of twinkling lights occupied most of the lobby. An ornate menorah sat proudly on the receptionist's counter, which was also hung with lights.

Kate and Bonnie were striking in what they called their "Pre-Emmy-Pulitzer-Prize Clothes." Kate wore a forest-green, velvet blazer with matching pants, and a cream-colored, silk blouse. High black boots completed her outfit. Bonnie wore designer jeans and a graphic T-shirt, accented with a pink silk scarf that matched her pink heels. With all their nervous energy, neither could sit, and both paced the room awaiting Billie.

Kate furrowed her brow. "Bon, I'm trying to remember the expression my grandmother used when I was a kid and couldn't calm down. Oh, yeah. She'd say, 'You're like a flea on a hot griddle.'"

"Well, I've got enough butterflies in my stomach for both of us, and I'm not the one who will be on camera."

Just then, a man in a dark suit and tie came walking toward them.

Kate's face lit up. "Oh, my God! Jay, it's you! I didn't expect to see you this morning."

"Billie let me know this was your big day, and I had to see you. I had to wish you luck, even though you don't need it. You're a star already!" He kissed her on the cheek and gave her a brief hug. Turning toward Bonnie, he said, "And you must be her best friend, Bonnie. Kate talks about you so much I feel like I already know you."

Bonnie smiled and extended her hand. He shook it warmly.

"She talks about you, too, but hasn't let me invite you over for dinner yet."

Jay grinned as much as he was able. "Well, maybe we can remedy that."

Billie came rushing toward them. "You look lovely, Kate. Perfect for today's shoot." She shook hands with Bonnie. "I'm Kate's boss, Billie. You must be Bonnie. I'm so pleased to meet you." She turned to Jay. "Why don't you show Bonnie into the green room?" Looking back at Bonnie, she said, "We've got a big monitor in there so you'll be able to see everything perfectly." To Kate she said, "Come with me, hon."

#

Bonnie and Jay sat at either end of the long green couch that gave the room its name. Perched on the wall directly in front of them was a 65-inch TV monitor. The end tables that flanked the couch were decorated with boughs of holly, and white-frosted wreaths adorned the other walls.

"What happens next?" asked Bonnie.

"They're probably going over the script, most of which Kate wrote herself. Of course, she'll have a teleprompter. They'll film her in front of a blue screen so they can add the images later, but I'm guessing they'll show Kate all the images first to get her in the right frame of mind."

Bonnie could hardly contain herself. "This is so exciting!"

"It's a really big deal for Kate and the network. A lot is riding on it. Big investments have been made." His half-smile beamed at her. "Everyone is sure it will be the number one hit of the season."

After what seemed to be an interminable amount of time, "Gimme Shelter" by the Rolling Stones began to play over the speakers. The song grew louder as the eerie wail of the chorus filled the small room. The monitor came to life. Kate stood before a blue background and started walking toward the camera.

Jay leaned over and whispered to Bonnie, "They'll probably show her walking on the shores of the lake, and it will look absolutely real. Magic!"

"My name is Kate Temperance, and I'm here to introduce you to a very special edition of Crime Story. *Tonight, we begin* The Lake Mead Murders. *Behind me, you see the largest man-made reservoir in the United States. At its height in 1983, Lake Mead was 1,225 feet above sea level. But the megadrought in the West has been relentless. As of May of 2022, the lake had dropped 176 feet. Areas that had been underwater, like the Hemenway boat launch behind me, are now shoreline.*

"The receding waters have exposed a World War II-era landing craft, a half-submerged B-29 plane, many sunken boats. And bodies.

"On May 1, 2022, human remains were found right here in a fifty-gallon drum. As if being found in a barrel weren't enough, the bullet hole in the skull confirmed it was a homicide.

"More skeletal remains were found on May 7, July 25, August 6, and August 18. And another offered clear proof of murder—two skeletons entangled in an anchor chain, one end of which was clamped to a leg bone and the other to a cinder block.

*"*The Lake Mead Murders *takes us on a globe-trotting journey from the glitz and glamor of Las Vegas to the busy streets of Paris, and finally to the bucolic vineyards of the Willamette Valley in Oregon. It tells the horrifying stories of these bodies and how a crime family in Las Vegas decades ago turned Lake Mead into a kind of Elephants' Graveyard for Gangsters. Our series will end in the present with a story ripped from today's headlines, the almost unbelievable tale of a murderous brother and sister who would stop at nothing to maintain their evil empire. I'm speaking, of course, about Bobby and Sofia Gemelli, children of the notorious Giancarlo Gemelli. Bobby, who had disappeared a half-century*

ago, was found this year in the vineyards of Oregon and has been charged with murder. Sofia, who had taken over the reins of her father's casino, the Florentine, was recently killed in a gunfight straight out of the annals of the Wild West.

"*The bodies in Lake Mead are rising. All the bodies do. They appear, they're discovered, they give up the ghosts they've been hiding for decades. Family secrets long buried—the affairs and adulteries, the lies and the scandals, even the murders—are one day revealed. No sins can remain covered forever. They all rise to the surface.*

"*All the bodies do.*"

The End

About the Author

William Cook is a Connecticut native transplanted to Oregon in 1989. He is a graduate of the State University of New York at Albany, where he received a Master's Degree in Social Work. Years of study in two Catholic seminaries and a long career as a mental health therapist have shaped (or warped!) his world view. He is spending his retirement with his artist wife Sharon, who paints her abstract expressionist work in the dining room, while he writes at a desk by the bay window in the kitchen. His fifteen grandchildren are now grown beyond their need for regular babysitting, but there are three great grandchildren so far...

He describes his first novel, *Songs for the Journey Home*, as a kind of spiritual journey. He has written three collections of short stories, *The Pieta in Ordinary Time and Other Stories*, *Catch of the Day*, and *Before Our House Fell into the Ocean: Stories of Love and Death*. His *Driftwood Mysteries*, include the novel, *Seal of Secrets*, the short story, *Eye of Newt*, the novel, *Woman in the Waves*, the novel, *Dungeness and Dragons*, the short story *Paper*, and the novel, *Gallery of Gangsters*.

Visit him at https://authorwilliamcook.com or at

https://www.facebook.com/writerwilliamjcook/

If you've enjoyed this book, please consider leaving a review on Amazon and Goodreads. Tell your friends about it on Facebook and Instagram. Word-of-mouth is the best sort of advertising!

Many thanks!

William Cook

Acknowledgements

As I noted in the dedication, this story never would have been written without the inspiration and encouragement of my daughter Julie. In addition, the constant support of my artist wife Sharon feeds my soul and keeps me going. Several of my writing friends have been tireless in their encouragement, especially Larry, Dennis, and Dallas.

The cliché is true—writing a book, like raising children, takes a village. My village includes my extraordinary extended family, who put up with this crazy old man who seems to be off in another world most of the time.

Other members of that village are my various writing groups—Writers Yesterday, Today, and Tomorrow (WYTT), the Northwest Independent Writers Association (NIWA), the Salem branch of Willamette Writers, and my faithful Critique Group. Thank you, one and all!

Finally, I would be remiss if I did not thank Jette Rainwater, Wine Ambassador for Willamette Valley Vineyards, who did not call the police or the FBI when I emailed her to ask, "Is it possible to murder someone by trapping them in one of the tanks used for the carbonic maceration of whole cluster Pinot Noir?" Her detailed descriptions of wine production (and the dangers thereof!) were immensely helpful. I credit her with Gavin's comment to Kate: "Oh, there are any number of ways to die at a winery!"

I think there is some truth to the idea that we are the stories we tell ourselves and others. My sincere hope is that I tell good ones.

Made in the USA
Middletown, DE
09 June 2024